# Hearts AND Hooves

# ALEXA ASTON

Summer Sutherland finished composing her email and attached the manuscript she had edited to it. She hit send and sat back, sighing. Over her eight years at Liberty House, she had worked her way up from editorial assistant to copy editor, then assistant editor, and now senior editor. She was partnering with several midlist authors and even had a dozen others who had hit bestseller lists. Her usual habit was to edit one manuscript at a time so that it had her full attention, adding suggestions and asking questions throughout it. She then wrote an overall letter to the author, giving her general impression of the work, always careful to praise the effort because writing a novel was hard work.

Some authors presented her with a clean manuscript which had few typos and flowed beautifully. These were the submissions where she had very few editorial notes, and they were a pleasure to edit. Most hit a middle ground, with work needed regarding grammar and typos and several notes to the author on ways to expand a scene, create a new one, or even delete a scene or entire chapter, working that content in somewhere else. These took more time to edit and involved more back-and-forth between editor and author before the manuscript was passed on to a line editor and then proofreader.

A few manuscripts she received were what her mom would call a genteel mess, with grammatical problems from run-on sentences to subject/verb agreement problems to atrocious spell-check errors. They also were the challenging ones which involved tearing the manuscript apart and giving the authors ideas for ways to put things back together in a coherent fashion.

This last one she had just worked on was the latter. The author was becoming well-known, and because of that, she didn't think she needed any editing. It was *because* she had great editing that her books sold so well. Summer almost wished she could turn this belligerent author over to another editor, but Dragon Lady would never go for that since she had specifically assigned Monica Sullivan to Summer. Her suspicion was that her boss believed working with Monica would push Summer to resign.

Dragon Lady was the nickname Summer had for Millicent Bennington, the editor-in-chief of Liberty House. For some reason, she had never liked Summer. It hadn't kept her from moving up the ranks, but Dragon Lady continually threw up roadblocks, creating new, ingenious ways to make certain that Summer failed. In the beginning, she was able to lie low and avoid Dragon Lady. Summer also had some great professionals at Liberty House who mentored her. They all had remarked on her talent for editing and coming up with creative ideas to improve a manuscript, and they even helped her move up the ladder at the publishing house. Now, however, Dragon Lady *was* her direct boss and would do her annual evaluation for the first time this year.

Her computer dinged, and she saw she had an email from Monica, the testy author she'd just emailed. Knowing Monica, she had been hovering at her computer, waiting for the manuscript and notes to be returned. There was no way that the author had had time to look over the notes Summer included with the manuscript because there were plenty of them. With dread, she opened the email.

Summer –

I just received your general notes. Glad that you enjoyed my latest creation. I think it's my best yet!

However, I opened the document and saw you have SO many notes attached. That is VERY disappointing to me. I always give Liberty House my BEST effort, but you never seem to recognize that and go out of your way to make my life miserable.

I wanted to do you the courtesy of giving you a heads up. I am going to ask Millicent to assign me to another editor. Our relationship is strained—at best—and I feel you are stifling my creativity.

Hope there are no hard feelings!

Hugs!
Monica

This would not bode well. Apprehension filled Summer as her eyes skimmed the email again, wincing at every exclamation mark. Dragon Lady would be pissed. Not at Monica.
At Summer.

She prepared herself, knowing she would be called in soon. She didn't want to start another manuscript at this point. That would be unfair to its author because she wouldn't be able to give the work her full attention. Instead, she scrolled through her emails, answering several. She made one phone call to an author who had left her a voicemail to call her.

"Hey, Celia. It's Summer. What can I do for you?"

"I hate to tell you this, Summer, but I'm not going to hit my March 1 deadline."

A sinking feeling filled her. Just another strike against her Dragon Lady would use.

"What's up, Celia? You're so reliable, usually turning in your submissions early."

The author began crying. "I'm sorry. I'm a mess right now. My husband was diagnosed with leukemia six weeks ago. Everything has been a blur since then. We've seen two oncologists. Started him on chemo and radiation. All of a sudden, my nice, quiet life of spending days in my office writing have flown out the window. I'm driving him from appointment to appointment. Caring for him when we get home because he's really ill from the chemo. And the few minutes I have to myself? I lock myself in my office and just cry. I can't be creative now, Summer. I just can't."

Her heart ached for Celia. "I'm so sorry you're going through this with Rob. Being ill yourself is bad enough, but when you see someone you love suffering, it's rough. I know you're the kind of person who is being the strong one in front of him."

"Exactly," Celia said, sniffing. "I don't want him to see how upset I am. We have two teenagers. They're also falling apart because of this. I've always been the glue in our family, and it's even more important for me to be that glue now, Summer."

"I get it."

"Writing is the last thing on my mind. I'm just too emotionally drained to do it right now. And I worry about what if Rob doesn't make it? I know my books are finally starting to sell well, but I don't make enough to take over our mortgage and send two kids to college."

Celia began sobbing. "What if I have to go back to being an accountant? My soul will dry up. I *adore* writing, Summer. I earn enough now to supplement what Rob makes, but ..." Her voice trailed off.

"Listen. What's important now is your mental and emotional health, as well as your family's. Take care of Rob and the kids." Summer paused. "How much do you have written?"

"All but the last five chapters," Celia told her. "I'm *so* close to finishing. I even know how to wrap it up. I just can't get myself in front of a keyboard to actually do it."

"Send me what you have."

"I haven't done my final read-through," Celia said. "You know I like to read from start to finish once the manuscript's done to check for inconsistencies."

"That'll be my job this time," Summer assured her. "And send me any notes for those last few chapters if you've written them down."

Celia sniffed. "Okay."

"I'll edit what you have. You know it doesn't take much to polish your work, Celia. You're one of my favorite authors to work with."

"I appreciate hearing that, Summer. I *needed* to hear that."

"Once I've done my part, I'll check in with you. If you

still are in a bad spot, I'll finish up for you. I know your style. Your voice."

"Oh, I couldn't ask you to do that."

"You didn't. I volunteered," she corrected. "And I may not even have to do that. You may hit a point where you'll need writing as an outlet. I had one author who accompanied her son to chemo and wrote during those four hours of his treatment because she knew he would need her once they got home. Her son put on his headphones and zoned out. She wrote. It turned out it was the only time she was able to write. You'll just have to play things by ear."

"Thank you for listening, Summer. You're not just my editor. You're my friend. I appreciate all that you do for me."

"Call if you need anything else."

"I will."

Summer hung up and said a little prayer for Rob's health, as well as Celia's peace of mind. She went to the restroom, needing a break from her office. When she returned, the assistant who sat outside her office and worked for her and three other editors looked at her hesitantly, biting her lip.

"I assume my presence is requested in the big office?" she asked lightly.

"Yes. ASAP."

"Heading there now," she said, steeling herself for what lay ahead.

When she reached Dragon Lady's office, her assistant took one look at Summer and quietly said, "You can go on in."

The look of pity on the woman's face had Summer's heart racing. She knocked lightly on the door and entered, closing it behind her, not wanting anyone to hear what went down between them.

Because Summer's gut told her she was about to be fired.

She lingered at the door because Dragon Lady was on the

phone, and she did not want to disturb her space or privacy. Her eyes roamed the room, however, landing on various pictures displayed of her boss and her husband, Ted Bennington, the owner and publisher of Liberty House. Ted had been very supportive of Summer, the complete opposite of his wife.

Dragon Lady laughed merrily. "We'll be there for drinks at seven. See you then."

The minute she placed the phone in its cradle, her real face came out. Gone was the fake, social smile. Instead, the crease between her brows deepened as she frowned at Summer.

Without waiting to be asked, Summer crossed the room and took a seat in front of the desk, knowing the ax would now fall.

"What were you *thinking*, alienating Monica Sullivan in that way? Monica is one of our top sellers."

"Only because she has solid editing," Summer said, not willing to roll over and play dead.

"She is a very talented writer."

"She is. I totally agree. But as her sales have grown, so has the size of her ego. Monica doesn't feel she needs to be edited anymore, and that's simply not the case. Her writing tends to be bloated."

"Why, I disagree. I read all her books, and they are streamlined."

Summer gazed levelly at her boss until Dragon Lady looked away.

"You can thank me for that. At least these last three novels I've worked on with her. I cut out the excess. I keep her from meandering all over the place. Monica is talented and creative, with great characters and plots, but she needs someone to rein her in. I've done that successfully."

She paused a moment, wanted her words to sink in before continuing.

"The hard truth is that Monica knows that she'll need to put a lot more work into her manuscript now that I've sent her my notes. She's gotten lazy. She doesn't want to put in the work necessary to make her words shine."

Dragon Lady shrugged nonchalantly. "We could fix it for her. She wouldn't even have to know. I doubt she bothers to go back and read what's been published. She's only interested in reviews."

Her brows shot up. "If you mean me as that we, the answer is no. I am not responsible for the necessary edits. Monica is the writer. I've recommended what she needs to do. She emailed me and told me she would request another editor, but I can tell you that she's already had a great edit. It would be foolish to have someone go through the manuscript again. I can forward you her original submission, along with my notes. That would give you a good idea of what I'm talking about."

"That's not necessary," Dragon Lady said haughtily. "I'll edit her myself."

Summer's stubbornness caused her to say, "You should still take my notes. It would save you some time. And at least I corrected all her typos, of which there were a ton. Anything else?"

Relief swept through her, knowing she could take Monica Sullivan off her plate. While it was nice to have a writer who pulled in that many sales, Monica had never wanted to be a team, as writer and editor usually were. Summer was also glad Dragon Lady would take Monica on herself. That way, she would see the problem. At least Monica wasn't Summer's problem anymore.

What she should do now is tell Dragon Lady that Celia's

manuscript would come in late, especially not knowing when it would be ready. A late manuscript shifted everything in production. Summer didn't think this was the right time to divulge that information, though. Already Dragon Lady's eyes were afire. She didn't need her spewing hate. Celia's delay could wait until tomorrow. Or the next day.

"You have an attitude problem," her boss declared. "If a writer of Monica Sullivan's caliber cannot be convinced to work with you, then obviously something is lacking on your part."

Summer kept silent, worried again where the conversation might go.

"This is just one of several instances which have arisen lately. I think it's time to part ways, Ms. Sutherland." Dragon Lady stared at her pointedly.

"You're firing me? On what grounds?" she demanded, not shying away from battle.

"I have found you lacking in numerous areas," Dragon Lady continued. "I have just cause to send you on your way."

She decided to call this woman's bluff. "No, you don't. My evaluations up until this point have been excellent. All eight years of them," she emphasized. "There is simply no just cause to fire me."

Her boss smiled slyly. "You haven't received *my* evaluation yet. It's due next week. I don't see the point in delaying the inevitable."

Digging in her heels, she said, "I don't see how I could work for Liberty House for eight years and receive outstanding evaluations and then suddenly, I'm worthless. Ask any of my previous supervisors and mentors." Summer paused and threw out. "Ask Ted."

Fire shot from Dragon Lady's eyes now. "That's Mr. Bennington to you," she snarled.

Suddenly, things became clear to Summer.

"You're ... *jealous*? Of me?"

"No," her boss said, far too quickly. "You simply do not fit in with the Liberty House philosophy."

Knowing her entire professional career was on the line, Summer said, "I won't go quietly. I'll file a wrongful termination suit. You are discriminating against me. You're retaliating against me. And knowing your reputation, you would be nasty enough to blackball me in the publishing industry. I won't allow that to happen, Millicent. I will call my lawyer so fast that your head will spin faster than that kid in *The Exorcist*."

Of course, the only lawyer she knew was her cousin Sawyer, and he was only licensed to practice law in Texas. Dragon Lady didn't need to know that particular bit of information, though.

Her boss' face had turned several shades of red. "I will speak to our in-house counsel immediately."

"Call him," she said coolly. "I'd like to be a part of the conversation. Call Mr. Bennington, too. Or I can call him," she threatened.

Ted Bennington had taken a shine to Summer from the moment she was hired. He wasn't in the offices often because he had several other business interests, but he had mentored her, giving her advice and guiding her throughout her time at Liberty House. Absolutely nothing sexual had ever taken place between them. Ted had been more like a smart uncle, sharing insight with Summer about the publishing industry and how to handle authors she edited. She was grateful for the time he had spent with her. The fact that this woman thought something inappropriate had occurred between Summer and Ted was ludicrous.

"Please leave," Dragon Lady said. "Remain available. I'll speak with Bill Larson and send for you when we're done."

Summer stood. "I'll be in my office."

She returned there, ignoring everyone looking at her. Word must have spread about Monica wanting to dump Summer as her editor.

Entering her office, she closed the door and pulled out her cell, not trusting the company line. She texted Sawyer.

> Can you talk? Call me when you can.
> Important.

He didn't reply immediately, and she knew he could be with a client. Or even in court. Then her phone rang, and she saw his smiling face light up her screen with a FaceTime call.

"Hey, Sawyer."

"What do I owe the honor of hearing from my lovely cousin in the middle of the workday?"

"It's bad. I'm about to get fired."

Immediately, he grew serious. "Tell me everything. Don't leave out any details. I'll decide what's important and what isn't."

For the next ten minutes, she outlined her rise at Liberty House, noting that it wasn't as if she'd been fast-tracked. She had served time in every job before moving up the food chain. She explained about her terrific evaluations and how the publisher had taken an interest in her years ago, helping guide her with advice.

"But Ted never got involved in any office politics or pushed to promote me. I know I earned every promotion I've received. Dragon Lady is just jealous."

"What was the straw that broke the camel's back today?"

Summer told him about Monica Sullivan's huge ego and how the author didn't want to put in the work, instead crying to the editor-in-chief that she didn't want to work with Summer.

"My evaluations have been terrific. My reputation is solid. I work long hours. All day here, and then I take home manuscripts to read at night and on the weekends. I used to have a thriving social life when I first came to New York, but it's dwindled to nothing over the years because I do put in so many hours."

She explained how she had threatened Dragon Lady with a wrongful termination suit if she were fired outright without cause.

"I didn't throw anything yet about an employee separation agreement. Dragon Lady is speaking to our in-house counsel now."

"You seem to know a lot about the law, Summer," Sawyer noted.

She laughed. "Last year, I edited a novel about an employee who was wrongfully terminated for being a whistleblower. He was murdered. I learned a lot working with that author on the book."

"You know I'm not able to practice in New York," he reminded her.

"I do. But if they want me to sign anything, will you read it first? Or do you know of someone who practices here who might help me?"

"I can read it, especially if they give it to you this afternoon. My gut is telling me that Dragon Lady is going to want to work fast and sweep you out the door before her husband hears anything about the decision."

"Should I text Ted?" she asked. "I don't want her to think I ran and tattled on her to him, but I do think he would want to know about this."

"I'd leave him out of it. You don't want to substantiate

any claim she has about something improper going on between the two of you. I know that's not the case, but we want to keep everything aboveboard. I'm going to let you go now. Call me the minute you have anything in hand, okay?"

"I owe you, Sawyer."

"I haven't done anything yet."

"But you were here to listen. I appreciate that. How is Hawthorne?"

"The same. I'm happy back here. I like being here again with Darby. West and Autumn. You're the only one who's missing."

"I know," she said softly.

Her cousin Darby had moved back to Hawthorne last fall, taking a teaching job at the high school after working with Cheer USA for a decade. She'd married Jace Tanner, a Dallas sports agent, over Christmas. Thankfully, Summer had gone home for Christmas in Texas and been able to attend the wedding.

Her twin had divorced her husband and left Houston, also returning to Hawthorne. Autumn had been named Director of Nursing at the new Hogan Health Hospital, known in the community as Triple H. Her sister had also remarried, and Summer's new brother-in-law was the medical director at Triple H, as well as Jace's brother.

West, her older brother, had retired from the NFL and taken a job as the head football coach and athletic director at their alma mater. He, too, had wed a local girl, Kelby Blackstone, who was Darby's best friend. Summer did feel left out, with so many of her family members moving back to their hometown the last two years. It made her long for a life in the sleepy North Texas town.

An hour went by, Summer pacing in her office, knowing

no work would get done while she was hanging in the balance. Then her phone rang.

"Summer Sutherland," she said.

"You can return to my office."

Hiding her trepidation, she left her office, head held high, and returned to the Dragon Lady's lair. This time, she had Bill Larson present. The portly attorney's face gave away nothing. Both were seated at a table, and Summer went and joined them.

Bill pushed a document of several pages across to her. "This is an employee separation agreement that Liberty House would like you to sign, Ms. Sutherland."

"I will need to read it first," she said. "I also want my attorney to go over it, as well." She handed Bill a piece of paper she'd brought with her. "Please email him the document at this address." To ensure Sawyer received it, she added, "I'll text him and tell him you're sending it now."

She did that and then picked up the separation agreement, blinking a few times because she didn't want any tears to spill onto it. The pages in front of her spelled the end of her editing career. She'd come to New York with high hopes, wanting to conquer the publishing world. While she had worked her way up to be a senior editor at an established publishing house, she still felt she was letting herself down.

After she finished reading it, Summer said, "I need to see what my attorney recommends. We'll wait to hear from him before I go a step farther."

The three of them sat in complete silence for eleven minutes. It was the most uncomfortable time she had ever spent in her life, and that included the one time she'd skipped school and gotten caught. She'd waited outside the principal's office while he met with her parents, and that had been awful.

*This* was agony.

Her cell buzzed, and she saw it was Sawyer. "This is Mr. Montgomery. I need to take this."

Instead of leaving the room, however, she answered it in front of them. "Hello, Mr. Montgomery. I hope you've had a chance to read the separation agreement."

"Yes, and they're jerking you around," her cousin said bluntly. "I've just sent a list of what I want the agreement to include. Have Larson check his email."

She instructed the attorney to do that and turned her attention back to her cousin. Briefly, Sawyer said the portion regarding the separation details and waiver of claims was fine, but he wanted more for her protection.

"I'm asking for a severance. While they stipulate they'll pay you for unused vacation days and through the end of this month, I want more incentives in order for you to sign this agreement, Summer."

"Such as?" she asked.

"In your case, benefits. Your insurance to be paid for one year, including medical, dental, and vision. Private insurance is expensive, and I want them on the hook for that. I want those benefits spelled out, plus the exact amount of compensation for the rest of February and its method of delivery placed in writing, along with the timeline when those monies are due."

"Got it."

"They want to get rid of you fast, so I'm asking apart from the severance that they offer you a set amount to sign this agreement. This isn't usually what employees ask for, much less what employers agree to. If Dragon Lady really wants you gone, however, she'll agree to this."

"Okay," she said, keeping her eyes on the pages before her.

"Do you care about the non-compete clause they included?"

"I don't think it should be there."

"Good. I agree with you. I also want to modify the non-disparagement clause they've inserted. It basically says that you won't trash talk Liberty House. I want that to be a two-way street, where they legally can't disparage you, as well."

"Agreed."

"I think if they agree to the one-time payment for you signing, they're going to insert a non-disclosure clause. You won't be allowed to share any details of this agreement with anyone, other than me."

"If you get the first, I can abide by the other," she told him.

"Look and see what their attorney is doing."

Summer looked up and saw Larson frowning at his tablet. He leaned over and whispered something to Dragon Lady.

"Larson has read it," she said quietly. "They're talking it over."

"I'll stay on the line. You're not alone in this, Cuz."

She watched as they went back and forth, Dragon Lady hissing at Bill several times. Finally, she nodded, and Summer knew they had reached a number.

"Put me on speaker so I can hear," Sawyer ordered.

"My attorney wishes to hear your counteroffer," she said, putting her cell on the table.

Larson cleared his throat. "We can agree to what Mr. Montgomery is asking for, but we wish to add a non-disclosure clause to the employee separation agreement."

Sawyer answered for the both of them. "Only if we receive the figure we asked for."

Summer saw Dragon Lady grimace, but she nodded, and Larson said, "Yes, we'll do that."

"Draw it up," Sawyer said. "Send it to me. I'll read over it and advise my client. Please take me off speaker phone."

She did so as Larson typed away. While she didn't say anything, Sawyer told her not to worry. Everything was working out for the best. He then told her about the latest basketball game he'd attended in the high school gym and some about last weekend's national cheer competition he'd gone to, where Darby's cheerleaders had taken first place.

The printer whirred, spitting out several pages. Bill retrieved them and said, "I just emailed the final agreement to Mr. Montgomery. You may look over this copy, Miss Sutherland."

Summer did so, seeing the changes Sawyer had asked for in print. She gritted her teeth so her jaw wouldn't fall open when she read the amount he had asked for as a general payment for separation.

It was half a million dollars.

*And Dragon Lady had signed off on that.*

Her mind began whirling. That was serious money. More importantly, it would give Summer the freedom to make a move she had longed to but hadn't been financially secure enough to make. She kept her composure.

In her ear, Sawyer said, "Back on speaker phone, please."

She did as he requested and heard her cousin say, "I am advising Miss Sutherland to sign this employee separation agreement."

Larson nodded at Dragon Lady, who left the table and went to the door. She spoke to her assistant, and a minute later, the assistant and a copy editor entered the office.

"You will act as witnesses as this document is signed," Bill told the pair. "Watch as we sign, and then you'll follow suit."

He offered Dragon Lady the pen first, and her boss

scrawled her name, her mouth set in stone. Summer signed next, followed by the two other employees. The four also signed a second copy of the agreement, with Bill telling Summer that one was hers to keep, and one would remain with him. He also promised to email her attorney a copy now.

Dragon Lady dismissed the two employees and turned to Summer. "Mr. Larson will escort you to your office. You will claim any personal items and turn in your employee badge. Provide him with the password to your email account. I will need to see what you are working on and reassign those authors."

"I keep a list of current projects and where I am in the editing process," she said coolly. "I'll share those with you."

She was glad she had updated the list after she spoke to Celia so it would be on record that Liberty House had granted the author an extension. She still planned to contact Celia because she meant what she'd said when she had offered to write the last few chapters of the book. She would need Celia to send what she had of the manuscript to Summer's personal email account.

As a parting remark, she said, "Please tell Ted goodbye for me. He always had thoughtful advice for me. I appreciate his counsel."

Dragon Lady practically bared her fangs at that remark, and Summer knew that was her cue to leave. She returned to her office without speaking to anyone, going to the copy room and claiming a small box. In it, she put the few personal things she had at the office, including pictures from her desk and an African violet.

She gave Larson her badge and showed him the list of where she was in her current workload, and then she walked out the doors of Liberty House for the final time. Going to the closest subway station, she took the train back to Brooklyn, knowing exactly what she was going to do now that she was financially secure.

Summer had edited several romance writers over the last few years, and she thought she could do better than they had. She'd read romance since her early teens, and over the last several months, she'd written the first book in a small-town romance series. Using West and Kelby's romance as inspiration, she had begun outlining the second book in the series, turning West into a hockey player instead of one who played football. Kelby had gone from a social media consultant to a photographer, but their love story had provided the seeds for the second book in the series. All her life, Summer had put her dream of wanting to be an author herself on the back burner, even more so once she left college because editing had taken up far too much time. Now that she had all the time in the world, she was going to work for herself.

And she was going to move back to Hawthorne, Texas. For good.

# CHAPTER

## *One*

BLACKSTONE RANCH—HAWTHORNE, TEXAS

Chance Blackstone dressed in jeans and a flannel shirt, not bothering to shave this Saturday morning. He went downstairs, finding Tammy sitting at the table, sipping a cup of coffee. It was only four-thirty, but she was up, as usual, and would be heading to the bunkhouse soon to cook breakfast for the cowboys on the ranch.

She smiled when she saw him. "Good morning, honey. I know you and West are going fishing this morning, so there's a thermos of coffee for each of you. I also made you a few sandwiches and placed them and some chips and cookies in the cooler."

He took a seat at the table. "That's thoughtful of you, Tammy. I'm sorry that we've always seemed to take you for granted. You do little things like this all the time which makes everyone's life easier."

Tammy had been his mother's best friend and had come to stay at the ranch after Chance's birth to help out for a couple of weeks. She had done the same thing a year later when his sister Kelby was born. This time, however, his mother experienced complications from that difficult birth, and she passed two days after bringing her daughter into the world. Tammy stayed on at the request of Chance's dad. Big Jim Blackstone had a ranch to run and had no idea how to care for two little ones. Tammy was more than willing to help out. A month became a year, and the years passed by, Tammy remaining with them. She had been the only mother Kelby and he had known. She ran the household, cleaning and paying all the bills, while also preparing all meals for their ranch hands.

He looked at her now with new eyes, seeing the gray streaking through the brown of her hair, wondering what kind of life Tammy would have had if she had been able to marry and raise her own family.

"I think I should hire a cook," he declared. "Someone to take on the meals for the cowboys. You cook for them seven days a week and never get a break."

An odd look came into Tammy's eyes, and she said, "I think that's a good idea, Chance. In fact, now that you've brought it up? There's something I need to discuss with you."

The pit of his stomach knotted. "What is it?"

"You know how I went to my high school reunion last fall in Waco? I ran into my old boyfriend during that weekend. He's a widower now. Lost his wife two years ago in a car accident. We've been in touch since then. Getting to know one another all over again."

Tammy hesitated. "I'm just going to spit it out, Chance. I have loved you and Kelby and every part of my life at this ranch, but it's time I finally did something for myself. We've been talking on a daily basis. He's written me the most beautiful letters, and we FaceTime every single night. I want a life with him, Chance. That means leaving Blackstone Ranch."

Her words hit him hard, but Chance said encouragingly, "You've sacrificed your entire life for this family, Tammy. You've been the person everyone leans on. Confides in. You've done more than your fair share of physical labor."

He smiled gently. "And you've been the best mom in the world to Kelby and me."

Chance leaned over and embraced her tightly, tears stinging his eyes.

"I'm glad this day has finally come," he told her. "We've been selfish, assuming you would always be here. What's your fellow's name?"

"Tommy," Tammy said, her face lighting up with that one word. "We dated all through high school, and then he joined the military, just like his daddy before him. I didn't want to sit around and wait for him, worrying if he was coming back to me or not. I wanted a life of my own and not one living through him. Fortunately, we parted as friends, but I've thought about Tommy many times over the years."

She took Chance's hands in hers. "Do I regret anything? Not a bit," she said convincingly. "I was lucky enough to go to college. Earn my degree and get a decent job after graduation. Meeting your mom and rooming with her those four years were some of the best parts of my life."

Tammy grew thoughtful. "Then I was needed here at the ranch. Your mama was like a sister to me, and I wanted to make certain that her children were raised right. Not that Big Jim couldn't have done a good job on his own, but he was faced with two little babies and a big ranch to run. He needed help, and I was all too happy to move to Hawthorne and love you two."

She reached out a hand and cupped his cheek. "You're doing a wonderful job with the ranch, Chance. Big Jim would be so proud of all you've accomplished. I know those were big shoes to fill, but you've done it admirably."

"I worry that Dad wouldn't like some of the things I've implemented," Chance admitted.

Her hand fell away. "It's *your* ranch now, Chance. Yours and Kelby's. You have to run it as you see fit. Times change. Big Jim wasn't always the best when it came to change," she said diplomatically.

Chance chuckled. "He would probably freak out if he saw all my spreadsheets, but seriously, Tammy, I'm happy for you and Tommy. Are you going to move to Waco? Is that where he is now? Or somewhere else?"

"He is back in Waco. Tommy stayed in the military thirty-five years, moving to bases all over the world. He and his wife never had children, though. After retiring from the military, they settled in Waco, wanting to put down some roots in a familiar place. Tommy has opened a body shop on Valley Mills, the main drag in town. I didn't know how to approach you about all of this, Chance. I don't want to leave you in the lurch."

"You won't, Tammy," he assured her. "Things have run smoothly all these years because of your steady hand. Just show me where everything is and what I need to know. I'll be fine."

"I've organized all the bills. I can walk you through those. The insurance, too. You will need to hire a cook, though, for the ranch hands. And have someone come in and clean the house once a week for you."

She smiled wistfully at him. "I was hoping before I left that I could see you happy with a woman, just as Kelby is happy with West now."

He shrugged, uncomfortable with the direction the conversation had now turned.

"You know I'm not dating anyone. The ranch keeps me pretty busy."

"Don't let life pass you by," Tammy advised. "I don't want you to wake up and be forty. Fifty. Even sixty—and still be by yourself. There's a girl out there for you, Chance. I feel it in my bones. The crowd you ran with as a teenager is starting to settle down now. West and Kelby. Darby and Jace. Even Autumn and Eli. I know that special someone will come into your life, maybe even sooner than you might expect. When she does, make time for her, Chance."

"When are you going to leave?" he asked, a lump in his throat.

"If you'd like, we can start interviewing cooks right away. I also want to do the same for a housekeeper."

"No live-in help," he said quickly. "You've been family, but it's just me at the house now. I like my privacy. I don't make too much of a mess. Having someone come in once a week will be good enough."

She rose. "Okay. I'm off to cook breakfast for the boys and make sandwiches for them to carry in their saddlebags for lunch. Don't forget your sandwiches and coffee."

"I won't," he told her, watching her as she went out the back door.

Chance knew that a different era was now dawning. With Big Jim gone and now Tammy moving away, he truly was on his own. Of course, he ran big decisions by Kelby since they were co-owners of Blackstone Ranch. His sister also handled their marketing and website, but he was in charge of the day-to-day operations with the cattle and horses. He spent half his day in the field with the cowboys, and the other half was spent in his office, handling the business end of things.

Tammy was the one who had finally insisted that he take

weekends off instead of working seven days a week. She had done that only two weeks ago, and he wondered if that had been in preparation of her leaving the ranch for good. Chance had no hobbies outside the ranch, other than reading. He enjoyed biographies and novels set during the Civil War and the years in the Old West after that war. He never watched TV. Didn't read any news online. Never turned on the radio, so he couldn't tell what songs were popular or who the artists who sang them were. He despised having an email account, preferring to do business in person with a handshake.

He definitely stayed off the computer once he finished his work. Chance had no social media accounts. He didn't care what was popular or what trends occurred. While the computer was a great tool for creating spreadsheets to keep track of everything from animals bought and sold to the amount of feed purchased, he wasn't glued to it as others were. Same with his phone. He had an old phone and only kept it on him so that if he needed to text a hand in the field, he could reach him quickly. The few times he went into town, he was amazed at how people were glued to their phones, ignoring everything and everybody around them.

Once Big Jim had allowed Chance to return to Blackstone Ranch three years ago, he had gone all in on the ranch itself, eschewing everything else. Maybe now it was time to work on that balance between managing the ranch and taking time for himself. At the end of a hard day, he was too tired to socialize, so he rarely left the ranch and didn't interact with many off the property. Maybe Darby could set him up with one of her teacher friends at the high school. Chance decided it was time to make himself get out and do a little living.

He grabbed the thermoses and cooler and went to his

truck, heading toward Lake Hawthorne to meet West. He had been best friends with West since they started kindergarten in Hawthorne. They had attended separate colleges, Chance going to SMU to earn a business degree, and West to A&M, where he played for the Aggies football team. They had stayed in touch as best as they could during those college years, but their friendship had cooled once they graduated. West had played ten years for the Dallas Cowboys, while Chance had moved to Chicago for work, followed by Denver and then Seattle, gaining experience in various aspects of business.

He had thought he would return to Hawthorne with his shiny business degree in hand, but Big Jim had told Chance he needed to see some of the world and work other places, away from his hometown. He'd enjoyed those years and cities, working hard and playing even harder. When his dad had finally agreed it was time for Chance to return and work on the family ranch, he had been glad, soothed by the tranquility of being out on the land and with the horses and cattle after so many years away.

Now West, too, had returned to Hawthorne, coaching the Hawks high school football team and marrying Kelby. The two of them had fallen back into an easy friendship, which Chance appreciated.

The only trouble was that he was slightly jealous of his sister and best friend. The pair had dated briefly in high school and had gone their separate ways after graduation. Both had wound up coming back to Hawthorne about the same time. The spark still existed between them, and they had married last April. Kelby was pregnant now with their first child, due in early June.

Chance wanted what they had.

He was happy for them. They were two of the most important people in his life, and he was thrilled they had found one another after so many years apart. Yet he envied them. The special looks he saw pass between them. The small, loving gestures toward one another. He yearned for that kind of relationship for himself. He'd partied hard in his twenties and had devoted his early thirties strictly to the ranch. At thirty-three, however, he felt that urge to settle down.

West and Kelby had him over for dinner at least once a week, and they invited others, as well. West's sister Autumn had returned to Hawthorne after a failed marriage, and she had gone to work for Triple H, the new hospital in town, marrying Eli, its medical director. Darby Montgomery, one of his closest friends from high school and Kelby's best friend, had also returned last year and now taught at their alma mater. She had married Jace Tanner, Eli's brother and West's sports agent. Seeing these three happy couples had made Chance realize time was passing him by. He wanted a family. To share his life with someone special.

But who?

He arrived at Lake Hawthorne and parked next to West's truck. He saw West had already carried the small fishing boat down to the water and stood waiting for Chance to arrive. Heading toward his friend, he held up what he'd brought.

"Tammy's provided a thermos of coffee for each of us and also some sandwiches."

West chuckled. "I brought two bottles of water. I sneaked out of bed as quietly as I could. Kelby needs as much rest as possible."

"She looked really good last weekend."

As they pushed the boat out into the water and climbed in, West said, "The first three months were pretty darn rough. The second trimester is the best for a mom-to-be. Kelby had more energy and began eating better. This last one, though, she's starting to tire more quickly. She hasn't slowed down, though, and I wish she would."

"Kelby mentioned to me that she was thinking about hiring someone to help out," Chance said. "Has that gone any further?"

"No. I want to nudge her more on that. Once the baby comes, she won't be able to keep up the breakneck pace she has since she started Social Synergy Creations. Now that it's off the ground and she's got a full roster of clients, she's going to need someone who can manage the business for her while she's on maternity leave and help take some of the load off her once she returns to work fulltime."

"Working out of your house will help some, I'd think. No commute, for starters."

"It should, but I still want her to hire an employee. As fast as the company is growing, she should also hire an assistant, as well. Maybe I'll bring that up tonight at dinner. You want to back me up on this, buddy?"

He was having dinner tonight at the Sutherlands' house, and they were going to watch the Dallas Mavericks basketball game after eating.

"I suppose the usual suspects will be there for dinner and the game tonight?" he asked.

"The usual couples and Sawyer," West replied, referring to Darby's brother, an attorney who had moved back to Hawthorne a year ago. Like him, Sawyer wasn't married and didn't seem to be dating anyone in particular.

"And I'm proud to say that we have a new addition to the group, as of tonight."

"Who?" Chance asked, curious because West usually kept a small, tight circle around him. His friend's days as a professional football player had taught West that most people only wanted to be friends with him as long as he could do something for them.

"Summer is going to be at dinner tonight."

West referred to his sister, Autumn's twin. Summer worked as a book editor in New York and only came to Hawthorne occasionally because of her busy schedule.

"She was just here at Christmas. I'm surprised she's already back for a visit," he said, his heart starting to speed up.

Summer and Autumn had always been on the periphery during his years growing up in Hawthorne. The twins were two years younger than West and Chance, so they had their own crowd of friends. He still thought of Summer as that outgoing girl who wore glasses and had a mouthful of braces. She had lost the braces and begun wearing contacts after he and West had graduated, though, and Chance recalled how Summer seemed to blossom after that. He had seen her sparingly over the years and talked to her for about twenty minutes the last time she had been in town a couple of months ago. He'd been impressed with the adult she had become. Summer was not only a beautiful woman, but she was very thoughtful and smart as a whip, with a great sense of humor. If Summer lived in Hawthorne, she would be the exact kind of woman he would want to date.

"How long will she be in town this time?" Chance asked.

West beamed. "There is no more visiting. All three Sutherland siblings have now returned to the fold, making Mom and Dad very happy."

Surprise rippled through him. "Summer is moving back from New York?"

His best friend nodded. "I don't know the particulars. She's been pretty tight-lipped since she arrived two days ago.

All I know is that she is back in Hawthorne for good. Naturally, Autumn is turning cartwheels."

Chance grew thoughtful. "Then we'll have to make Summer feel welcome now that she's back in Hawthorne."

And he would start by being a welcome wagon of one.

# CHAPTER
## Two

Summer placed the last pair of pants into her suitcase and zipped it closed. Her mom stood in the bedroom doorway, shaking her head.

"I'm so sorry, honey," Meg Sutherland said. "This is your home, and you aren't even going to be able to stay here."

She laughed easily. "Mom, this hasn't been my home for eight years. I've been living in Brooklyn that whole time. And I was at college the four years before that."

Mom looked at her pointedly. "You will always have a home with us, Summer. We are here whenever you need us."

She went and hugged her mom tightly. "I know that. I appreciate all the support you and Dad have given me over the years. I just need peace and quiet to write, however, and I'm sure not going to be able to get that around here."

When she had arrived home two days ago, her parents had welcomed her with open arms. Then they had revealed they were having house renovations done, starting the middle of next week. They were both reaching the age where they were considering retirement, and so they wanted to get the house in tip-top shape before they did so, while they still had a steady stream of income to pay for any renovations and updates. A new roof would be placed on the house. The kitchen was being redone, with new countertops and backsplash. The floors were also being replaced. Even the powder room downstairs and the primary suite's bathroom were being redone.

It would be impossible to work with all that noise going on for an indefinite amount of time, so she was going to stay with Autumn and Eli for a while. Once the dust settled at her parents' house, she might return and stay here until she could find a place of her own, or she might even go over to her parents' house to write during the day while they were at work. It was nice to be in a position where she could be so flexible, with both her work hours and where her writing would take place.

"I can't believe that everything you own fits into these two suitcases," Mom marveled. "Your closet used to be stuffed with clothes back in high school."

Summer picked up her backpack from the floor. "Don't forget this. My life is in here. It has my laptop. Tablet. Kindle. Chargers." She grinned. "And my favorite pair of shoes. You saw how small my apartment in Brooklyn was. I just didn't have a lot of room for clothes or possessions. Thank goodness books have gone the digital route. All I have to do is pull out my trusty Kindle or use the Kindle app on my phone to read. That's something I look forward to doing because I never got to read for pleasure as an editor."

Mom laughed. "As a librarian, I will never give up the feel of a real book in my hands. Turning a page and smoothing it."

"I still like that, too," she said. "But I know it's not practical for most readers to own a ton of books. The days are long gone of packing a carryon with five or six books in it for a week at the beach. You can tote around hundreds of books on your Kindle and slide it into your purse."

Her dad appeared at the door. "Can I help carry your suitcases down?"

"You grab that one, and I'll take this one," Summer told him, slinging her backpack over one shoulder and rolling one piece of luggage to the stairs.

They placed her bags in the foyer just as the doorbell rang. Mom opened the door and greeted Autumn and Eli.

"We can't stay," Eli shared. "Got a call on the way over. A small crisis is unfolding at Triple H, and I need to get over there ASAP."

Dad volunteered, "Then you go to the hospital, Eli. I'll drive the girls back to your house."

"Thanks, Joe," Eli said gratefully. "I really appreciate it."

He kissed Autumn goodbye and waved to them before rushing to his car.

"Are things going to be okay?" Mom asked worriedly.

"It's nothing that Eli can't handle," Autumn said confidently. "Thanks for driving us home, Dad."

They moved Summer's luggage to her father's truck, placing it in the bed. They were at Autumn's house in less than ten minutes, and Summer felt good about how close her family would be now that she was back in Hawthorne. The only thing she would need to do immediately was buy a car. She was used to being close to a subway station or even using a rideshare app in a pinch to get around. With the wide-open spaces of Texas, she would definitely need to invest in a car. At least she had the cushion to do so, thanks to Sawyer.

Dad helped bring in her suitcases and even carried them upstairs to the bedroom Autumn directed him to.

"This is our only guest room," her sister said. "We still

have a few other rooms to furnish up here. We're taking our time, though."

"Well, I know you girls are dying to gab, so I'm off," Dad told them. "Don't be a stranger, Summer."

"I won't. I may not be staying at your house, Dad, but you'll be seeing a lot of me. I promise."

Once he left, Autumn asked if Summer might like something to drink.

"I'd love a cup of hot tea," she told her twin.

Autumn pulled the tea caddy from the pantry. "Pick out whatever you want."

She chose a blackberry herbal tea, and Autumn told her to make it two while she heated mugs of water for them in the microwave. Soon, they were sitting at the kitchen table, dunking their teabags in steaming water, nibbling on oatmeal cookies.

"Okay. I need the full scoop now that you're here and we're alone. You never indicated to me that you were thinking about leaving Liberty House, and then suddenly, here you are back in Hawthorne. What's the deal, Summer?"

"I decided that I wanted to write full-time," she said honestly. "While being a book editor was always my career goal from the time I graduated from college, the dream has always been to write fiction. I told you I had been writing a small-town romance." She paused and then grinned. "I finished it."

Her sister's eyes lit up. "Are you going to let me read it?"

"I would be honored if you did so. I appreciate any feedback you have for me. I know that I need to line up a few beta readers to help me polish my manuscript. I'm ready to start the second book in the series. I've got my cast of characters, and I've outlined about fifteen pages of the entire plot. Right now, I'm planning on it being a trilogy, but you never know."

"You know you can stay with Eli and me for as long as you want," Autumn assured her. "You would definitely have more privacy here than with Mom and Dad. I'm curious, though. Are you going to need to get a job while you're writing? You've talked in the past about how hard it was to save money because everything in New York was so expensive."

"Don't worry about that. I'm set. I have a decent amount in savings. I'm going to give myself a year, dedicating myself to nothing but my writing. If I haven't sold the first book during this coming year, I may even go the indie route and self-publish. I'll evaluate things this time next year and figure out what I need to do professionally. My goal is to finish the trilogy and try to sell it as a series." Summer sighed. "We'll have to see."

Autumn pressed her. "There's something you're not telling me. And you still haven't answered why the sudden move from Liberty House. We tell each other everything, Summer."

She couldn't hide everything from her twin, and so she said, "I would if I could, Autumn. The fact is, I signed an NDA. A nondisclosure agreement. It was part of the employee separation agreement when I left."

Her twin's eyes widened. "This sounds serious. You weren't discriminated against, were you? Or sexually harassed?"

"Even if that had happened, I couldn't tell you about it. Just know that the time had come for me to leave Liberty House, and I was able to do so with a nice package. It will give me the freedom to be a full-time writer and see if I've got the talent to make a living by writing."

Autumn took Summer's hand. "I hate that you can't tell me anything, but at least I know you're okay. You seem like you're in a good place."

"I am," she assured her twin. "I decided since I was going to take the leap into writing full-time, I might as well do it in a familiar place. I saw no reason to stay in New York when I could come home to Hawthorne and be around family. My series is set in a small town in the Panhandle. I hope I can draw inspiration being back in Texas."

Her sister squeezed Summer's fingers. "Selfishly, I'm glad you're back. Not just for me." She smiled. "I have some news. We'll be sharing it soon, but I wanted you to know." Autumn beamed. "Eli and I are going to have a baby!"

Joy filled Summer, and she grabbed her twin, hugging her tightly.

"This is the best news ever!" she exclaimed. "I'm going to be an aunt. You're going to be a mom. Oh, Autumn, you're going to rock as a mom. And Eli is so kind and steady. He'll be a great dad."

"Thank you. He's a little nervous about it because he didn't have a father growing up. He worries that he won't know how to be a father, but I told him he's a natural. Eli has also become friends with West. Now that West will be a dad in a few months, I think Eli will get a taste of what it's like by observing West."

Autumn hugged her again. "I'm so happy you came home, Summer. To have us both back in Hawthorne feels right."

"Tell me the details," she urged. "I need to get ready for the baby's arrival."

"I'm ten weeks along now, which means he or she will come around the beginning of September. We'll probably start telling people soon, once I get through this first trimester. Right now, we've been keeping the news to ourselves." Autumn paused. "As a nurse, I'm also aware of the possibility of a miscarriage during this first tri, so we don't want to share our good news and then find there won't be a baby after all."

"Have you told Mom and Dad yet? Wait, I already know the answer to that. It's no. Mom wouldn't be able to keep something like this to herself."

Her sister laughed. "Mom and Dad will be over the moon once they hear. They already are because of West and Kelby's little girl arriving soon. Dad keeps suggesting names to them, and West and Kelby just smile like Cheshire cats. I'm sure they've already picked out a name and are keeping quiet about it for now."

"When can you learn the gender?"

"They have a blood test I can take soon, but it's not always one hundred perfect accurate. We've decided to wait until the eighteen-week mark and do a sonogram. It will definitely let us know if we're having a boy or girl, and we can plan from there. One of those rooms upstairs will become the nursery. I hope you'll help me decorate it."

"I don't know about that. I have to be honest, Autumn. I know nothing about babies. You were the one who always did the babysitting growing up. I never wanted to burp babies or change their diapers. That's why I chose to work at Sonic. At least there, I had a chance at tips. Of the two of us, you've always been the more maternal."

She took her sister's hand, seeing tears misting in Autumn's eyes.

"I am so grateful that you got out of your marriage with Flint Ferris and found Eli. He's such a good man, Autumn. I know he's a wonderful husband because I see how happy you are, and he'll be a terrific father."

"I realize now that I was in a dead-end marriage for so many years," her twin said quietly. "I was like a loyal little puppy that Flint kept kicking, and I just kept coming back for more, starved for affection. If I would have known he was cheating on me, I would have left a lot sooner. I understand, though, that I was meant to come to Hawthorne when I did. To get my job at Triple H and meet Eli. I'm just so happy in this marriage, Summer. I hope you can find someone here, too."

"Whoa, Sis. You're moving pretty fast there. Yes, I hope I can make a go of writing here in Hawthorne, but I don't know if here is where I'll stay. If I can't earn a living writing novels, I may have to move somewhere else and take a full-time job while I write on the side."

A stubborn look came into her sister's eyes. "We're not going to think like that," she declared. "My baby needs her aunt close by, and I need my twin. Period. All these years apart, I felt a piece of me was missing. You coming back to Hawthorne completes me, Summer. You simply have to be a success. And I'm going to do everything I can to keep you here. I'll even look for someone for you to date. So many new people have moved to town because of Triple H. I might be able to find you a handsome doctor or nurse. And with West and Darby at the high school, that's a large pool of prospective teachers and coaches they could introduce you to."

Autumn gazed steadily at Summer. "I want you to be as happy as I am with Eli. I want you to have a rich, happy life, just as I have now. With a man who is your soulmate."

She was touched by her twin's words, but Summer was the more independent of the twins. Autumn had always been the one who needed a man in her life. She was glad that her sister had found Eli and that they were so happy together, but Summer didn't need a guy to make her happy. She could be fulfilled on her own.

Of course, she wouldn't push away anyone who appeared and appealed to her. She was open to the idea of dating. Even marriage. Maybe even kids. At thirty, she was comfortable in her own skin but could see that sharing her life with someone could make it richer and more fulfilling.

"I'm going to unpack now," she announced. Taking her tea bag and dumping it the trash, she placed her mug in the dishwasher.

"Remember, we're having dinner at West and Kelby's tonight to celebrate your return to Hawthorne," Autumn reminded.

"I haven't forgotten. What time are we leaving?"

Her sister glanced at her watch. "Hopefully, in ninety minutes. I assume Eli will have taken care of the emergency and calmed everyone's fears by then. If not, we'll go without him, and he can meet us there."

"Okay. I'll be downstairs in a little bit."

She returned to the guestroom she would be staying in, glad that it was en suite. The first thing she did was plug in her laptop and tablet so they could charge. Then she took her cosmetics bag and placed items from it in the medicine cabinet and drawers and then unpacked both suitcases. Some clothes were hung in the closet, while others were folded and went into the dresser.

As she got settled, Summer thought about what she might do for Sawyer. He had been the one who had helped set her free from Dragon Lady. The least she could do would be to take him out for a nice dinner. She didn't even know what restaurants were in Hawthorne anymore, other than places such as Sonny's Sports Bar and BBQ Bliss. Pulling out her phone, she clicked on her Around Me app to look up restaurants and discovered a new steakhouse had opened in town. Clicking on its website, Summer perused the menu, deciding this would be where she offered to take Sawyer.

She returned downstairs and chatted with Autumn as she put together a taco salad

"I guess I should've offered to bring something."

"No," her sister said. "You're the guest of honor. You aren't supposed to bring anything. We're celebrating you."

Eli came through the door, saying, "Everything's solved. Looks like it's close to time to head out."

"I just need to grab the dressing from the fridge," Autumn said, covering the bowl with foil and placing it in a basket. "Then we can be on our way."

"I'll get it," he said, handing over the bottle he retrieved. "Your chariot awaits, my ladies," causing them both to laugh. "That's as Bridgerton as I can get. Autumn had us binge-watch every season. Let's just say I'm glad I don't have to wear a frockcoat or waltz at balls."

They drove to West and Kelby's house, which sat just outside of Hawthorne proper. West had wanted to build on several acres so their kids could run around freely. Summer also knew how much her famous brother liked his privacy. She figured West would be recognized for years to come. He had been one of the highest profile athletes in Dallas, and he still had several endorsement deals in place. She had seen magazine ads of West wearing certain watches and apparel and knew he also appeared in commercials.

TV hadn't been a part of her life in years. The higher up the literary ladder she had climbed at Liberty House, the less time she'd had for herself. Summer barely knew who the president was these days, much less what was going on in the world. She vowed to herself to make a change in that regard. It would be impossible to write fourteen hours a day, even though that had usually been the amount of time she spent editing manuscripts, both at work and her apartment. She would have to pace herself, taking frequent breaks along the way. She had walked a lot in New York, and she might want to think about taking an exercise class now or downloading a couple of apps so she could work out at home. Maybe that would be the way to reward herself. Write a chapter and then the perk would be to get in a workout.

Excitement filled her at the prospect of being her own boss and making her own hours. She had planted seeds in the first book she had written, introducing several characters in the small town in that first romance. Hopefully, readers would want to see some of their stories, as well. She would take tomorrow off and relax and then come Monday morning, she would begin her career as a full-time author in earnest.

They arrived at the Sutherlands' spread, and a truck pulled in behind them. Sawyer got out of it, and Summer ran to him, flinging herself at him.

"Nice greeting, Cuz," Sawyer said.

"I'm taking you out for a steak dinner at Great Steak," she informed him. "And you can't say no."

"I've never said no to steak, especially if someone else is paying. But why?"

"You're my knight in shining armor, Sawyer. I owe you. Big time. Plus, you need to send me a bill for your time."

"I didn't spend much time at all," he protested. "No bill is coming, Summer. You're family."

Summer slipped her arm through his. "Then I'm glad you won't turn down the steak dinner. Let me know when it's convenient for you."

"Any night is good for me."

"We'll talk later. We better go inside. It's already been hard enough avoiding Autumn's questions. I've got to stick to the parameters set by the NDA."

They headed to the door, where West and Kelby were

greeting Autumn and Eli. Both her brother and sister-in-law gave Summer a huge hug and kiss.

"Look at that baby bump," she said, smiling at Kelby. "And you're one of those women who glow."

"Being pregnant has been awesome for my nails and hair," Kelby informed her. "My hair has grown twice as fast, and my nails are hard as a rock. I think there's something in the prenatal vitamins that help. Come on in."

As they entered the kitchen, West said, "We've got your favorite. Chicken enchiladas. Plus, Darby's bringing Spanish rice and beans."

"And I've got a taco salad," Autumn chimed in.

"Gotta go back to the truck," Sawyer said. "I forgot the dessert." He looked at Summer. "It's a German chocolate cake from Luscious Layers."

"Quick!" she cried. "Give me a fork. I'm heading to the truck with Sawyer. That cake is all the supper I'll need."

Everyone laughed as the doorbell chimed. Soon, Darby and Jace had joined them. She greeted her cousin and Jace and chatted with them, learning that while they were living in a new apartment complex near Triple H, they had bought the land adjacent to West and Kelby.

"The construction crew broke ground yesterday," Jace said proudly. "It's too dark now, but you'll have to come over and walk the property."

"We share a tank with West and Kelby," Darby said. "It straddles both our properties. Jace has been doing some fishing with Eli, so I'm sure the guys and future kids will be down at the pond fishing."

The doorbell rang again, and Summer wondered who else might be coming. "I'll get it," she volunteered, heading to the front door.

When she opened it, her heart stopped.

Chance Blackstone stood there, cowboy hat in hand. His unruly, coal-black hair had been tamed into place, and his gray eyes were steady as they looked at her.

"Hey, Summer," he drawled. "I hear you're back in Hawthorne for good."

She swallowed, her heart now beating wildly against her ribs. "Yes. I'm going to try my hand at writing." She paused. "Come on in."

He stepped into the foyer, which suddenly seemed small. She also got a whiff of his cologne, mixed with the scent of leather. The combination was intoxicating.

"You didn't say anything at Christmas when we talked about you leaving New York."

"It wasn't in the cards then," she replied. "I did tell you I was working on a small-town romance novel. I'm proud to say I've completed it and will be starting another one come Monday."

"I suppose Monday is a good day to start a romance," he said, his gaze steady.

Summer swallowed, the butterflies madly flapping away in her belly. She had always had a crush on Chance Blackstone. He had been West's best friend since kindergarten and two years her senior. She had always looked up to him, thinking him smart, funny, and hot as hell.

Chance had never given her the time of day.

She didn't know if part of the reason was guy code. How a best friend's little sister should be off-limits. At least, that was one of the big tropes in romance. She'd edited a few of those over the years. Chance was polite and friendly to her. Then again, he was that way with everyone. Summer also thought he had never been attracted to her. She had been all legs and arms and awkward as all get out before she hit her teens. She'd also had a mouthful of braces and thick glasses. By the time the braces came off and she'd gotten contacts, Chance had moved on, graduating from Hawthorne High School.

Her choice of college had been SMU in Dallas. Not because it was where Chance was, but because Summer had entered and won a writing contest. The grand prize paid for a year's tuition at SMU. Her parents never could have afforded to send her to the private school, but the scholarship had made all the difference. Once there, counselors at the university had helped Summer in applying for other scholarships, and about three-quarters of her tuition and fees had been paid for by these scholarships during her next three years.

She hadn't rushed a sorority, though. Membership fees to those exclusive Greek clubs were expensive. And Chance was president of one of the most popular fraternities on campus. They had existed on the same turf, but they had lived in different worlds during their college years. She had seen Chance on the SMU campus maybe four or five times during the two years they overlapped. He had never seen her before, mostly because he was always with some beautiful Kappa or Tri Delt.

Summer knew even though they were now adults, Chance had no interest in her. The most she could hope for was that they could continue to be friendly toward one another. Maybe even become friends someday.

"Mondays are the best day to begin a romance," she replied saucily. "I plan for my hero and heroine to meet, and I promise that sparks will fly. That's what a romance novel is all about."

Chance studied her a long moment. "I wonder if real-life romances begin on Mondays?"

Was he *flirting* with her?

"I wouldn't know," she said breezily. "It's been too long since I've been in one."

"So, no brokenhearted guys left behind in the Big Apple?"

"Nope," Summer said cheerfully, stepping around him to head to the kitchen, her knees a little wobbly.

Then his fingers closed around her elbow. A tingle shot through her so fast, her head began to spin.

"Then maybe we can meet up for coffee," Chance suggested. "I'd like to hear about your time in New York."

She shook her head. "I know you only think of me as West's kid sister. You don't have to be so nice, Chance."

His fingers felt warm against her elbow as he said, "You haven't been a kid for a long time, Summer. I realized that back at Christmas when we talked. And I'm asking to take you to coffee because I want to. Not out of any sense of obligation."

"Really?" she asked, her butterflies high-fiving one another inside her.

"Really. That is, if you have time on Monday to do that. Starting a romance ... novel must be pretty time-consuming."

"I can take breaks," she said, trying to calm herself. "I wrote a lot of my first book in coffeehouses. Write. Sip. Edit. Write. Sip. Edit. I've got the pattern down."

"Sounds like you do. There's a new coffeehouse on the square. Not a chain. It's called Coffee Hour. They serve you coffee in big, white porcelain mugs. Could we meet at two? Maybe you'd have enough writing done by then and can take a break."

"Two is good," she heard herself say, thinking how surreal things had turned. She was going to have a coffee date with Chance Blackstone. *The* Chance Blackstone.

One of the most popular kids who had walked the halls of HHS.

And he had matured into a devastatingly handsome guy.

"Good. Two it is. That'll give me plenty of time in the field early in the day."

"We should go into the kitchen. Dinner's almost ready. Some of my favorites. I love chicken enchiladas. Don't you?"

She winced inwardly, knowing she was babbling now. But how could she remain calm when Chance Blackstone was paying attention to her? As if he were seeing her for the first time ever.

They returned to the kitchen, and West handed her a margarita. He passed one along to Chance, too, and then held up one of his own.

"Here's to Summer's return to Hawthorne. May she take the romance world by storm as she renews old friendships in her hometown."

"Hear-hear," said everyone, holding up glasses. She noted Kelby and Autumn toasted with bottled waters and wondered if anyone else picked up that Autumn wasn't drinking a margarita, a particular favorite of hers.

She took a sip of her own margarita and sighed. "Oh, it's sweet to be back in Texas. Thanks for welcoming me home."

The entire time Summer spoke, she was aware of Chance standing next to her, heat radiating from him, his cologne enticing her.

Tempting her.

"Everyone take a plate and circle around the island," Kelby instructed. "We're eating in the dining room. It's too chilly to be outside tonight."

As Summer filled her plate, she wondered why Chance had really asked her to join him for coffee. If she were reading too much into the situation. Or if he felt some of the sparks she had felt back at Christmas—and he was now acting on them.

Returning to Hawthorne was proving to be very interesting.

# Three

As they all sat down for the meal, Chance felt grateful to be at this table with these people. He realized he had isolated himself the last few years, pouring heart and soul into Blackstone Ranch. Especially now that his dad was gone, Chance felt the heavy mantle of responsibility on his shoulders.

He knew, though, that he had put his personal life on hold for too long for the ranch. As Tammy had told him, it was running smoothly now. Maybe he could aim for more of a balance in his life, working and seeing friends and family. Even doing a few things for himself.

He looked to Kelby, who was telling a story about an Instagram account she was handling for her social media and marketing business. He was proud of his sister for all that she had accomplished, but even more for what she had survived. She and Darby had been the best of friends forever, the same as he and West. The four of them had been a tight foursome in high school.

Gazing around the table, he saw the newcomers who had been added to their circle. Darby's husband, Jace. Jace's brother, Eli. He wanted to get to know these two men better. The same was true for Sawyer. Sawyer Montgomery had been two years ahead of Chance in school and a first-class athlete. He had been an All-State basketball player and had won an athletic scholarship to the University of North Texas. Chance believed Sawyer could have gone to the NBA and made his mark there, but a devastating injury had brought his college basketball days to a close. Sawyer had turned all his passion for basketball toward law school, graduating at the top of his class.

Chance wasn't certain why Sawyer had left Dallas since he'd had a promising career there in the district attorney's office. Then again, he looked at how many around this table had returned to Hawthorne after a decade or more away. Something about this town brought people back to it.

Autumn was speaking, so he focused on her for a moment. While she and her twin favored one another in the face and both possessed the same, unique turquoise eyes which West also had, Autumn was petite and curvy, with long auburn hair.

His eyes flicked to Summer, who was listening carefully to her sister's story. Again, Chance was struck by Summer's natural beauty. She must be about five-eight, with a willowy frame, her honey blond hair falling in long, soft waves below her shoulders.

The fact that she would be residing now in Hawthorne made him all the more determined to get to know her better. Their coffee date on Monday would be a start. That is, if you could call it a date. He wasn't quite ready to put a label on what he wanted with Summer. Chance just knew they were both aware of the spark between them. They owed it to themselves to explore it.

Summer said, "I can't thank you enough for coming and having dinner here tonight. I've missed so much about Hawthorne over the years. Despite being happy during the years I worked in the New York publishing world, I've felt the pull back to Hawthorne. Apparently, a lot of you felt the same. At least those who grew up here."

"Let's catch each other up on where we've been and what we've done," Kelby suggested. "Not in a boring way, though." She paused, thinking, and then added, "Why don't we talk about our favorite meal in the place we've lived? Darby, will you start us off?"

Darby smiled widely. "I think all of you know that I worked for Cheer USA for over ten years before I came back to teach in Hawthorne. I was able to travel to all of the lower forty-eight states, conducting cheer workshops. I was based out of Kansas City, which is known for its barbeque."

Her nose crinkled. "It is *not* Texas barbeque. Instead, I think my favorite meal in all those years was one in Charleston, a town I highly recommend people visit, not only for the food, but the great architecture and history. The best meal I got there was in a restaurant which used to be an old church. The stained-glass windows are impressive. I'll never forget the mussels. They came with andouille sausage, roasted peppers, and a smoked cream sauce on sourdough bread. And that was just the appetizer. I split my entrée of crab cakes with a friend who got steak so we could try both items. I don't remember what the dessert was, only that it was divine."

Darby turned to her husband. "What about you? With all your fancy meals in Dallas and beyond?"

Jace threaded his fingers through hers. "I've been a sports

agent ever since I graduated from Texas A&M. I've represented clients all across the country and have definitely taken them to some of the best restaurants, including several with a Michelin star. Even in Dallas, I only dined at the finest places for years."

Jace lifted their joined hands and kissed Darby's fingers tenderly. "But the best meal I ever ate in Dallas was the first one I shared with this beautiful lady. We went to Adelina's, a mom-and-pop Mexican joint in a strip shopping center. Hands down, it's the best food I've ever eaten. And the best company."

West asked, "What about you, Autumn? Houston has a lot of great restaurants."

Autumn smiled shyly. "Houston may have a lot of terrific places to eat, but I was usually working double shifts at the hospital and didn't get to go to any of them." Looking at West, she added, "I think my favorite meal is when we were in New Orleans last year for the Super Bowl. You took us to Brennan's. The bananas foster alone was worth the trip there, not to mention seeing you walk away as Co-MVP of the game."

Autumn looked at her husband. "What about you, Eli? You also lived in Houston a long time, even if we never crossed paths there."

He shrugged. "I worked eighteen-hour days in the ER, so a lot of my meals came out of a vending machine. Peanut butter crackers were my go-to. If I had time, I would eat in the hospital cafeteria, and that was nothing to brag about."

Eli grew thoughtful. "The best meals I have these days are the ones Autumn and I cook together. She started me out on the basics, such as spaghetti and fried chicken, and we've become a little more adventurous in our cooking. Wait. I will say the best meal I've eaten in Hawthorne was the first day I came here for my interview regarding the Triple H job. I went to Dizzy's Diner, and Dizzy himself seated me. Took my order. Chatted me up and brought me what was—up until then—the best meal of my life. It was pure diner food, which I'd never had before. I knew it, Dizzy, the diner, and this town were all something special. I'm proud to be a resident of Hawthorne."

Kelby chuckled. "Maybe I should put that on the Chamber of Commerce's website. The City of Hawthorne is one of my new clients at Social Synergy Creations. That's a wonderful testament to your new hometown, Eli."

"There's just something about Hawthorne. The warmth of the people. Everyone so friendly and giving. I can't imagine living anywhere else but here." Eli glanced to Autumn. "Or raising a child anywhere else."

Chance saw the look passing between them, with Autumn nodding slightly.

Eli looked around the table. "We've been keeping this under our hats, but it's about time that we start sharing our news. Autumn and I are going to have a baby."

The room grew festive with the announcement, people leaping to their feet and hugging both Autumn and Eli.

Chance shook hands with Eli. "You're right. Hawthorne is the best place to raise a family. Your kids will be better for growing up in a small town, where everyone seems to know one another. They'll have an entire town watching out for them."

He then brushed a kiss along Autumn's cheek. "You're going to be a great mom, Autumn. Your mom is a shining example of what a mother should be to her kids. Just do everything Meg did, and this baby will turn out better than fine."

They seated themselves again, and Kelby said, "Baby

news is hard to top. But let's get back to food." She looked to her husband. "West, what about you?"

"I did travel a lot during my NFL days, but we never really got to know the cities we played in or see much of them. We would go straight from the plane to the practice field. Then check into a hotel and have a team meeting. Almost every meal was eaten in that hotel. Some of the guys would go out and grab a bite, but I was never interested in doing that. I concentrated on the game and playing my best. I knew my contributions on offense would be important, so that's where my focus stayed."

West leaned back, crossing his hands behind his head. "But if we're talking great food? I think it's right here in Hawthorne. You can't get a better slice than at Pizza Palace. Eli's right in saying that Dizzy's Diner has the best home-cooked meals. If I never went anywhere else, I would be happy to stay in Hawthorne the rest of my life."

He looked to Kelby. "What about you, honey? You traveled around a lot yourself before coming back to Hawthorne."

Sympathy filled Chance, knowing his sister had been a nomad because of her worthless first husband. After being cut from one NFL team, Bax Porter would sign with another. And then another, resulting in multiple moves across the country for him and Kelby. His alcohol and drug use escalated, and Kelby had finally divorced him. Bax had been murdered in jail while awaiting to be tried for a murder he himself had committed.

Chance now looked to Kelby with interest, wondering what she would say.

"I think during my time in Dallas, I ate at some wonderful places. I worked for a clothing company in North-Park Center, and it has not only world-class shopping but terrific restaurants."

She named her favorite place there, where she used to meet some of her former sorority sisters for dinner and then said, "But my favorite meals these days are the ones when we all get together. Everybody bringing something, like tonight. I'm especially fond of Sawyer's chili and cornbread. That leads us to you, Sawyer, my fellow, former Dallasite. What was your favorite meal in Dallas during your years as an assistant DA?"

"Let's put it this way. I didn't travel in the same circles that Jace did," he said, causing them all to laugh. "As an ADA, I didn't rake in the cash the way attorneys in private practice do. I do recall one meal, though, which stands out above all the others."

Sawyer dabbed his mouth with his napkin. "I was prosecuting a man on a first-degree murder charge. I always try to get to know everything I can about the victim. In this case, I learned that DeMarvian was a kind man, one who would give you the shirt off his back. He was in his mid-thirties when he was robbed and killed. Had three little girls and a wife who worked as a nurse at Parkland. DeMarvian had worked in his parents' restaurant since graduating from high school. I ate there several times, both before and during the trial. His mom did most of the cooking. His dad seated customers and made the place feel like a home away from home.

"The day the guilty verdict came in, I saw no joy on his family's faces. They were good people who were trying their best to wrap their heads around losing their son. Husband. Father. They invited me back to the restaurant, which they closed. We ate ham, black-eyed peas, glazed carrots, and mashed potatoes with cream gravy. Dessert was pecan pie, with a thin, flaky, golden crust. DeMarvian's mother told me that this had been his favorite meal, and she was serving his favorite dishes in his memory. It was a solemn occasion.

They were hoping to be able to move on with their lives. I appreciated being included that day, but I never went back to the restaurant. Much as I wanted to, I knew I was a reminder of the most painful thing that had happened to them."

Sawyer placed his napkin on the table. "Sorry to bring down the mood."

"No, don't be," Summer told him. "We're all here for each other. It's one of the reasons I'm happy to be back in Hawthorne. To have the love and support of my family and hopefully make some new friends."

Sawyer smiled gratefully at his cousin. "Thanks, Sum. Okay, Ms. New Yorker. What was your favorite meal while you were living on the East Coast?"

She smiled, causing Chance's heart to beat a little faster.

"I'm afraid I was in your boat, Sawyer. Publishing houses aren't known for being overly generous when paying their employees, so I was always pinching pennies. I'd grab a frank from a Nathan's vendor as a splurge at lunch, but I usually packed one and brought it from home."

Summer paused. "A frank is a hot dog to you uninitiated. I did live in Brooklyn, however, and it's home to the best pizza in the world."

She told them about a place which was mere steps away from the foot of the Brooklyn Bridge, which crossed over into Manhattan.

"There are only about eight or ten tables in the place, packed tightly together, but it's literally the best pizza I've ever eaten. I'm just thankful that Pizza Palace here in Hawthorne is run by New Yorkers who understand what makes up a great crust. I'll have to get my pizza hankerings satisfied there. Or maybe I'll go to Italy one day and see if their pizza tops ours."

Summer's eyes flicked to Chance. "How about you, Cowboy? What's been your favorite meal?"

"I've had a good many of them," he began. "Not everyone may know this, but Big Jim wouldn't let me come back to Blackstone Ranch once I graduated from SMU. He told me I needed seasoning. I should gain experience at other companies and see something of the world. So, I worked and lived in different places, from Chicago to Denver to Seattle. All those cities have their share of foodies and great restaurants. I ate my fill, paying through the nose at some of those eating establishments.

"Then Dad said it was time for me to return home. The first meal I ate the night I got back was cooked by Tammy."

Chance looked at Eli and then Jace. "Tammy Carruthers is like a mom to Kelby and me. We lost our mom when Kelby was only a few days old. Tammy was Mom's best friend. She came to help out—and never left. Tammy became the loving woman who raised us, as well as serving as housekeeper, cook, and chief bottle washer.

"That night, Tammy made me pork chops, my absolute favorite meal. They were so tender that you could cut them with a fork. She also added green beans and mac and cheese, along with some of her jalapeño cornbread. We ended the meal with banana pudding. *That* was the best dinner I've ever eaten."

His gaze met Summer's, and she said, "I want to learn how to cook. Maybe Tammy would be willing to share her pork chop recipe with me. And I could try it out on all of you as a thanks for tonight."

"If you want it from her, you'll have to move quickly." Chance's gaze turned to Kelby. "I just found this out today, Kel. I know Tammy wants to talk to you about it, but she's leaving the ranch."

"What?" Kelby cried. "Where on earth is she going?"

Chance explained how Tammy had reconnected with Tommy, her high school love.

"Tommy retired after over thirty years in the military. He's a widower with no kids. Owns a body shop in Waco, where he and Tammy grew up. They still love each other after all these years and aren't willing to waste any more time being apart."

Kelby's eyes misted with tears. She looked to West. "I'm glad I came back to Hawthorne when I did. I can't imagine going a day—much less decades—without you in my life." She stroked her burgeoning belly.

West beamed at his wife. "I'm glad it didn't take over thirty years to track you down, babe. My life would be empty without you in it."

For a moment, everyone at the table was silent, lost in their own thoughts, and then Kelby said, "The Mavericks game is about to start. Why don't we give our food time to settle? We can serve dessert at halftime."

Everyone agreed, collecting dishes and returning them to the kitchen. When they went to the great room, Chance made certain that he took a seat next to Summer. She was very into the game, yelling at the refs and cheering when the Mavs made a great play. She even applauded when a Lakers guard hit a shot from mid-court as the buzzer sounded for halftime.

"That's pretty decent of you, cheering our opponents, Sutherland."

"Just because I'm a Mavs fan doesn't mean that I can't acknowledge a talented shot." She sighed. "I'm so happy to be back. Now, I can watch my teams on a regular basis."

"Do you like other sports besides basketball?" he asked.

"I like all sports," she declared. "Football will always be

number one in my heart, but give me a good hockey game or F1 race, and I'm happy as a clam."

Chance decided he wanted to take Summer to a game in Dallas. He wouldn't hit her up with that idea just yet. He would wait and see how their coffee date unfolded on Monday.

But in his heart, Chance knew that he was already falling for Summer Sutherland.

# CHAPTER
## Four

"I hate that you're going to be stuck in town all day," Autumn said as she and Summer got into Autumn's car.

"Don't worry about me," Summer told her twin. "I plan to get a ton of writing done today. First, though, I'm going to stop and have breakfast at the diner. Then I'll walk over to Coffee Hour. I wrote a lot of my first novel in coffeehouses in New York. There's just something soothing about sitting in one. It's usually quiet. People leave you alone. I think I'll get a lot done today."

She looked out the window. "This development is really coming up. You and Eli are going to be having all kinds of neighbors soon."

"We're lucky that we're on a cul-de-sac, so we don't get through traffic. The house was already built by the time Eli got the job offer from Hogan Health. It's actually part of his compensation package. We were allowed to decorate however we chose, but Hogan Health pays the mortgage on it."

Autumn talked a little about a new nurse she had just

hired for the cardiac unit, and Summer could tell how much her sister was enjoying her new position as Director of Nursing for Triple H.

They reached the town square, and Autumn pulled into a parking spot opposite Dizzy's Diner.

Summer turned and said, "I won't be able to write the entire time you're at work. I'll probably take a couple of breaks. Walk around the square and visit some of the new shops. A lot has changed since we went away to college."

"If you need me to run you home, just call."

"I may wind up walking over to the library," she said. "It's only about a mile or so from here. I do some of my best thinking when I'm walking. Text me when you're leaving work, and I'll let you know where I am, so you'll know where to pick me up."

She hadn't mentioned her coffee date to Autumn. Summer had no idea how long she and Chance would talk. As laconic as he could be at times, it might be over in ten minutes. She didn't know if she'd hang around Coffee Hour after Chance left or head to the library. She would play things by ear.

And try hard not to get her hopes up when it came to a certain cowboy.

Autum grinned. "You sure you want to be writing sexy scenes with Mom in view?"

"Surely, I could find somewhere out of her line of sight," Summer said, chuckling. "And I promise that I'm going to look at cars soon. I can't depend upon you or Eli for rides all the time. Have a good day. See you tonight."

Summer climbed from the vehicle and lifted her backpack, tossing it over one shoulder. She waved as Autumn drove off and then crossed the street, entering the diner.

Dizzy himself greeted her with a huge hug.

"Summer Sutherland, it's about time you came home. Your two siblings figured out Hawthorne is the place to be. I'm glad you've joined them. I know your folks are thrilled to have all their ducklings back."

"It's good to see you, Dizzy. I can't tell you how much I've missed your biscuits and gravy."

Dizzy grabbed a menu and said, "Then let's get you a plate of them and whatever else you'd like. Booth or table?"

"Booth," she told him, following the diner owner to a row of booths next to the windows looking out on the square. She set her backpack on the cushion and slid in beside it as he placed a menu on the table.

Knowing she would drink a couple of cups of coffee while writing today at the coffeehouse, she said, "I'd like a tall glass of ice water, please."

She handed him the menu. "I don't need to look at this unless you've changed it up."

He laughed. "Why would I change it when everything's just the way folks like?"

"Then I'll take a number two. Eggs over easy. Bacon crisp. And some of your glorious hash browns."

"Be right back, Summer," Dizzy said.

She had decided that she would most likely eat a big breakfast each day. That way, she could work through lunch, maybe snacking on a yogurt and a handful of almonds. She was eager to begin work on this second book in the trilogy. Her small town in the series was located in the Panhandle and had really taken shape in the first book. Summer had discovered through her editing job that setting could actually be an interesting character in itself, and she had made the town and surrounding area shine in book one, introducing different residents. She would use the first book's hero and heroine as her anchor couple, and they would appear in the next two books.

Summer was starting to rethink things, though. The small town and all its inhabitants might make for more than a trilogy. Of course, readers would have to buy the first book or two in order to give the series traction, but she could see this entire town coming to life in her mind, bringing new residents in to mix with the old, allowing different romances to blossom.

Dizzy returned with her food and water, and Summer put aside thoughts of plotting for the moment. Instead, she soaked up the atmosphere of the diner as she enjoyed her breakfast. The biscuits were her favorite part of it, so light and flaky. The white gravy, speckled with black pepper, gave just the right kick to things.

A few people stopped by her table, wanting to speak to her, telling Summer how glad they were that she'd returned home. As much as she had enjoyed living in New York, there was nothing like the friendliness of a small town in Texas. Since everyone seemed to mention her writing, she supposed her parents had spread the word. She only hoped she would be able to live up to her own hopes, as well as those of her parents.

Once she finished eating, she paid her bill and left the diner to walk a lap around the square so she could see which shops were still familiar to her and what new ones had opened during her years away from Hawthorne. She would try to write for a couple of hours and then take a break and go inside a few of them.

Summer headed for Coffee Hour and entered it. It was almost nine o'clock, and she saw a group of elderly gentlemen sitting at a table in the back. From the sound of their laughter, they were having the time of their lives. Most likely, they were all retired now and had been friends for decades. She would have to think about including a similar group in this upcoming book.

Going to the counter, a man in his mid-fifties with silver streaking his temples greeted her.

"Good morning. Welcome to Coffee Hour. I'm Ben Craft, the owner. What can I get you?"

"It's nice to meet you, Ben. I'm Summer Sutherland. I grew up in Hawthorne and have been away for several years now. I've just moved back, though, and will be working on a novel. I'll probably be a frequent flyer here and do a lot of writing."

"Ah, you're Joe and Meg's girl. I heard that you were coming home. It was New York where you were living?"

She nodded. "I worked as a book editor at Liberty House. Now, I'm going to try my hand at writing novels myself."

Summer asked for a hazelnut latte, and Ben rang her up, telling her to have a seat.

"I'll bring it to you."

She thanked him and went to a chair in the corner, opening her backpack and taking out her laptop. She also removed a notebook and pen. She had jotted down a few ideas and read over them before her coffee arrived.

Ben placed the oversized mug on the table in front of her and took the chair opposite her.

"Your mom tells me that you're writing a romance novel. If you ever need to know what's gone wrong in a marriage—and then what's gone right—ask away."

Summer was always looking for new ideas, and so she said encouragingly, "Tell me your story, Ben."

"In a nutshell, I ruined my first marriage. I spent my twenties as a roughneck in the oil fields of West Texas, working my way up to a field manager. Someone in the front office thought I had potential and tapped me to join them in corporate down in Houston. I married a gal who was the sweetest thing on earth, and she put up with a lot. Too much, as I quickly climbed the corporate ladder. Unfortunately, I chose to be married to the job first and her second. She got tired of the long, lonely hours. She left me—and I barely noticed."

Ben sat back in his chair, shaking his head. "I spent my entire thirties and forties at that oil company, making myself indispensable. Eventually, leading it as its president. And then the day came when I had a heart attack. I'd ballooned up to two-fifty. Never exercised. Ate too much and drank even more, and that didn't even include the chain smoking."

Her eyes widened. "You look so fit now. A picture of good health."

"Now, yes. Back then, I was a disaster," he told her. "The heart attack happened at my desk. Late at night. I fell to the floor and blacked out. No one found me until the next morning. I was rushed to the hospital. Had triple bypass surgery."

Ben looked her in the eyes. "I came out of that experience a different man, Summer. I'm one of those people who died on the operating table. Floated up. Saw myself and those trying desperately to save me. I told myself that if I had a second chance, I would make the most of it. Next thing I knew, I was back in my body. I'd always been about numbers and profits, even building myself a tidy fortune in the process. But I realized that I had no one to share it or my life with. No one was there for the highs, and they sure weren't present for the lows. My goal at first was to go back to work. That's all I wanted to do, despite what I'd said while out of my body. I wanted to show people I was still the same sharp, decisive leader."

She was intrigued by his story and could already see putting her own spin on it.

"But during my rehab, my perspective began to change. The therapists and nurses who worked with me showed me— a stranger—so much kindness and patience. I didn't have anyone else in my life doing that. It made me remember that promise of what I'd do with a second chance in life."

Ben leaned forward, bracing his arms on his thighs. "I decided that I was going to be a people person. I wanted to give back to others without asking for anything in return. I knew I could easily retire because I had plenty of money to do so. A week after I returned to work full-time, I told the company I was ready to leave and turned the reins over to new, younger leadership. I was given a very generous compensation package and took my time, about four months, deciding what I wanted to do next. I ate better. Exercised, trying things like tai chi and meditation, along with strength training and walking. And I decided I'd like to be someone who lived in a small town. Someone who became a part of his community. I started driving to various towns around the state and would stay a day or two, walking around, talking to people. I knew how there was a Starbucks on every corner in Houston. The coffee culture has definitely taken over. I thought opening a coffeehouse would be ideal, so that's what I did."

"So, you chose Hawthorne as your new home."

He nodded. "One of my first customers at Coffee Hour was a kind, attractive woman named Becky. She's a counselor at the high school. Never married. Ten years younger than I am. We hit it off. Friendship quickly turned to love. We've been married two years now, and those have been the happiest of my life. I have a loving woman to share my ups and downs with each day. I have a new purpose in life, taking care of those who come into my coffeehouse. I know I'm where I'm supposed to be, with the woman who is my soulmate, and I make certain that she knows every day just how much I love her."

"It's a beautiful story, Ben," Summer said, blinking back tears. "Thank you for being so open and sharing it with me."

"I don't want to say that I wasted the other part of my life. I worked in an important industry. I helped hire a lot of people and made a lot of money for our investors. My life is richer now, though, living in Hawthorne and giving residents a place to gather. I have people who stop by for coffee before they head to work. Carpooling moms who drop off their kids at school and head over to socialize here for an hour."

Ben paused and indicated the group of old men laughing. "You see those guys? They come in every weekday morning. Talking over old times and sharing their memories. I give people like them a place to go. A home away from home."

He rose. "I need to let you get busy now. That book isn't going to write itself. Feel free to use any little part of my story down the line."

Summer had already decided to do that very thing. There was a need in the world of romance for books featuring older couples. She decided Ben and Becky's story would be worth fictionalizing.

"Thanks for sharing with me, Ben. At some point, I'd like to talk with you and Becky together and hear more about your love story from her perspective. I don't know when I will write this, but what you told me has really intrigued me. I'd love to put my own twist on it."

"Just let me know when you want to get together, Summer. I can't wait to share this with Becky. She'll be thrilled to meet you."

She opened her laptop and signed in and then created a

new document. Quickly, she bullet pointed the basics of Ben and Becky's love story and then closed the file. She would need to mull over an older couple romance and decide if she wanted to include it in the series she was now writing or make it completely separate.

Going to a document which contained her outline for the new book, she read through the first page before starting the prologue. She was only two paragraphs into it when she was interrupted.

"Summer Sutherland. I hear you're a big-time author now."

It was a one of the members of her mom's book club, and Summer politely chatted with her for a few minutes.

She went back to work, reading the two paragraphs she'd written to get back into her story. This time, she only completed two new sentences before she was interrupted again by a busybody from her parents' Sunday school class. The woman talked for over ten minutes, asking Summer a question and then proceeding to talk instead of waiting for a reply. By the end of their conversation, Summer was ready to scream. The woman would probably have talked another hour, but Summer told her she needed to get back to her prologue.

Two hours later, she had written less than two pages. Ben Craft had created a warm, homey atmosphere at Coffee Hour, and plenty of people dropped by it. Summer knew far too many of them, and with Hawthorne being a small, friendly place, every single person had felt the need to come and chat with her. It frustrated her that she had so little to show for the entire morning. She decided she would have to leave the coffeehouse and find another place to work.

Slipping on her jacket, she gathered her things and placed her backpack on her shoulder. She waved goodbye to

Ben and stepped outside. She could walk the mile or so to the library now, but she was afraid the same thing would happen there. Plus, she would have to walk the mile back to meet Chance at Coffee Hour by two. Frustration filled her. She supposed she could stay home and write at Autumn and Eli's house each day. Eli had even offered his office to her. Summer had actually gone in and sat at his desk, but she decided it wasn't a place conducive to creativity. She preferred sitting somewhere casual, in a chair, with her feet propped up, if possible.

She decided to go into a few of the stores along the square and allow her temper to cool a bit, stopping at stores with clothing, antiques, and crafts. She left the square and walked a half mile to one of the local parks. With it being near noon on a February weekday, only a couple of moms were present with strollers and four toddlers, sliding and swinging.

Summer found a bench away from the playground and opened her laptop again, calmer now. Surrounded by the quiet of nature, she was able to begin writing again. The sun was so bright that even wearing her sunglasses, she couldn't read what was on her screen, so she closed her eyes and ran a movie in her head, capturing with her fingers what she saw in her mind's eye.

She finished the short prologue quickly and now felt creatively on fire, hitting return several times and typing Chapter One. She could worry about correct spacing later. Summer immersed herself in her story, new details coming to her about her characters. She knew the more she wrote, the better she would get to know them. At least, that was how her first book had turned out. It had caused her to go back and rewrite a few of the earlier chapters, but she felt that first book was stronger for having done so.

When she completed that chapter, she realized she was a

little chilly and thought she might head back to Ben's coffee-house now and get a cup of hot chocolate to warm her up before meeting Chance. Having dived deeply into her story, she hadn't thought about him, which was a good thing. She had been distracted by thoughts about him all yesterday. Maybe they would talk now, and nothing would come of it. Or they might decide simply to be friends.

What she really wanted, though, was to see if he might be feeling the same connection she did.

As she closed her laptop, she heard the bells from First Methodist Church, a few blocks away, beginning to ring. Once. Twice.

Summer realized it was already two o'clock now, and she was half a mile from the place where she was meeting Chance. Panic seized her as she jammed her laptop inside her backpack and zipped it up, slinging it on her shoulder as she took off running.

Hoping that Chance would still be waiting for her.

Chance dressed in his usual winter attire of flannel shirt, jeans, and boots. He would clean up before he went into town to meet Summer. Venturing downstairs, he saw Tammy putting her coffee cup into the dishwasher.

"How did your talk with Kelby go last night?" he asked, pouring himself a cup of coffee from the pot.

"Better than I would have expected," Tammy replied. "Then again, Kelby is madly in love with West, so she understands why I need to leave the ranch and be with Tommy. She hopes I'll come back once she has the baby and help out for a week or so. I promised her that I would." She hesitated. "I'd like to bring Tommy with me when I do. I want you to meet him, Chance."

He embraced her. "I'd like that, Tammy. Tommy is going to be a part of our family now since he's with you."

"Once I get to Waco, we're going to go to the courthouse and get hitched. No fanfare. Just say our vows and start our life together. Finally."

Chance took her hand and squeezed it. "I'm glad you're

getting your happily ever after, Tammy. I'm just sorry it took this long for it to happen."

She smiled. "I'm not. Tommy and I needed to live the lives we did, him serving his country and me here at the ranch with you and Kelby. It will be nice to finally be together, though."

"Does he have any family?" Chance asked.

"Not really. His late wife had a sister, but she's up in Wichita Falls and is pretty ornery. He hasn't seen her since the funeral. Tommy's folks are gone now, same as mine. We'll have each other."

"I hope you'll consider coming to the ranch for some of the holidays. Thanksgiving. Christmas."

Tammy kissed his cheek. "We'll work it out, honey. Don't you fret."

"I know you'll probably want to stay at Kelby's when the baby comes, but the door is always open here."

She squeezed his arm and slipped into her coat, heading down to the bunkhouse to cook for the hands. Chance began taking out items to make himself pancakes. Breakfast was the only thing he knew how to cook. Eggs. French toast. Bacon and sausage. During his years away from Texas, when he was partying a little too hard, he frequently woke up with a hangover. He'd found a solid meal helped both his head and belly. Once he'd returned to the ranch, he had eaten with the other hands, wanting to get to know them better and build strong relationships.

Now that he owned Blackstone Ranch, though, he made it a point to eat away from the men. They didn't need the boss hanging over them, listening to every word they said. They needed the freedom to relax and enjoy one another's company, even blow off a little steam. As for him, Chance enjoyed starting his day making breakfast and eating in solitude.

As he ate his short stack, maple syrup poured over it, he thought about what needed to be tackled for the week. He had trouble concentrating, though.

Because his thoughts kept returning to Summer.

He feared he was pinning too many hopes on this casual coffee date. It was hard for him to understand how he could go from not even thinking about settling down to suddenly wanting to desperately. Chance blamed the happy couples around him for this sudden change of heart. Seeing his friends and their happiness had spilled over to him, and he was wanting things he'd never had. He wondered if Summer Sutherland would be the girl for him. No, woman. He had to stop thinking of her as West's kid sister. She was thirty now. He knew because he'd gone to a party celebrating Autumn's thirtieth birthday last September.

"Get your head out of the clouds, Blackstone," he chided aloud, rinsing his dishes and putting them into the dishwasher. He would focus on the ranch, his priority, and let this afternoon's time with Summer work itself out later.

Chance went to the stables and saddled Rebel. The horse had become his favorite mount once he'd returned to Texas. Rebel had a coal-black coat and was as feisty as they came. Most of the ranch hands had given up trying to ride him by the time Chance had moved back to the ranch. He'd always loved a challenge and made it his business to make Rebel his horse. They understood one another, and he could count on Rebel in a pinch.

Monday mornings were reserved for riding the land. Chance rode to the front gate and went around the entire perimeter, eyeballing the property, checking to see if any of the fencing needed to be mended. He made note of where the different herds were and the water levels in the ponds. It always felt good to be out on the land his family had owned for five generations.

Once he finished his ride, he headed to where the hands would be having lunch. Since they ate at five every morning, they usually broke for lunch around eleven. Tammy always packed thermoses of coffee and provided thick sandwiches of meat and cheese, along with fruit and homemade cookies. He found the hands gathered near the cattle herd, sitting on the ground, eating.

He nodded to Buck Overton, who rose and came over as Chance dismounted.

"Anything new to report?"

"Still working on improving the pasture," Buck told him. "We've got the brush under control, but we're still trying to get rid of a few of those invasive plants. We need to get a better handle on them. I don't want them to spread."

"Got it. If you need another pair of hands, I can be in the field all day tomorrow."

"We do," Buck told him.

"Then I'll join you after breakfast," he assured Buck.

Buck was the only college graduate among the ranch hands, with a degree in farm and ranch management from A&M. He'd previously been a hand at two other ranches, and Chance knew they were lucky to have him at Blackstone Ranch now. With more of Chance's time being devoted to the business end of things, he knew the time was coming when he would need to have eyes and ears in the field for him. He wanted to mull over the offer he would give Buck, though. Right now, he served as head hand, but it was time to give Buck a better title and more responsibility, else he could see losing him in the near future.

As he started to mount Rebel again, one of the hands stood and approached him.

"You need to talk about something, Joaquin?"

"Yes, Mr. Chance."

He wished the ranch hands would simply address him as Chance, but he knew they were showing a sign of respect for his position as the owner of the ranch.

"Then let's take a walk." Chance handed his reins to Buck. "Be right back."

They moved away from the other hands, and Joaquin said, "Miss Tammy told us at breakfast that she's leaving the ranch."

"She is," he confirmed.

"You will need a new cook," Joaquin said. "And someone to clean for you at the big house. The bunkhouse, too. I know Miss Tammy didn't clean it. That we do it." The ranch hand shook his head. "We could do better, Mr. Chance, but we're tired after a long day on the land."

He had never thought of that and would mention it to Tammy. Maybe whoever she hired to clean his house once a week could also go down to the bunkhouse a day or two a week and keep it in shape.

"I have someone to tell you about," Joaquin continued. "My cousin Zeke and his wife Maria. They would be good for Blackstone Ranch."

"Tell me about them," he encouraged, always preferring a personal recommendation over cold interviews.

Joaquin briefly described the experience the couple had, Zeke as a cook and Maria as a housekeeper, and how they were now out of a job.

"Their boss sold his ranch," Joaquin explained. "It won't be a ranch anymore. They're going to build on the land. The horses have been sold off. You bought one of their horses, Mr. Chance. Moonlight."

Chance knew the ranch Joaquin referred to. He had purchased one of their studs for his own small breeding program. If this couple had worked for Bart Nelson, Moonlight's owner, that was recommendation enough. The man was a picky perfectionist and would have expected a lot from his hired help.

"How soon do you think they could be here?" he asked, knowing Nelson's ranch was down in the Hill Country.

"They are in Ft. Worth now, visiting relatives and looking for work." Joaquin paused. "But they have two little ones, Mr. Chance."

He had never hired a couple and knew a family couldn't stay in the bunkhouse with the other hands. He certainly wasn't willing to have them in the big house since one day, he'd be raising his own family there. There was a cabin on Blackstone land, but he had been thinking that Buck might move into it when Chance promoted him. The need for an immediate cook, however, was more pressing than separate housing for Buck. He decided this couple could move into the cabin, and he could deal with housing for Buck later.

"Give me Zeke's contact information," Chance said, retrieving his phone from his pocket.

Joaquin did the same, pulling up his cousin's number. Chance entered Zeke Benevides into his cell's contact list.

"Give your cousin a call now and tell him I'm interested in speaking to him and Maria about working for me. I'll wait an hour before I call. That way, they can talk over anything you tell them about Blackstone Ranch."

The ranch hand beamed at him. "Thank you, Mr. Chance. Thank you. I promise you they are hard workers, just like me."

He clapped Joaquin on the back. "I appreciate you letting me know. Now, go make that call."

Joaquin stepped away as Chance headed back to claim Rebel.

"He tell you about his cousin?" Buck asked.

"He did. I'm going to interview Zeke and Maria by phone, but I can tell you now, I'm going to hire them. Joaquin has vouched for them, and if they have half his work ethic, it'll be good move."

Buck nodded. "After Tammy let us know this morning that she was leaving, Joaquin came to me and asked if he could talk to you about someone who might be a good replacement for her. I told him I'd let him approach you, which is why I didn't say anything before."

"I'm glad he spoke up. I hope this'll solve a big problem for me." Chance paused. "He let me know they have two kids, so I was thinking about letting them stay in that old cottage. It will need a little fixing up, though. Tammy can help supervise a couple of the hands. It definitely needs to be painted. Aired out. Floors scrubbed."

"Just tell Tammy to let us know what needs to be done. We'll handle it," Buck assured him.

He took the reins from Buck and climbed atop Rebel. Joaquin came running toward him.

"You can call anytime, Mr. Chance. They already know I'm happy here."

"Okay, I'll head back to the house and do that. Thanks again, Joaquin."

He went to the stables and handed off Rebel to Hank, the hand who worked with the horses. Returning to the house, he found Tammy in the kitchen, baking cookies. One batch had already come out of the oven and cooled on racks.

Snagging one, he bit into it. "Yum. There's nothing like a

peanut butter cookie. Hey, do you have time to do an interview with me?"

"Sure," she said. "You've already got someone coming by?"

Quickly, he explained Joaquin's pitch for his cousin and wife to take over the cooking and cleaning. He mentioned how the bunkhouse also needed more cleaning, and Tammy agreed.

"I keep the kitchen sparkling, but I know those boys can be a little lax regarding the rest of the place. Let's just say that I wait to hit the restroom until I'm back here since their aim is not always the best."

Chance laughed. "Let me grab my tablet—and another cookie—and then we'll call them."

The call went even better than he had expected. Tammy peppered the couple with questions and then told him that she was satisfied with what she'd heard.

"If Tammy is happy, that means my hands will be, too," Chance told the pair, whose hopeful faces now bore smiles.

He named a salary and explained how they would be allowed to live in a three-bedroom house on the property, not far from the bunkhouse.

"I know you have two kids, and while my hands are respectful, their language is a little salty at times. Besides, this will give your family privacy and time together."

Zeke said, "We are so grateful, Mr. Chance. This means everything to us. We liked working with Mr. Bart, but there's no place for us now with him."

"How soon can you get here?" Chance asked.

"The day after tomorrow," Maria said. "It will give us time to pack and say goodbye to our family. They have been kind enough to let us stay with them."

"Sounds good." He gave them directions to Blackstone

Ranch and added, "Tammy will be here for a couple of days to walk you through everything, but then you'll be on our own."

They ended the call, and Tammy said, "I can't believe how fast we solved that problem, Chance. They'll be here on Wednesday. I'll stay through Friday. I'll be in Waco by Saturday."

She hugged him. "I need to start doing some packing. And I still have a few lists to compose to give to you. First thing, though, is to tackle the cabin."

"Buck can pull as many men as you need to get it fixed. You'll need to move quickly, though, especially since I think it needs painting."

"Then I'll go see him right now. We can move the furniture out and sweep and mop. I'll send Hank into town for paint and anything else once I've had eyes on the place."

He glanced at his watch. "I'm going to get cleaned up. I need to go into town for a bit myself."

"See you later."

Chance got into the shower, washing the smell of horse from him. He dabbed on a bit of cologne and then shaved. He wondered what to wear and then laughed. Summer knew who he was, a cowboy, through and through. No need to wear anything different from what he usually did, so he slipped into a fresh flannel shirt and clean jeans before tugging on a nicer pair of boots than those he wore in the field.

He tamed his hair as best he could and grabbed his cowboy hat and jacket, going to his truck. The drive into town only took ten minutes, and he parked on the square, finding a spot only two doors down from Coffee Hour.

When he entered, he waved at Ben, the owner, and said, "I'm meeting someone. We'll order once she gets here."

Ben's brows shot up. Chance had been coming here ever since Ben opened the place.

And he had never met anyone. Much less a woman.

"Sounds good," Ben replied, going back to polishing the counter, biting back a smile.

Chance glanced around, surprised that Summer wasn't here. She'd left him with the impression that she would be working on her novel at Coffee Hour before they met. He looked at his watch, seeing it was five till two. Big Jim had always said if you were five minutes early, that was barely on time, and Chance had lived by that his entire life.

He moved to the rear of the coffeehouse and took a seat facing the door so he could see Summer come in. Two o'clock came.

No Summer.

Five after.

Still no Summer.

Disappointment flooded him. He had looked forward to spending some time with her, getting to know the adult Summer Sutherland better. They had chatted a bit this past Christmas, the first time he'd seen her in several years. He'd found her interesting and funny. Maybe she had changed her mind.

Chance decided his time was too valuable to wait around for anyone, and he stood. Just as he did, the door to Coffee Hour opened, and Summer came flying in. She spied him and practically galloped across the room to him, her face flushed, breathing heavily.

"I ran," she got out. "I couldn't write here. They wouldn't leave me alone, so I went to the park and I started writing and I got caught up and then the church bells rang and I was late and I'm sorry, Chance."

All of that came out in a rush.

Summer looked directly into his eyes. "I was so afraid you wouldn't wait. That you'd already be gone." Then she sighed, a radiant smile spreading across her face. "But you did wait. And my heart is still racing. Partly from running.

"And mostly because I was eager to see you."

Something inside him began to glow. It spread like wildfire through him. Chance stepped to her, resting his hands on her shoulders.

"I will always wait for you, Summer. I'm just glad you're here now."

# CHAPTER
## Six

Embarrassment washed over Summer, knowing she had babbled away. Heat burned in her cheeks.

But Chance's hands rested on her shoulders now, his gaze intent. A calm descended upon her. Her breathing slowed, even as her pulse began to speed up.

Because of his touch.

Nervously, she wet her lips, catching the flare of desire that sprang to his eyes. Suddenly, she felt feminine power filling her. She was aware of the electricity between them.

She hadn't been wrong.

*He felt it, too.*

"Let's get your backpack off," he said, turning her so he could remove it, gently pulling the straps down her shoulders. He set it so that the backpack leaned on the chair next to her.

"Thank you," she said, her mouth going dry.

Summer had never experienced such a rush of potent feelings before. She was afraid to put a name to it. Scared it was mere lust.

When she wanted more from him.

"Don't rush it," she said under her breath, causing Chance to frown.

"Nothing," she said more loudly. "I'm just worn out. It has been a heck of a day."

He reached for her hands, taking them in his. She didn't realize how cold they had been until surrounded by his warmth.

"You've been outside a long time—without wearing gloves," he lightly chastised.

"I can't type in gloves. Mine are too thick. I used to have thinner ones that let me use my cell phone, but New York winters are frigid. I gave away the thin pair and bought bulkier ones."

"You should've kept both."

She laughed. "I'll bet you've never been to New York before."

He smiled. "You'd lose that bet. I went on several business trips during my twenties."

Chance still held her hands, and she wasn't about to break the spell and make him aware of that fact.

"Then you stayed in some fancy hotel with a great view and a big closet."

"That about sums it up."

"My apartment, if you could call it that, probably would've fit inside that hotel closet."

The corners of his mouth turned up. "You're exaggerating."

"I rented a place just under four hundred square feet. I didn't even have a bed. I slept on the couch. Which I could sit on and reach out and touch the kitchen counter, where I had a microwave and tiny fridge. No oven. And it only took about five steps to get to the bathroom. The sink inside it also served as the kitchen sink. As big as you are, you wouldn't have even fit inside my shower. And the hot water would run out after two minutes. I learned to take the fastest showers of my life."

He squeezed her hands. "I want to hear more about your life in New York." Chance glanced down at their joined hands and then back up at her. "I think your hands have warmed up now."

They certainly had—as well as her cheeks.

"Let me get us something to drink."

Summer pulled her hands from his. "No, the coffee's on me. I almost stood you up, so I need to make it up to you."

"But I asked you to meet for coffee. I should be the one paying."

"Not a chance, Blackstone," she said, sitting on the chair and reaching into her backpack, extracting her wallet. "What's your order?"

"Coffee black," he told her.

She frowned at him. "No way. This is a coffeehouse, Chance. You can get anything you want here. Lattes. Expressos. Even—"

"What's wrong with my order?"

"It's ... not fun."

His dark brows shot up. "Not fun?"

"You know what I mean. Like I usually eat cereal or oatmeal for breakfast. If we went out to brunch, would I get that? Absolutely not. That's the boring, regular stuff I eat every day. Brunch is *fun*. It's Belgian waffles and French toast and eggs Benedict and mimosas. The same rule applies at a coffeehouse. You get something you normally wouldn't drink at home."

He studied her wordlessly, taking in what she said. "Surprise me."

"Okay. I will."

Summer headed to the counter, seeing Ben was the only barista present.

"Hey, Ben. I'm back. I'm going to need a large hazelnut latte and large caramel macchiato."

"He won't drink that. Chance. He's never ordered anything but a black house coffee."

She smiled confidently. "I am broadening Mr. Blackstone's horizons."

Ben laughed. "This ought to be good. Coming right up, Summer."

She returned to where Chance waited. He rose again as she arrived and waited for her to take a seat. She had forgotten that's what a gentleman was taught to do in Hawthorne. It made her feel good to be back in her small Texas hometown.

Slipping off her coat, Summer placed it on the back of her chair. She saw Chance had also removed his jacket but left his cowboy hat on.

"Do you mind removing your hat?" she asked. "I'd like to be able to see your eyes better."

She loved their unusual gray color, which only added to his sex appeal. That included his unruly hair, black as midnight, and cheekbones which could cut glass. She was five-eight, but he had least half a foot on her. He was lean yet muscular, toughened by life on a working ranch. Summer couldn't help but wonder what he looked like under his cowboy clothes.

Chance removed his hat. "Sorry. Should've done that before—being indoors. I'm not often in town, around people. My hat just is a part of me."

"Well, you look good in it," she said brightly, hoping that didn't sound too flirtatious. "What do you want to know about New York? You told me back in December that you've lived in big cities. I think while they all must have their own personalities, they also must feel alike in many ways."

"Chicago is frenetic," he shared. "Fast-paced like Manhattan. Everyone in a hurry. And that wind whipping off Lake Michigan can be a booger bear come winter. Seattle is the exact opposite. Laid back. Funky. A Starbucks or some other coffeehouse on every corner. Denver has those amazing views and a huge beer culture. They say beer is the new gold in Denver. Just like Seattle has an abundance of coffeehouses, Denver has a ton of microbreweries."

He raked a hand through his hair. "If they were people, I'd say Chicago would be a Wall Street trader, always in motion, making the deal, with a deep-dish pizza ready to devour when the trading day ends. Seattle is an old hippie, freethinking, dressed in Birkenstocks and a shirt from a secondhand clothing store, sipping a coffee and smoking a joint. Denver is a guy in his late twenties, cutting a deal one minute and tasting a flight of craft beers the next before heading out for a long hike."

"I've never been to any of those places," she admitted. "You make me want to see them."

"Maybe we'll go one day."

She couldn't quite read the look in his eyes. "Maybe."

"How would you classify New York?" he asked.

"I assume you mean the city, and when you say the city, most people think of Manhattan. The five boroughs are all very different. Manhattan is that guy who's always in a hurry, brushing past people and bumping them, never stopping to apologize. But it's got the bright lights. The great restaurants, from Michelin star places to little holes in the wall. And I enjoyed going to all the museums. They have a museum for everything. I really liked spending time at The Cloisters, which housed medieval art and tapestries. Its grounds overlook the Hudson. Fall is the best time at The Cloisters."

Summer laughed. "They even have a museum dedicated to ice cream."

"Now you're talking my love language," Chance teased.

Ben appeared, two large mugs in hand. "Who gets what?"

"Give him the macchiato first," she suggested. "He doesn't know it, but he's going to try both."

"I am?" Chance asked, arching one brow, causing her to laugh.

Ben set the mugs down. "Holler if you need a refill."

"Will do," Summer said as he left. To Chance, she said, "I'm eager to see what you think, sampling two new, different coffees."

He picked up the mug in front of him, frowning slightly as he peered down at it. "What is this exactly?"

"A caramel macchiato starts with a shot of espresso and a little vanilla syrup. Then you pour steamed milk over that and finish with a drizzle of caramel sauce. The caramel adds not only sweetness, but it caramelizes the flavor. Try it," she encouraged.

He brought the mug to his lips, and suddenly, Summer wanted to take the mug from his hands and climb into his lap so she could explore those sensual lips with her own.

She had gone off the deep end. These kinds of thoughts had to stop.

Instead, she watched Chance taste the brew. Swallow. Then he smiled.

"Not half bad." He took another sip.

"Better than coffee black?" she teased, causing him to give her a mock frown.

Sliding the other mug toward him, she said, "Give this one a try now. It's a hazelnut latte." Before he could ask, she added, "It also has espresso, along with steamed milk and sweetened with hazelnut syrup. It'll taste rich and nutty."

Cautiously, he lifted the second mug, staring into it. Then he took a sip. Paused. Took another one.

"I like this better. Don't get me wrong. The first one was really good. This is more to my taste, though."

"Then you keep it. I'll take the macchiato," she said, her fingers curling around the handle so she could bring it closer. "See, isn't this more fun than a boring house blend? I've opened a whole new world to you. Next thing you know, you'll be ordering flat whites and peppermint mochas. Maybe even pumpkin spice lattes next fall."

"You just think you've enticed me to the dark side, Sutherland. The minute we leave Coffee Hour, I'll be back to my tried-and-true black coffee."

"I'm not saying never drink black coffee again. Just when you find yourself at a place which specializes in coffees, have a little fun with it. Loosen up."

"Hmm." Chance took another sip of his latte. "I guess I could get used to this. Away from the house. I'm not ordering any fancy machine for the kitchen at the ranch, though."

"It's enough to know that if you come in here again that you'll spice up your order."

"Only if I have someone to drink it with. Like you."

Was she reading too much into his words? Summer couldn't figure Chance out. Then again, she'd never really known him.

And she decided to speak up and say so.

"I guess I don't really know you well enough to know what you like to drink. Or eat. Or do. You were always West's friend. Hanging with him. You were the brother he never had. When I think back to my childhood, you were always around, but I never really knew much about you. Yes, you played football. You loved to ride horses. West always said you were really smart. But that's it. I guess I'm ready to know the man you are now, Chance."

"Ditto," he said. "You were West's pesky little sister, with a mouthful of metal and thick glasses. I do remember you were funny. And popular. You always had a lot of friends around."

"Thank goodness I finally got those braces off." She smiled at him, deliberately showing her teeth. "They did their job. And I got contacts, too, which made a world of difference. Especially in cheerleading. After college, I had Lasik eye surgery done. It was able to correct my nearsightedness and astigmatism. No more cleaning contacts and having different solutions lined up on the bathroom counter."

She took a sip of her coffee. "Let's start from scratch then. I mean, I know a little about where you lived after college. You've heard about my apartment in Brooklyn. Let's just go from there and see if we have enough in common to become friends."

Chance held her gaze a long moment and then said, "What if I want to be more than friends?"

# CHAPTER
## Seven

Summer forgot to breathe. She was lost in Chance Blackstone's eyes. Then she gulped air.

"Really?" she squeaked.

"Maybe," he said, and she heard the tiny bit of hesitation.

"I don't want to mess this up," she said, placing her cards on the table. "I might want a little more, too, but I think it would be smarter to get to know one another before we make a decision like that. After all, we have a lot of people in common. It would be awkward to leap into something and then discover we weren't a good fit for one another."

"So, try on friendship first to see how it fits?" he asked. "And then if that feels good, go a little deeper?"

All Summer could think of was him thrusting into her, her begging him to go deeper and harder and faster. She sensed the blush spreading across her cheeks and hoped he would never discover where her mind had just gone.

"Yes. Try things as friends. Then ... see where things might lead."

"I could do that," he said agreeably. Then he grinned. "Especially if we sip hazelnut lattes together."

She laughed. "Oh, you are *so* hooked. I can tell."

He might be hooked on lattes, but she was fast becoming addicted to him.

And that scared the hell out of her.

Trying to keep things light, she said, "What did you do after SMU? In those cities you talked about?"

He talked a few minutes about the different jobs he'd held. Accounting. Finance. Marketing. Logistics.

"I dipped my toe into several ponds. It was what my dad wanted for me. He wouldn't let me go to A&M with West. I had thought I'd major in farm and land management or agribusiness, to better prepare me to work on the ranch. While Big Jim was set in his ways, he knew the world of ranching was changing, and he wanted me prepared for that. He told me to work in various fields. Take jobs with different responsibilities and ways of thinking."

Chance looked sheepish. "And to enjoy myself. He said a small town like Hawthorne could stifle a young man. He encouraged me to sow my wild oats, so I did."

"Were you like West when he played for the Cowboys?" she asked. "A different woman every week?"

"Pretty much," he admitted. "I worked long hours at my various jobs. I had a great work ethic and did my best to be indispensable and creative. I also played hard after hours, Summer. But like West, I never had any serious relationships. Then I got the call from Dad that I had been waiting for, and I was able to come home to Hawthorne. Back to the ranch. And I've pretty much lived like a monk since. I'm up at four-thirty. In bed by nine at the latest. I work with the ranch hands, doing physical labor for half a day, then I return to the house, where I keep an office, and I deal with the business end of things"

"You really haven't dated anyone since you've been back?" she asked, curious.

"Nope. Well, I have had two dates. Both the first month I came back, and that was three years ago. They were a bust. Ever since then, I've kept my head down. Worked hard." He sighed. "Worked even harder since Dad's death."

Sympathy filled her. "Big Jim was a great man, Chance, but you don't have to fill his shoes. Walk in your own instead. You'll make your mark in your own way. He wanted you to experience other places and businesses. That way, you could bring back new ideas to Blackstone Ranch. Like you said before, your dad was known for being set in his ways, but the world is changing. As the owner of Blackstone Ranch now, you'll have the flexibility to change with the times."

"Thank you," he said, sincerity shining in his eyes. "I have a tendency to doubt myself at times."

"A little doubt is good. It keeps you on your toes."

"What about you?" he asked. "You came home pretty abruptly. Were you unhappy in your job? Or with New York? You've already told me you didn't leave any broken-hearted guys behind."

Summer paused a moment, collecting her thoughts. "Have you ever loved and hated something at the same time? That describes my time at Liberty House. I started as an editorial assistant straight out of college. I worked with senior staff from the planning stages to the actual production of a book. That meant helping various departments, from creative to editorial, production, and even marketing. I helped coordinate the activities between these departments. I even acted as a liaison to authors and handled things such as their copyrights.

"That was in addition to getting in a little proofreading when asked. I also had to handle tasks any admin would— answer the phone. Managing calendars for the higher ups. Doing their expense reports."

"Sounds like you hit the ground running," Chance said.

"I was fortunate to have some good people mentoring me. I moved up to being a copy editor, where I assisted in a book's marketing campaign. I'd write the copy for the book's blurb and get author quotes endorsing it. I'd also write author bios, website copy, and handle press releases and social media posts for authors assigned to me."

She took a sip of her macchiato. "But my objective was to be an editor. Eventually, I became one. I would seek out manuscripts and review the promising ones from the slush pile, as well as work with authors assigned to me. I would edit all their content. I read each manuscript with a fine-tooth comb, giving them notes on how to improve scenes."

"Like what?" he asked, clearly interested.

"Oh, maybe having the characters show more emotion. Maybe extending a conversation. Beefing up their reaction to something which had occurred. Or if I thought a transition was lacking from one scene to another or one chapter to another, helping the author to figure how to smooth things out. Sometimes, I would even suggest adding a scene to firm up the plot. Other times, I would ask for a scene to be deleted, especially if it repeated information previously given in the book. I tried to help each of my authors find their voice. Then with a finished, polished, proofed manuscript, I would work hand-in-hand with the production and marketing staffs to support all promotions on behalf of the author and book."

"It sounds like a lot of intense work," he noted.

"It was. I was juggling all kinds of authors. Baby ones

with a debut book. Midlist authors, ones who sell steadily but aren't those who make their publishing houses millions. I even edited a few authors who'd made a bestseller list. It was a hodgepodge, but it eventually became draining. When I moved to New York, I was young and had a pretty active social life. That began to fizzle the higher I climbed the ladder at Liberty House. By the end, I'd put in ten-to-twelve-hour days at work and then go home and edit for another two to three hours. I had no life and was starting to burn out."

"Then why stay in the book world?" he challenged. "I know you're working on a novel of you own."

"That's different. For now, I make my own hours. Have complete creative control. If something doesn't get done, I have only myself to blame. To liken it to the navy, I was a top officer on a nuclear sub. Now, I'm the captain of my very small fishing boat. I can sail into uncharted waters, going wherever I want to go."

"Eventually, you'll have to submit your work to a publishing house. Will you try your old place of employment?"

Summer stifled a laugh, coughing into her hand. "No. I don't think they'd be a good fit for what I'm writing."

"Which is?" he pressed.

It wasn't that Liberty House didn't buy romance. They bought quite a few authors in that genre, but after the way things ended with Dragon Lady and the NDA, she would be radioactive to them.

"I'm writing a romance series about a small town in the Texas Panhandle. I've already finished the first book. I'm going to try to write two over this next year. I've planned it as a trilogy, but this town is really coming alive, both in my head and on the page. Maybe it'll be more books. As to whether I submit to a traditional publishing house or not, that remains to be seen. I've discovered that readers don't really care who publishes a book. If they're interested, they simply want to read the book. There's a possibility I might go the indie route and publish it on my own. Of course, that means hiring a team to help me with that. A cover designer. An editor. A proofreader. It's early days, though."

She laughed. "And I will have to find a place to write. I wrote in coffeehouses in New York, simply to get out of my tiny, cramped apartment. I'd order a coffee and write for several hours without being disturbed."

"When you rushed in, you said people wouldn't leave you alone. What did you mean by that?"

She shook her head. "I think my parents are almost too proud of me. They might as well have taken out a front-page ad in the newspaper which announced I was moving home and would be working on a book. I would write a sentence, and someone would come up to chat with me. Welcome me home. Tell me about their family. Ask me what I was writing. Five, ten minutes would go by. Then I'd excuse myself, they'd leave, I'd get two lines written, and it happened all over again. And again. And again." Summer chuckled. "Hawthorne is just too friendly."

"That's when you went outside to write?"

"I was afraid to go to the library. Mom being there. Also, people would probably feel free to come up and interrupt me, just like they did here at Coffee Hour. I walked to the park closest to the square, found a bench, opened up my laptop, and escaped into my own world."

Summer bit her lip and then gave Chance a rueful smile. "I was so wrapped up in my writing, that I lost track of time. When I finished a chapter and began packing up, I heard the

Methodist bells ring twice. Then I ran like hell from the park to Coffee Hour."

"I almost left," he admitted. "My dad was a stickler about time. If something started at seven and you showed up at seven, then it was as if you were ten minutes late." He hesitated and then added, "I thought you might have changed your mind. About meeting with me."

"No," she said firmly. "I wanted to be here today. I enjoyed being around you the other night. I ... wanted to see where this might go. And now we know. We're going to aim for friendship first. Maybe we'll stay in the friend zone. Maybe we won't."

His gaze met hers. "Does my new friend need a refill?"

"No. I don't drink caffeine after three in the afternoon. I like that it pumps me up and gets me going in the morning. Keeps me sharp when I'm writing. But it can cause havoc with my sleep."

"I get that. I switch to decaf once I get home from working with the hands. Or I drink water. Are you at least happy with the pages you wrote at the park?"

"Very satisfied," she confirmed. "I'll read through them tonight and tweak it a little, but right now, I'm definitely on the right track."

"If you don't write at Coffee Hour, where will you go? You can't sit outside every day. At least not until the weather warms up. And then you know how brutal summers can be here in Texas. You might die of heatstroke come July, even if you're sitting in the shade."

"I'm staying with Autumn and Eli right now. Eli offered me his office, but it's so spartan. I had wanted to go somewhere else to write because I don't want to associate home with work. I'd go to my parents, but they're starting some very noisy renovations this week, and they're likely to go on for a while."

"How about coming to the ranch? I'll be the only one living there once Tammy leaves this coming weekend. I'm gone until a little before noon each day, then I spend the rest of the afternoon in my office. Occasionally, I come out for a snack, but you could write wherever you were comfortable."

"That's a very generous offer, Chance, but I'll have to pass. I don't even have a car now, so walking to the ranch would be too far."

"I could come get you."

Summer shook her head. "I won't mess up your day. Although I suppose Autumn could drop me off. No, that's out of her way. I just need to buy a car as soon as possible so that I can get around on my own. I was thinking of asking her if she would ride with Eli to work tomorrow so I could borrow hers and go car shopping."

"Do you know what you want to buy?" he asked.

"I'm open to a good deal. I don't have my eye on any particular make or model." She giggled. "I haven't even been behind the wheel of a car in years. I used the subway to get to work and around New York, throwing in an occasional rideshare. I applied for a New York driver's license once I got there, but all I've ever used it for is identification purposes."

"You'll need to get a Texas license."

"Not yet. I don't have a permanent address. Autumn said I could stay with her for as long as I wanted, but with her being pregnant, I need to get out long before the baby comes. I don't want to be a fifth wheel to her happy family."

"I'll take you car shopping," Chance said. "You want to go tomorrow? Let's do it."

"Could you be away from the ranch on a weekday?"

He laughed easily. "Cattle and horses don't know the

difference between a weekday and weekend. Ranching is a seven day a week business, Summer. I'm the boss, though. I can do what I want. In fact, I can put in three or so hours and then come get you. Think about where you want to shop."

"You'd know better than I would."

"Okay, I'll think about where to go. Your homework assignment is to get online and look at cars. New and used. See what appeals to you and be able to let me know by tomorrow. The closest dealerships are in Decatur. We'll start there and see how it goes. Okay? We'll make a day of it."

How could she say no to spending an entire day with Chance Blackstone?

"All right," she agreed.

"I'll pick you up at nine-thirty. We can be in Decatur by ten." He paused. "How are you getting home from town?"

"Autumn said she'd text me when she's leaving work. I'll tell her I'm here."

"Nope. Text her now that you've got a ride home."

Her stomach exploded with a mass of butterflies. "Okay."

She dug her cell from her backpack and saw she had a voicemail from Celia Cameron. She would call her later. Summer texted Autumn.

> Getting a ride from Chance. See you when you get home.

Autumn had already given her a key to the house, so she wouldn't be locked out when they got there.

Her phone dinged, and Summer saw a thumbs up from her twin.

"Okay, Autumn knows. Are you ready to leave now?"

Chance looked at her a long moment, causing her heart to bump against her ribs. "Yeah. Let's go."

They slipped into their coats, and he reached for her

backpack, slinging it over his shoulder. As they moved away from the table, his hand went to the small of her back, guiding her through Coffee Hour. A thrill shot through her. For the first time ever, Chance Blackstone was finally seeing her.

And it felt really, really good.

# Eight

Chance dropped Summer at her twin's house, declining an invitation to come in.

"I've got lots to do if I'm going to be gone a good chunk of tomorrow," he told her. "I'll see you in the morning."

He watched as she went to the front door and unlocked it. Summer turned and waved before heading inside. It took everything he had not to get out of the car and go in after her.

He returned to the ranch, thinking about how he would need to rearrange his day as he went to his office. Chance decided to call one of his old fraternity brothers from SMU. Buzz Penniwell's father had owned a few luxury car dealerships, and Chance figured that Buzz had probably gone into the family business. He had lousy grades but a winning personality and would be great in sales.

"Where the hell have you been, Chance Blackstone?" Buzz asked, answering his phone. "I lost track of you after you went to Chicago. I think someone said you went west after that?"

"I worked for businesses in Denver and then Seattle. I

moved back to Texas a couple of years ago, returning to help on my family's ranch in Texas. My dad passed last spring, and I've been running Blackstone Ranch on my own since then."

"Sorry to hear about your old man. Big Jim was the life of the party."

Chance had invited his father to one of the parents' weekends the university held. His dad had stayed for the partying after the football game and family functions. Everywhere he went, Big Jim Blackstone had made friends, even if they were decades younger than he was. His dad had outdrunk every Greek at a pretty wild fraternity party. It had made Chance feel odd, watching his dad, almost as if he were outside a house, looking in. After that, he stopped asking his dad to come to parents' weekends.

"I wanted to see if your family still owned car dealerships in Dallas," he told Buzz.

Buzz laughed. "You just have to Google it to find out, Chance. Dad runs the BMW and Cadillac ones. My older brother is in charge of the Lexus one. My sister is managing one which carries Audis. Since I'm the youngest, I'm in charge of the Nissan dealership, not anything fancy. Why? You in the market for a new car? I would think you ranchers would drive big ass trucks."

"I do. I'm happy with the one I have, but I have a friend who just moved back to Texas from New York. Obviously, without any subways to take to get around, she's going to need a car. I told her I'd help her look for one."

"Hmm, a lady friend. I remember you being a real player in college."

"Summer is my best friend's little sister," Chance said defensively. "West Sutherland. He used to play for the Cowboys."

"I didn't know you were best friends with West Suther-land," Buzz said excitedly. "He's driven cars from dad's dealerships for years. He turned the last one in, though, after he retired. Said he was moving back to his hometown and was going to coach football."

"He is doing that exact thing. West is head coach for the Hawthorne Hawks and driving a pickup truck."

"West was a solid guy. Not pretentious at all. Some of these celebs that we get in the dealerships act as if they own everything and everyone around them. Not West, though. He was a great guy to work with. Did some print ads and commercials for us in exchange for leasing a new model each year. So, it's West's little sister who needs help."

"Yes," Chance said, feeling very protective of Summer because he remembered what a womanizer Buzz Penniwell had been. "If you're going to be in tomorrow, we'd like to drop by. I'm not sure what Summer is looking for, but—"

"We'll get her fixed up, Chance. I promise you that. Dad will want West's sister taken care of."

"We probably won't be there until about eleven. Does that work for you?"

"I'm usually in from about ten to seven on Tuesdays. I'll see you then."

"Sounds good, Buzz," he said, ending the call.

Hopefully, Buzz would respect West enough to allow that respect to roll over Summer's way. If not, he would step in and make certain that Buzz knew Summer was off-limits.

Chance went to the kitchen and fixed himself a sandwich, bringing it back to his office and working until almost eight. He liked to wind down the hour before bed, so he closed out of the program he was working in and headed to the library. It was a small room, with floor to ceiling bookshelves lining two of its four walls. It had a comfortable couch with a TV on the wall in front of it and a great reading chair that he settled into now. This room had been his mother's refuge, and Chance liked to come here every night, wanting to feel close to the woman he couldn't remember but still loved.

On the table sat a biography of Ulysses S. Grant. He picked it up and read for an hour before setting it aside and going upstairs to get ready for bed. He was still sleeping in the room which had been his growing up. Tammy had wanted him to take over his dad's bedroom, but it didn't feel right to him just yet. Still, Tammy had cleaned out the drawers and closets, and the bedroom was his for the taking whenever he decided he wanted to sleep there.

He didn't need to set an alarm. His internal clock always seemed to go off at the same time each morning. When it did, Chance rose and dressed, going to the kitchen. He had even beat Tammy downstairs today, and so he started a pot of coffee for the two of them. He scrambled himself four eggs and fried up bacon to go with it. Two slices of sourdough toast, slathered in butter, completed his meal.

Chance was halfway through breakfast when Tammy appeared, pouring herself a cup of coffee and taking a seat at the table beside him.

"You're an early bird today," she noted, stirring sugar into her cup.

"I'm going to take Summer Sutherland car shopping later. I want to get in as much work as I can before I pick her up."

"Summer was always such a sweet girl. Autumn, too. I know Meg and Joe are so glad the girls and West have come back to live in Hawthorne."

Tammy looked at him as she sipped her coffee. "Any

particular reason why you're helping Summer out with car shopping instead of West? Or Joe?"

He had always been able to talk to Tammy about anything. His dad was all business, with the only other topic he was interested in talking about being sports, especially football. Tammy had been the one Chance had poured his heart out to from the time he was a young boy.

"With you leaving, I'm not sure who I'm going to bounce ideas off," he began. "I haven't said this to anyone—not even Kelby—but I may be interested in Summer. More than interested," he admitted.

She smiled gently. "I haven't seen Summer for years, but I know the Sutherlands raised their kids right. West and Autumn are such lovely adults, and I'm sure Summer is the same. Have you asked her on a date yet?"

He shrugged. "We had coffee yesterday afternoon at Coffee Hour. Talked for a couple of hours."

Tammy beamed. "You saying more than two sentences tells me that you are definitely interested in her. I don't know the last time you sat down with a woman for that long."

Chance raked his hands through his hair. "It's been a good while." He grinned sheepishly. "Maybe ... never? Things are just so easy with her, Tammy. Our conversation flows back and forth. It's like she was always there, yet I never realized it."

"Well, she was younger than you, honey. And she was West's little sister. I know guy code usually declares that a hands-off situation."

"Do you think I should tell West that I'm interested in her?" he asked.

"You don't need anyone's permission to be seeing Summer. She's a grown woman. But if you do start dating, I think it would be the courteous thing to let West know. I believe he would be all for it."

He finished his last bite of bacon and rinsed his plate, putting it in the dishwasher. He had already cleaned the cast iron frying pan he used to cook the bacon and eggs.

"I'll see you tonight," he told Tammy.

"I've got my book club in town," she reminded him. "There's some leftover meatloaf in the fridge if you want to heat that for your dinner."

He grinned. "The only purpose of meatloaf is to have leftovers the next day so you can make a cold meatloaf sandwich, smothering the meatloaf in ketchup."

Tammy laughed merrily. "You and Kelby and your ketchup."

Placing his hat on his head, he lifted his jacket from the hook by the door and slipped into it. "Bye."

The early morning hours went by quickly, and he returned to the house, showering and shaving. For once, he put on a shirt other than flannel but still wore his jeans and boots. He decided to leave his hat at home and then went to his truck. He texted Summer to let her know that he was on his way, and she replied with a thumbs up. Already, his heart was speeding up at the thought of seeing her again. Spending today in her company.

When he pulled into the cul-de-sac, he saw Summer sitting in a rocker on the large porch. She stood and came down the porch stairs to meet him as he pulled into the driveway.

She got into his truck. "Good morning. Or since you've been up for so long, it must feel like afternoon for you."

He laughed. "This'll be a nice change to my day." As he backed out of the driveway, he asked, "Did you look at cars online? Find anything you like?"

"You're talking to the girl who always did her homework, Blackstone. I also drove both Eli and Autumn's cars when they got home from work. Then I went over to Mom and Dad's and drove her SUV. That's what I think I want, an SUV. I like riding up higher. I can see more of the road that way."

She bit her lip, and he noticed it must be a habit of hers when she felt unsure about something.

"I've never owned a car. I haven't even driven since I was in college."

"What?"

"None of us had cars in high school. Mom or Dad would drop us off or in a pinch, we were close enough that we could walk. With them having salaries paid by the public, cars and insurance for three kids were out of the question, especially needing to pay for three kids in college. West was lucky enough to earn his athletic scholarship. I had most of my college covered by academic scholarships and working part-time, but SMU was expensive. I didn't have enough from my job to buy a car and pay the insurance."

"You went to SMU? When I did?" he asked, surprised at hearing they'd been at SMU at the same time.

"Yes. We ran in very different circles. You were always seen with girls named as Rotunda beauties. You lived the Greek life. Let's be honest, Chance. Greeks didn't acknowledge anyone who was a non-Greek. We didn't orbit in your hallowed universe."

He felt terrible that they had hooven at the same university, and he'd never known that. Sure, he had gotten together with West when they had a break from school and seen Summer in passing, but he had never asked what the twins were doing or where they were going to college. He realized that Summer was right. His focus had been on Greek life and all the parties, mixers, and formals. He went to football games with his fraternity brothers and played intramural sports with girls from sororities.

"I apologize, Summer. I was pretty shallow then. If I would've known you were at SMU, I would've looked after you more. Had lunch with you each week. That kind of thing."

She shrugged. "It's all in the past, Chance. Don't worry about it. Changing subjects, you have to know more about SUVs than I do. Do you know a good make? I saw some online that I liked, but Decatur only has a couple of dealerships. We might need to go beyond it. Ft. Worth. Dallas. Or at least the suburbs surrounding them, I suppose."

"We're actually heading to Dallas now," he shared. "I have an old fraternity brother whose family owns several dealerships there. I told him we'd come by this morning. Since you're interested in SUVs, look up Nissan."

"That's one of the ones I liked. They had a Pathfinder. A Rogue. A Murano. Will I be able to test drive one?"

"You're with me, Summer. You'll be able to do whatever you want."

She laughed, a deep, rich, warm laugh.

One that Chance wanted to keep hearing for the rest of his life.

"Tell me about this friend of yours. Do you think he can help me get a good deal? I read online all about dealer sticker prices and markups and blue book values. What to ask and how much to go above sticker."

"You did do your homework," he said, impressed. "Buzz will do right by you."

"Buzz? What kind of name is that for a grown man?"

Chance laughed. "He's actually the third in his family with the same, stuffy name. I remember his grandfather was

Stanton. His dad goes by Stan. He's Buzz because back when he was really little, maybe three, he found his dad's electric razor and buzzed his hair. The nickname just stuck."

"Oh, that sounds familiar," Summer said, shaking her head, a smile playing about her lips.

"What are you talking about? Do you have a buzz story, Sutherland?"

"Close. Mom bought Autumn and me American Girl dolls for our fifth birthdays. She had just started reading us the stories. I don't know if Kelby was into American Girl or not, but they had books about girls in certain times of history. The Colonial Era. World War II. That kind of thing. You could buy dolls and paper dolls. All kinds of accessories. Mom didn't buy dolls which were characters from the series, such as Felicity or Addie. Instead, she custom ordered ones which resembled us. Auburn hair for Autumn and blond for me. As close to turquoise eyes as she could get.

"One of us—probably me—got the brilliant idea to cut both dolls' hair. Autumn and I had hair which was halfway down our backs, same as the dolls. We cut her doll's hair first and then mine. Then I said that we needed to have matching hair like our dolls, so she cut my hair, and I cut hers. You should have seen the look on Mom's face when we went to show her what we had done. Dad just laughed, though. He told Mom to take us to the Style Shack, and Betty Jo trimmed and shaped our hair so that we looked fairly normal. She even did the same for our dolls. I thought we would be in a lot of trouble, but Mom and Dad sat us down. Told us it was okay to be curious about wanting to try new things. They encouraged us to check with them if we wanted to do anything like that in the future. Autumn cried and apologized, but I never did. Guess that was my stubborn streak. Gosh, I haven't thought about that in ages."

"I always think of the two of you with long hair."

"After that, we both let it grow out again. Neither of us wanted to cut it for many years. Even now, we just trim it."

Chance felt her eyes on him. "I'm sure you have some kind of story like that from your past. You and West probably got into a ton of trouble that none of us ever knew about."

"Well, I think the statute of limitations has lapsed for this. Do you remember that big, plastic cow that used to sit on top of the old butcher shop back in high school?"

He glanced over and saw Summer's eyes widen. "No! You and West were the ones who stole it? I remember coming to school sophomore year. Everyone was talking about the cow in the courtyard. How on earth did the two of you get it down from the roof of the butcher shop and into the school's courtyard?"

He laughed easily. "That's on a need-to-know basis, and you don't need to know our trade secrets. Nobody ever found out, though, and West and I made a pact never to talk about it."

"And you just broke it. For me," she said softly.

"I wouldn't say I broke it," he said breezily. "You're in the family. You would never testify against your brother. Like I said, the statute of limitations is way beyond being charged. Besides, Mr. Peterson got his cow back." He grinned. "Even though it did have HHS branded on its rump."

"I bet Mr. Peterson would be interested in knowing who took his cow even though it was a long time ago," she told him. "I think you're going to have to buy my silence, Blackstone."

He put on his turn signal, moving from the left lane to the right and then slowing down, stopping on the shoulder of the road. Chance then turned on his flashers and slipped his palm behind Summer's nape.

Her turquoise eyes grew large as he said, "I'm past the point of slicing my palm open and rubbing my blood against yours, like West and I did long ago, declaring ourselves to be blood brothers. We're going to seal your silence with a kiss, Summer Sutherland. Is that all right with you?"

She wet her lips nervously, and desire rippled through him.

"Yes," she whispered.

Chance unbuckled his seatbelt and leaned closer.

Then he pressed his mouth to hers.

# Nine

As Chance's lips met Summer's, electricity shot through her body. In her wildest dreams, she never would have thought her long-ago crush would actually kiss her. But it seemed as if Chance was finally seeing her.

*And liking what he saw.*

The kiss started slowly. He didn't rush it. His lips, soft yet firm, pressed against hers and backed off, only to return, again and again. She liked that he wasn't hurrying the kiss, giving her time to become used to him. Gradually, though, his kisses became harder. More demanding of her. And Summer responded, every fiber of her being on high alert now.

His thumb gently caressed her neck, his fingers still warm against her nape. He slowly teased her mouth open, and she was all too willing to give him entrance, allowing him to explore her leisurely. His fingers moved up her neck, pushing into her hair, then tugging slightly on it. Her head tilted back, giving him better access now, and the kiss deepened, becoming even more electric. All her yearnings for this man from so many years ago now flooded her. She knew he was different. So was she. Years had passed since she'd had a girlhood crush on him, but he was even more devastatingly attractive to her now as a mature adult.

Her hands went out, grabbing his jacket, pulling him closer to her. She began fighting him now for control of the kiss, excitement rippling through her. This kiss was one she would never forget. No matter what happened in the near—or far—future, she would take the memory of this kiss with her to her grave.

Suddenly, a pounding sounded on the driver's window. They sprang apart like guilty teenagers caught making out by a parent. Summer looked up and saw a police officer standing beside Chance's truck, peering into the vehicle.

Immediately, Chance rolled down his window and said, "Good morning, Officer."

"I saw your flashers, son, and thought you needed help." He eyed them disapprovingly. "Doesn't look as if you're having any car troubles, though."

"No, sir. No trouble. I just needed to stop and let this woman know exactly how I feel about her."

The cop's stern look disappeared, and he began to smile. "May I see your license, sir?"

"Yes. Let me get it for you."

Chance reached into his back pocket and pulled out his wallet. Opening it, he removed the license and handed it to the patrol officer.

The cop skimmed it, saying, "Well, Mr. Blackstone, there are better places to kiss a lady. The shoulder of a public highway is not one of them. I understand you believed that time was of the essence, but I want you two to be safe." He paused and then grinned at them. "Besides me stopping to assist you, this is Texas. It was only a matter of time before a Good Samaritan or two also stopped to offer a helping hand.

If you want to kiss this little lady, I suggest you do it in private in the future, now that she knows how you feel about her."

"Yes, Officer," Chance said respectfully. "I do plan to do a lot of kissing with her in the future. I've staked my claim, and I promise I won't be pulling over impulsively in the future."

The cop handed Chance's license back to him. "Y'all have a good day, now, Mr. Blackstone. Ma'am," he added, touching his fingers to his hat.

Summer called out, "You, too, Officer," partly mortified at what the cop had seen, yet her emotions soaring on a natural high.

*Chance Blackstone wanted to keep kissing her.*

Chance returned his license into his wallet and slipped it into his back pocket again. He buckled his seatbelt and turned off the truck's flashers. Glancing into the mirror, he gave a wave as he started the vehicle again, moving along the shoulder and picking up speed. He smoothly merged back into traffic.

As he did so, he reached out a hand, his fingers seeking hers, lacing them together. A warmth spread through Summer.

"I feel properly chastised," Chance said drily. Then he glanced to her and back at the road. "I meant what I told him, Summer. I plan to be kissing you a lot. I hope that's okay with you."

She swallowed. "I'd like that, Chance. I've dreamed about kissing you for years."

He cut his eyes quickly to her. "You have?" he asked, wonder in his tone as he looked back to the road.

"If we're being honest, I had a crush on you back in the day. It started in seventh grade. You and West were freshmen. I thought you were the best-looking guy in school, and you were always so kind and polite to everyone."

She bit her lip and caught herself doing it, quickly releasing it.

"But you never gave me the time of day. I was lucky if you glanced in my direction when you came over to the house."

His fingers tightened around hers. "You've got to understand, Summer, that you were West's little sister. I wouldn't have looked at you in any other way except a brotherly one back then. Besides, there was a gap in our ages. I would've felt like I were robbing the cradle if I would've thought about kissing you. Now, though? A couple of years don't mean much of anything when you reach your thirties. And I am very interested in you, Summer. I wasn't just BS-ing that cop. I enjoyed talking with you when you came home last Christmas. To be honest, it was the first time I really saw you. Heard you. Was attracted to you.

"And when I learned you had moved back to Hawthorne, it gave me hope."

"Hope?" she asked, her own hope running through her.

"Yeah. I thought there was something there between us. A spark I wanted to investigate. It was still there at dinner the other night. It definitely was present during our coffee date yesterday. I'm ready to explore it with you now."

She saw him smile, and she couldn't keep her own smile from spreading.

"I plan to get to know you very well, Summer. In my mind, that means not only talking, but kissing." He glanced quickly to her. "And more. If you're up for it."

A rush of emotions flitted through her. She squeezed his fingers.

"I would like the same, Chance. I'm not that gawky teenager anymore, thank goodness."

"You *were* pretty gawky," he said, a smile playing about his sensual lips. "It took a while for the rest of you to catch up to those long legs. And those braces? You seemed to have more metal in your mouth than a suspension bridge."

They both laughed, and she said, "It's so easy talking to you. I don't think I've ever been more comfortable in a guy's company before. You may not believe this, but once the braces and glasses were gone, I turned out to be pretty popular."

"You were popular before, Summer. I remember you always had a lot of friends. You were really outgoing. Maybe you blossomed physically once you lost the braces and glasses, but your essence never changed." He paused. "I said the same thing to Tammy. That you're easy to talk to."

Surprise filled her. "You told Tammy about us?"

He nodded. "I've told Tammy everything that was important to me my entire life."

The fact that he had spoken to Tammy about her—and that he believed what they were feeling about one another was important—meant a great deal to her.

"Tammy knows that I have feelings for you. I wanted to make certain she did before she leaves for Waco on Saturday."

"That's fast. I better get that pork chop recipe from her quickly," Summer teased. Then she grew serious, asking, "Where do you think this is going, Chance? This thing between us. I'll be honest. I've dated a lot in the past, but this feels different."

"I don't want to make any kind of predictions now, Summer. I want things between us to unfold naturally, but I can already tell you that my feelings for you are pretty damn strong. I'm no longer that guy you seemed to worship back in high school. I've done a lot and been through a lot since then. I know you're the same for having lived away from Hawthorne all these years. I do think we have the same values, as well as having a lot in common. I want to see as much of you as I can. I know we'll also be thrown together because of family and friends."

"What if this thing between us doesn't work out?" she asked. "As you just said, we'll be around each other a lot. Kelby's my sister-in-law. West is your brother-in-law. If things don't work out between us, it could be pretty awkward for us and everyone else."

He raised their joined hands, kissing her fingers tenderly.

"I'm willing to take that risk, Summer. I'd rather explore what's between us than not. I hope it'll work out, but if it doesn't, I still would want to be your friend."

"Okay," she said softly, knowing that she'd be a fool to pass up the opportunity to have a relationship with this man. "Let's take things slowly then. See what direction it goes. And if it doesn't work, let's don't let it drag on forever, neither of us voicing the obvious. We should admit it isn't working and move on."

She hoped that this connection between them would grow, though. That Chance Blackstone would turn out to be her soulmate.

After that, their conversation grew much less serious, and they reached Dallas and his friend's dealership.

As Chance opened the door to the dealership for her, he placed his palm on the small of her back, guiding her inside. Not only did little tingles run through her, but Summer appreciated the gesture. It made her feel protected.

She saw a salesman head their way, but another man waved him off, coming to meet them. She figured this must be

Buzz. Even though he was in his early thirties, he still looked like the frat boy he had been.

Buzz held out a hand, and Chance took it.

"Chance Blackstone. It's so good to finally see you again in the flesh." Buzz's eyes turned to her. "And you must be West's sister. Good to meet you, Summer."

"Do you know West?" she asked.

He looked at her slyly, and Summer felt Chance's hand press more firmly into her back.

Buzz gave her a million-dollar salesman smile. "Do I know West? You betcha. My family owns several car dealerships. Your brother was a spokesman for a couple of them for several years. He even drove some of our cars and did ads for us. We're going to take good care of you, Summer."

Already, she didn't like the slimy Buzz. If it had been up to her, they would leave right now. Still, she didn't want to embarrass Chance by doing that. What Summer decided to do was take charge of the situation. This was a guy who didn't think women had a brain in their heads.

She was ready to prove him wrong.

"I'm here to look at your SUV inventory, Buzz," she said brightly. "I'm leaning toward either the Murano or Rogue and would like to test drive both models."

"Ah, the little lady knows her own mind," Buzz said almost condescendingly.

"I do," she said firmly, unwilling to be pushed around by this guy. "I've already studied both models online, but I'd like to hear from you. Compare both and tell me the advantages and disadvantages of each model," she said, her tone businesslike.

Chance's thumb stroked her back in approval, while Buzz seemed to be flustered for a moment. She believed he was more of a figurehead at his family's business.

Diplomatically, she said, "You are more of a big picture guy, I assume, running this dealership. You may not know all those particulars about every model."

Summer looked to the salesman who had started to greet them and waved him over.

"Why don't you let this gentleman answer my questions?"

He reached them, and she thrust out her hand. "I'm Summer Sutherland. I'd like to hear your expert opinions about the Murano and Rogue."

"I'm Jim Hamilton." The salesman's eyes flicked to his boss, and she saw Buzz nod. "I'd be happy to walk you through both cars, Summer."

She turned to Chance. "Why don't you and Buzz catch up? Jim and I will look at the cars before I test drive each."

As she and the salesman walked away, she heard Buzz's low whistle, and heard him say, "She's a firecracker, Chance."

"Summer definitely knows her mind," Chance replied. "I like that in a woman. Especially my girlfriend."

Hearing him call her that caused her spirits to skyrocket. It took everything not to rush back to him and throw her arms about him, giving him a big kiss. She played it cool, though, letting Jim do his spiel. Summer turned her attention to him and even stopped him a few times, asking questions.

"You've done your homework, Summer," the salesman said approvingly after he'd answered everything for her. "I wish more shoppers did the same. Which car would you like to drive first?"

"Let's go with the Murano," she told him, and then she looked to Chance. "Want to go out with me?"

"Nope," he said. "You're the one buying the vehicle. You're the one who should decide. You don't need my input."

Jim said, "I'll need to get your license, Summer."

"Not necessary," Buzz told his employee. "Just give her the key fob, Jim."

The salesman quickly returned with both fobs, and he told Summer to try both city streets surrounding the dealership and then take the car on the highway for a couple of exits, saying, "You want to see how it performs at both low and high speeds."

She accepted the keys to the Murano and did as he suggested, returning about twenty minutes later. Chance gave her a look that told her he needed rescuing.

Summer traded fobs with Jim and then motioned to Chance. "Come on, Cowboy. Let me take you for a ride."

As he came toward her, a slow smile spreading across his face, she realized the innuendo of her words, and her face flamed.

They got into the Rogue, and Summer drove the same route she had before, assessing the Rogue's performance versus the Murano's.

"What are you thinking?" he asked after a few minutes. "Like one over the other?"

"They both handle well. I think the Rogue is actually giving a slightly smoother ride. And it's a bit smaller but still a decent size. It's the one I want."

She glanced his way and smiled. "Besides, I think it's pretty funny that a romance writer would choose to drive a Rogue."

He looked baffled. "Why so?"

"I guess you've never read a romance," Summer said, laughing.

"Nope. Never have. I like Louis L'Amour novels and read him and biographies, mostly."

"I've edited my fair share of both historical and contemporary romances. Historical heroes are often rogues. Contemporary romance authors simply call them bad boys. Women seem to be consistently drawn to a rogue or bad boy. The heroines, though, whether they're strong personalities or a little meeker in nature, always seem to smooth out the rough edges on a rogue, and those rogues find they're crazy about the heroine. They find their happily ever afters together."

She pulled back into the dealership and said, "I'm going to buy this Rogue."

"I can't wait to see you at the bargaining table," he said, his gray eyes dancing with mischief.

Summer grinned. "Watch and learn, Cowboy. I've had my fair share of dealings with ornery authors. Dealing with Buzz and Jim will be a piece of cake."

They exited the Rogue, and she handed the fob back to a waiting Jim.

"Let's go talk numbers," she told the salesman, and he led her inside the building to an office with Buzz's name on the door. The dealership owner quickly joined them, and they all took a seat.

Though Summer had read online that a buyer was never supposed to admit to a car salesman that you wanted a car, her strategy was a bit different.

"I'd like to buy this Rogue. It only has twenty miles on it, and I like the dark gray color. It also has the exact options I'm looking for. I'm not interested in financing. I'll pay cash for it."

She saw the surprised looks coming from all three men.

"We usually finance cars," Buzz said, frowning.

"That won't be necessary," Summer emphasized. "I've researched sticker prices for Rogues, and I know you've marked it up significantly for your MSRP," referring to the manufacturer's suggested retail price. "I'm willing to pay above costs by a thousand dollars."

Summer named the figure and added, "You can take my offer or leave it, gentlemen. If I were you, though, I wouldn't walk away from a cash deal. Your profit will be slim, but you won't have to fret about moving the car, plus you don't have to worry about getting the price of the car spread out over four or five years."

She smiled brightly. "So, what's it going to be? Do you want my business or not?"

Jim swallowed, looking hesitantly to Buzz, who said, "You drive a hard bargain, Summer. I was willing to make you a good deal since you're related to West, but what you're offering barely covers—"

"That's fine, Buzz," she said, cutting him off and rising. "We'll go somewhere else." Then to make certain the fact she was leaving stuck in his craw, she added, "I'm sorry I'll have to tell West how disappointed I was that you refused to do business with me."

"Wait," Buzz said, and she waited for him to capitulate. "That won't be necessary. We want you to be happy, Summer." He looked to Jim. "Write it up."

"Yes, sir," Jim said, leaving the office, and she noticed he bit back a smile.

"How long will that take?" she asked Buzz sweetly.

"Not long."

She looked to Chance, who said, "I'd like to take my girlfriend out to lunch to celebrate her new car. We'll be back in a couple of hours."

"Thanks for your time, Buzz," Summer said breezily.

He looked unhappy but said perfunctorily, "Thank you for coming in. I hope you'll be happy with your Rogue."

Looking to Chance, she said, "Oh, I'm very happy with my rogue." She winked at Chance, who chuckled.

They went to his truck, and he opened the door for her. Before she could get in, his hands captured her waist.

"You are a smooth operator, Sutherland," he complimented. "Are you certain *you're* not the rogue in this scenario? You handled him with ease, making Buzz dance to your tune."

Summer smiled at him. "It felt pretty darn good," she admitted.

"Holding you this way feels pretty darn good to me," he said, his voice husky, causing those tingles to ripple through her again.

Then Chance kissed her possessively. Summer didn't care who saw. She merely reveled in the kiss. In the feel of his hands on her. The scent of his cologne, crisp and clean.

He broke the kiss. "Now, you can get in."

"Where are you taking me to lunch?" she asked, getting into the truck.

"Wherever you want to go, babe."

Ooh. She liked him calling her babe. She liked him kissing her. Touching her. Summer liked everything about Chance Blackstone.

And she ready for whatever came next.

Summer followed Chance home from Dallas in her brand-new Rogue, getting used to driving again. She had cautioned him that she would be a little tentative since she hadn't been behind the wheel of a car in years, and he had kept his truck at the speed limit or slightly under. She could feel her confidence returning as they left the heavy traffic of Dallas behind and headed toward Hawthorne.

When they had returned to Buzz's dealership, the paperwork had been complete. She contacted her bank, which had branches across the country, even one in Hawthorne, which had proved to be convenient. She assumed things went so smoothly because Chance was a personal friend of Buzz's, plus the fact that Buzz seemed to want to wash his hands of her.

Jim had been a peach, though, taking Summer through the car and pointing out all its features. He paired her cell with the Rogue, even helping her set her radio to stations she might enjoy. By the time she drove off the lot, she knew exactly how all the bells and whistles worked. Jim told her he would text her when her license plates came in, and she had thanked him for spending so much time with her.

Chance texted her, and she touched her screen, hearing a voice read the message aloud to her. He wanted her to pull into the Sonic which would be coming up soon on the right. She followed him down the exit ramp, pulling into the space next to his. He motioned for her to join him in his truck.

When she did, he said, "I thought we could take advantage of happy hour," causing her to giggle. Sonic happy hour at the burger place offered half-priced soft drinks and slushes. She and Autumn had been big fans of happy hour when they were growing up.

"I know you used to order a cherry slush," he said.

"How do you remember that?" she asked.

Chance shrugged. Then mischief lit his eyes. "Maybe I was paying more attention than you thought."

He touched the button and ordered a large Dr Pepper for himself and a cherry slush for her.

As they waited, he told her, "You'll need to get the Sonic app for your phone. If you do, you get half-priced slushes and drinks all day."

"Really?" She frowned. "So, happy hour isn't all that special anymore. I guess I'll have to roll with the changes. I'm thrilled to be near a Sonic again, though. They have the best crushed ice in the world. I don't feel a bit guilty eating it. You know how the dentist always warns you not to crunch ice? Well, Sonic ice doesn't count," she declared, causing Chance to laugh heartily.

"How do you like your new SUV?" he asked. "Are you feeling more comfortable behind the wheel now?"

"More since we left Dallas. The traffic there is way worse than I remember. It's almost New York-like, and that's not a compliment."

"It's worse everywhere in the state. Houston is a down-right nightmare. At least they've built a loop around Austin. You go out of your way a bit and have to pay a toll, but it's worth every penny to do so. If you stay on I-35 and get near downtown Austin, things slow to a crawl and then become a standstill. Like a parking lot."

The carhop brought their drinks, and Chance handed her a few dollars for a tip since he had already paid.

"Thank you for doing that," Summer said. "I remember when you and West used to come to Sonic when I was carhopping. You always left me a generous tip."

"You were working hard. You've always had a great work ethic, Summer. That's why I think you'll be successful as a novelist. You're disciplined. You'll get your writing done." He grinned. "I might even ask to read what you write. Or maybe you could work out your romantic scenes with me. Practice on me."

His words caused her to blush, knowing what she had written in her first novel. The thought of having sex with Chance caused her pulse to race.

He smiled knowingly. "I see your characters must do more than kiss by the look on your face."

She nodded. "There are different kinds of romances. Sweet ones, where there's barely a kiss. Then some where the door is closed to more intimate action between characters."

"And I gather that your door stays wide open?"

"It does," she said, feeling her face burning now.

"Well, if you need a research partner to help you work anything out, you know you can text me anytime."

She laughed. "Now it sounds as if you want booty texts from me."

His eyes darkened to a stormy gray. "Maybe I do."

A shiver ran through her. She caught the heat in his eyes and wondered if the same might be reflected in her own.

"Slow down, Cowboy," she said. "We've just gotten started. I'm not ready to jump into bed with you yet."

Actually, she was ready. At least her body was telling her that was the case, but Summer wanted more than a physical relationship with Chance. She wanted the whole package.

"I know," he said. "We're taking it slowly. We'll have to agree to step things up at the same time. For now, we'll stick to kissing." He took a sip of his DP. "Ready to hit the road again?"

"Sure."

Summer turned to open the door, but Chance took her chin in his hand. He leaned over and gave her a sweet, soft kiss.

"How about you come back to the ranch with me? See if you can get Tammy to show you how to cook a pork chop?"

"I'd like that. Let me text Autumn and tell her not to expect me for dinner."

He moved close and brushed his lips against hers again. "Okay. Get out of the truck, Summer. If you don't, I'm afraid we won't make it back to Hawthorne anytime soon."

She looked at him, searching him. "Do you really mean that?"

"That I'm heavily attracted to you and would be willing to sit at Sonic and kiss you ravenously for hours? Absolutely."

A warmth spread within her. "Good answer, Cowboy."

Summer returned to her Rogue, taking her drink with her. She placed it in one of the cupholders and started her car. As they got back on the highway, she used voice text to let Autumn know she'd be at Blackstone Ranch for dinner. Autumn replied that she was interested in hearing all about

Summer's day. She read into the text that her twin wanted to know more than about the SUV her sister had bought.

They arrived back in Hawthorne, and happiness flooded her as they drove through town. She hadn't realized how much she'd missed her hometown until she'd moved back permanently. She'd been a little homesick when she'd graduated from college and moved to New York, but everything had been new and exciting then. The job. The people. Her neighbors. Making new friends. Dating. Hawthorne had always simmered in the back of her mind, and each trip she'd made home had caused the pull toward home to grow stronger. Although she still hated the way her career at Liberty House had ended, Summer knew things were working out for the best.

Especially since Chance Blackstone was a growing part of her life in Hawthorne.

They went through town and exited the other side. Blackstone Ranch was slightly north of Hawthorne, and she followed Chance through the front gates, heading toward what he'd always called the big house. She could see cattle grazing in the distance.

He pulled up in front of the house, and she parked behind him. Before she could get out, he was already at her door, opening it, helping her from it.

"Thank you," she said. "I'd forgotten how gentlemanly you were."

He threaded his fingers through hers. "Or how possessive I can be. I hated the way Buzz looked at you. As if he wanted to jump your bones right on the showroom floor."

"Is that why you referred to me as your girlfriend?" she asked coyly.

"Damn straight. And I don't want you to think we're friends. I haven't seen him since I left SMU. I called him out of the blue last night. Buzz and I may have been fraternity brothers, but we weren't close back then. I thought he was really immature. From the looks of it, he still hasn't grown up."

"Agreed. I almost wanted to leave when we got there."

"I'm glad we didn't," he told her. "I liked how you worked him. You knew what you wanted and went for it. You were ready to walk out if you didn't get what you wanted. That was *very* sexy, Sutherland."

"It was?" she said, batting her eyelashes in an exaggerated manner.

"Definitely a turn on." He kissed her hard, once, and said, "Let's go inside."

She was still reeling from the quick, possessive kiss when they entered the house.

"Something smells good," she said.

"Tammy's a terrific cook. Seems like she's already started dinner." He paused. "I called her the minute we left the dealership and told her I was bringing you home for dinner. We only had cold meatloaf, so I guess she decided to make something better for us."

Chance led her to the kitchen, where Tammy was standing at the stove, placing chicken in a cast iron pan.

"Hey, Tammy," Chance said, causing her to turn.

Tammy smiled at Summer. "I hear you bought a car today."

"I sure did," she said proudly.

"Chance told me about it," Tammy said. "He also said you were coming for dinner. I hear you're interested in learning about how to cook pork chops."

"I am. I love them, and Chance says yours are the most tender and tastiest he's ever had."

"How long before we eat?" Chance asked.

"About twenty minutes," Tammy replied.

"Okay. I'm going to go send a few emails. I'll be back."

He released Summer's hand and kissed her. "Be back in a few."

She watched him go and then turned, seeing the satisfied smile on Tammy's face. Suddenly, the woman wrapped her in a tight embrace.

"Thank you," Tammy said, releasing her. "It's been hard, planning on leaving the ranch for good. I know Kelby is taken care of. West is a wonderful man, and Kelby is deeply in love with him. I've worried about Chance, though. He's so quiet. Stoic. Never shows much emotion."

Tammy clasped Summer's hands in hers. "But when he talked to me about you, I saw something in his eyes. Heard something in his voice. Chance has avoided commitment for a long time, but my gut tells me he's ready to embrace it now."

"That's nice to hear, Tammy, but Chance and I are just getting to know one another," she protested.

The older woman shook her head. "You've known each other your entire lives. Yes, you've gone different directions, but fate has led you both back to Hawthorne. I can already tell that the years are melting away. That Chance is seeing you for *you* this time, Summer. You're not West's little sister. You're a beautiful, interesting, confident woman in your own right. The question is, do you think you could have a future with my boy?"

Her throat thickened with emotion. "Yes," she said simply. "I worshiped him as a kid. Desperately wanted him to pay attention to me, but he never showed the slightest interest in me. I get that I was West's sister—and younger— and that made me off-limits in his mind. I assure you that I understand he's different from when I had a crush on him. I'm different, too. We've had a lot of different life experiences, but I'm eager to explore what we could have if we made a commitment to one another."

"I'm so happy hearing that," Tammy said. "Chance has lived for the ranch since he came home. He wanted to please Big Jim more than anything. After his father passed, he concentrated even harder on the ranch, wanting to prove to himself that he could run it well. He's focused so long and hard on this place that I worried he'd grown tunnel vision and wouldn't be able to see himself as a husband and father."

Tammy smoothed Summer's hair. "You're the first woman who's come along that he's been interested in since he came back to Hawthorne. I know he was sowing a lot of wild oats during college and his years away from Hawthorne, but Chance is, in his heart, a one-woman, settling down kind of guy. I hope that he'll do so with you."

"Me, too," she said, her vision blurring with tears.

Tammy whipped a tissue from her pocket and dabbed at Summer's eyes. "No tears. Just be yourself with him, honey. Everything'll work out just fine. Let's talk pork chops now. If a way to man's stomach is through food, you'll have Chance fall at your feet if you can perfect my pork chops recipe. That boy could eat his weight in them."

Summer laughed, feeling relaxed with Tammy, who pulled out a cookbook and opened it to a certain page.

"This is a write your own cookbook. Every recipe in here is one I already know by heart. I'm going to give this to you, Summer."

"No, I can't take it," she protested.

Tammy pressed it into Summer's hands. "I want you to have it. Try some recipes. See what you like. Change things up a bit to make them your own."

"I don't really know how to cook," she admitted.

Tammy smiled, patting the cookbook. "Then this baby

will help you learn," she promised. "Read over the pork chop recipe, and let me know if you have any questions.

While Tammy busied herself in finishing dinner, Summer studied the pork chop recipe. It surprised her that they weren't cooked in a cast iron skillet. Instead, they were oven-baked. Tammy had noted the different times in baking boneless versus bone-in pork chops. She also indicated to use a meat thermometer to make certain the chops were at a certain temperature.

"The spice rub is the key," Tammy told her.

Summer noted the rub included both garlic and onion powder, paprika, oregano, sea salt, and pepper. She saw in parentheses that Tammy had marked that oregano could be replaced with Italian seasoning and thought that an interesting swap.

As Tammy mashed potatoes by hand, she told Summer, "Lots of pork chop recipes call for brown sugar, but I've found this rub is better and healthier. And always make sure you drizzle the olive oil on first, then sprinkle my spice mix on top and rub it in. In fact, I make up a good amount of the spice mix and keep it on hand. I sprinkle it on other meats and sometimes over chicken or fish. Even potatoes."

"This reads really easy. I know this recipe is something I can follow," she said.

"The resting for five minutes after they come out of the oven is important," Tammy told her. "Resting any kind of meat for a few minutes lets the juices soak in. And I don't note this on the recipe, but don't let your baking dish be too big. You don't want too much space between chops, or the juice will evaporate faster, and they'll dry out and toughen up."

Tammy added milk to the potatoes, as well as more salt and pepper, while Summer flipped through the cookbook.

She saw recipes for everything from peach cobbler to potato salad to Texas sheet cake.

"Are you sure you want me to take this?" she asked. "What if ... Chance and I don't stay together?"

"I know you will," Tammy predicted. "But regardless, the cookbook is yours."

Summer decided that she would take it for now and make copies of the recipes.

Just in case she needed to return it in the future.

Chance entered the kitchen again. "It smells heavenly, Tammy. Can I do anything?"

"Grab some plates for us. Silverware and napkins are already on the table."

Tammy didn't bother putting anything in bowls and setting the food on the table. Instead, they spooned up food directly from the pans and bowls. Summer put crisply fried chicken, mashed potatoes, and butter beans on her plate as Tammy pulled a cookie sheet filled with biscuits from the oven.

Her stomach gurgled. "Oh, my. Those are golden brown and calling my name."

"Butter's on the table," Tammy said. "Honey and syrup if you want to add that."

Chance leaned close, his lips brushing her ear. "I like syrup on mine. I think I'd also like syrup on you."

A hot blush flooded her cheeks. "Behave," she said quietly, causing him to chuckle low.

Summer enjoyed the meal with the pair. Chance told her about their FaceTime interview with Zeke Benevides and his wife, Maria, and how the couple would be cooking all the meals for the ranch hands, as well as keeping the big house and bunkhouse clean.

"They'll be bringing their two kids with them," he said.

"We're fixing up the old cabin for them. Remember, we used to play in it when we were kids."

"I do," she said. "It's great they won't have to be in the bunkhouse with the other cowboys." Summer looked to Tammy. "Chance says you're leaving on Saturday."

"Yes. The Benevides family will arrive tomorrow afternoon. I'll help them get settled and then walk them through things on Thursday and Friday. After that, I'm eager to head to Waco and my Tommy."

When they finished dinner, Chance said, "I'll clean up. Just let me tell Summer goodbye."

Tammy said, "Say your goodbyes here. I'll walk Summer out." She left the kitchen, giving them a moment of privacy.

Chance wrapped his arms around her, and she said, "I know how much you're going to miss Tammy."

"I will. She's a mom to me. I'm just happy she's got a chance for personal happiness now. It seems there was always a part of her which loved Tommy."

He bent, giving her a long, slow, absolutely delicious kiss which made Summer's head spin.

"Go," he urged. "I'll see you tomorrow."

"I'm having dinner with Sawyer tomorrow night," she told him. "I'm treating him to a steak dinner at Great Steak. He did me a huge favor, and I want to pay him back."

"Then maybe after dinner?" he asked hopefully.

She laughed. "Our reservation isn't until seven. It'll take a good two hours probably. I know you go to bed really early."

He looked disappointed but said, "Then I'll call you tomorrow. I just need to hear your voice."

Already, she craved hearing his voice. Needing his touch. Summer was tumbling, hard and fast, and knew she was already half in love with Chance.

"Okay," she agreed.

He walked her to the door and kissed her lightly. "Bye, Badass. If I need anyone negotiating for me anytime soon, I know who to call."

"Bye, yourself," she said saucily, secretly pleased that he'd thought her taking a firm stance with Buzz was a turn-on.

Tammy was walking around Summer's new SUV, admiring it. "You picked a beauty," she said.

"I'm really pleased with it."

Tammy smiled. "I may not see you again before I leave for Waco." She took the cookbook Summer carried and slipped a pen from her pocket. "I'm giving you my cell number. Call if you have any questions about the recipes. Or if you just want to talk."

"Thank you. I'd like that, Tammy."

The older woman hugged her. "Take care of my boy, Summer."

"I will," she promised.

Summer drove back to Autumn and Eli's house, riding a natural high. She had a boyfriend, one who'd kissed her a good number of times today. It was as if everything she'd dreamed of was coming true.

Autumn met her at the door, and she called for Eli. They came out to look at her new vehicle, both complimenting her on her choice. She had them get in and took them for a ride, stopping at her parents so they, too, could see her new purchase.

After she'd driven back to Autumn's, her twin followed her upstairs, closing the door to the guestroom.

"Spill it. Everything," Autumn said. "You look different—and I think I know why."

Not holding back, Summer said, "I think I'm in love with Chance Blackstone."

# Eleven

Summer awoke early and went for a long walk. She had read an article which described how movement spurred creativity, and she had begun walking in New York each time before she sat down to write. All kinds of ideas popped into her head as she did so, and she often used her voice memo app to make notes of what came to her. By the time she returned to the house, Autumn and Eli had left for Triple H.

She would try to work from their house today. Coffee Hour had proved that it wasn't conducive for her getting much of anything done. She wouldn't have to sit behind Eli's desk, though. Instead, she would sit in the great room, which got a lot of natural light and would be a cheery place to work from. If she were still here when the weather grew warmer, she might even work from the screened-in back porch, so she could soak up nature as she wrote.

Summer showered and dressed, putting her hair up in a ponytail to keep it away from her face so it wouldn't distract her as she wrote. She brought her laptop to the great room and had just settled in when her cell rang. That was a rare occurrence. Her generation texted instead of calling. The only people she had ever called on a regular basis when she was living in New York were her parents and Autumn, and she FaceTimed them.

Glancing down at her phone now, it surprised her to see Jen Adelstein's name flashing across the screen. Jen had been a fellow editor and Summer's closest friend at Liberty House. When Summer was let go, she had texted Jen and a few of her other friends at the publishing house, telling them that she was returning to Texas and going to try her hand at being a full-time novelist. She kept the text vague and said it would be better if no one contacted her for a while, hoping those she contacted would read between the lines and know not to associate themselves with her. She had received a few texts in reply, wishing her well, and a longer one from Jen, who told her how much she had appreciated Summer's friendship. Jen even said she'd like to visit her in Texas someday.

Answering her phone, Summer said, "Hey, Jen. It's good to hear from you. What are you up to?"

"I'm in the office supply closet with the light off and the door locked," her friend said quietly. "All kinds of rumors are swirling about your departure from Liberty House, Summer, and I figured you signed something that wouldn't allow you to talk about why you left so fast. I'm calling because Celia Cameron needs you."

With her quick packing and move to Texas, Summer had almost forgotten about Celia and her promise to help the author finish her manuscript. While she had waited a couple of hours at the airport for her flight and then on the flight itself, she had read the manuscript Celia had sent to her, correcting a few typos and adding a handful of notes to it. The manuscript was in terrific shape, and it hadn't needed much tweaking.

Once she had arrived home, however, she had forgotten to email her notes to Celia. It struck her now that she didn't even have the author's email address since she hadn't been able to take anything with her, other than a few personal items, from Liberty House.

"What's going on with her?" she asked, worried about the situation.

"I was passing the receptionist's desk when I heard Sarah telling Celia that you were no longer with Liberty House. Celia must have asked for your phone number or personal email, and Sarah said she couldn't provide any information to her. I got Celia's number from Sarah so I could pass it along to you. I know she was one of your favorite authors to work with. Maybe you can tell her more than what you were able to tell the rest of us."

Summer could hear the hurt in Jen's voice and said, "You guessed right. I had to sign a non-disclosure agreement, so I can't discuss the exact reasons I left Liberty House with anyone other than my attorney. It's better if none of you get involved in this matter or stay in contact with me for a while. I don't want to jeopardize any of your jobs."

"I knew that had to be the case," Jen said, sounding relieved. "I'm going to text you Celia's number. Call her and calm her down. And I meant what I said, Summer. I would like to come and see you sometime. I'm getting fed up with a lot of things here at Liberty House. In the short time you've been gone, Millicent has been on a tear."

"Go back to your desk. Call me tonight when you're home. No, I'm going to dinner with my cousin. I probably won't be home until about nine, which is ten your time. Can we talk then?"

Jen laughed. "It's not as if I'll be in bed. I'm editing until midnight or later these days. Millicent is demanding more and more from her editors, and I'm fast on the road to burnout."

"Talk to you later," Summer said, ending the call.

A moment later, a text from Jen appeared, providing Celia's phone number. With a bit of trepidation, she dialed the number.

"Hello?" Celia said tentatively.

"Hey, Celia. It's Summer Sutherland."

"Summer! What on earth has happened? I sent you an email because I did what you suggested. I actually wrote during Rob's chemo session. Since I had everything outlined, two chapters just flowed from me. I wanted to email them to you so you could also look at them when you perused the rest of the manuscript. But the email bounced back. I tried it again, and it still wouldn't go through. That's when I called your extension at Liberty House, but my call wouldn't go through. I called the main number, and the receptionist said that you no longer were working for them. I left her my number in the hopes she might pass it along to you. What's going on?" Celia wailed.

"It's a long story, and I'm not going to burden you with it, especially with all that you have on your plate," Summer told the author. "I did read the manuscript you sent to me. Corrected a few grammar mistakes and added my editorial notes. Celia, this is the best novel you've ever written, even though I haven't seen the end of it. And I still want to help you finish it, despite the fact I'm no longer employed by Liberty House."

"I got a voicemail just before you called," Celia said. "From someone named Lauren at Liberty House. She told me that she was my new editor and that I needed to meet my March first deadline. That no matter what I'd been told previously, I had to honor the contract."

"You still have two chapters and an epilogue to write, correct?"

"Yes," Celia said, desperation in her voice. "Rob is so sick right now, Summer. I don't think I can get that written, not caring for him and my kids at the same time."

"If I sent you the manuscript with my notes, do you think you could work on making those corrections and additions?"

"Yes, if it's not a lot," Celia said, sounding unsure.

"I guarantee you, it's not. What you sent is clean as a whistle. Text me your email address. Make sure you add the number I called you on to your contacts. It's my personal cell number. I'll also text you my email address. I'll look at the outline for the remaining chapters that you sent to me, and I'll knock out those two chapters and the epilogue by Monday. It'll give you time to read through them, and then you can send in the manuscript to Lauren. Who is a great editor, by the way. You're lucky you were placed with her and not someone else."

Today was Wednesday. Summer would need to put aside her own writing in order to help Celia out of this bind.

Celia began crying. "Oh, Summer, I can't thank you enough. I was going to dedicate this book to you anyway, but I'll definitely do so now."

She wanted to tell Celia not to send in that dedication, but it would be a year or so before the book saw print. By then, she might be able to talk Celia into dedicating her book to someone else. She didn't want the author's career at Liberty House tainted—or even tanked—because of Celia's association with her former editor.

"Hanging up now. Text me your email while I print out your outline notes. I'll send you what I've edited for you to clean up. You can handle it, Celia. Talk soon. Bye."

Eli had kindly paired Summer's laptop with his printer so

that she could print anything she needed during her stay. Summer opened the file she had saved with Celia's outline on how to finish those last few chapters. By the time the pages were printed, Celia had texted Summer her email address, and she turned around and sent what she had edited to the author, telling her that she would read over the latest two chapters now and send notes on them before she started writing the remainder of the book herself.

An hour later, Summer had read both chapters, made her suggestions and corrections, and sent the document back to Celia. Immediately, Celia had texted back, saying she had gotten the email.

Now that she was caught up in the manuscript, Summer looked over the notes for the upcoming chapter, glad that she had a blueprint for where Celia was going. It didn't surprise her that Millicent had instructed Lauren to bring the hammer down on Celia and demand that the manuscript be turned in on time. Summer might not be able to help all her authors in this way, but at least she could help Celia, especially since her attention needed to be devoted to her husband and children more than on her writing.

Familiar with Celia's voice after having edited several of her books, Summer found it relatively easy to imitate the author's voice, keeping with Celia's style and sentence structure. By noon, she had the first chapter written. She took a break, having forgotten to eat breakfast after she got home from her walk, and made herself a sandwich. She also peeled a banana and opened a container of Greek yogurt to round out the meal.

She worked for two hours after lunch and then took a break, glad she did so when she checked her phone and saw that she'd missed a call from Chance. Summer always silenced her phone when she was writing. Instead of texting, she returned the call.

He answered on the first ring. "Hey, beautiful. You working hard on that novel of yours?"

"Working hard—but not on my stuff."

"I don't get it."

"I'll explain the next time I see you. When is that?" she asked, hoping he might have time for her this afternoon since she would be with Sawyer this evening.

"I had to come into town to the feed store to pick up a part for some equipment that the hands are repairing. I'm about to finish up. Can I grab a couple of coffees and stop by to see you for a few minutes?"

She knew that would be more convenient for her than driving into town and meeting him at Coffee Hour. "Yes, I'd love to see you. The coffee will just be a bonus."

Chance chuckled. "What's your order?"

"I'll take a skinny French vanilla latte."

"Skinny, huh? Do you think I would like it?"

"I do."

"Okay, I'm trusting you. I'll bring two. See you in a few."

Although she knew she should try to get in some more writing before Chance arrived, Summer was too excited to see him to concentrate on the chapter she was in the midst of writing. Instead, she went and brushed her teeth and put on a fresh coat of lipstick, fluffing her hair and also spritzing on some perfume.

While waiting, she scrolled through her emails. A text from Sawyer came in as she did so.

Are we still on for Great Steak tonight?

She texted him back.

Yes. I'll pick you up in my NEW SUV! 6:45?

His reply was quick.

I see you're putting some of your settlement money to good use. I could get used to this. A lady picking me up. Buying me dinner. See you later, Cuz.

The doorbell rang, and Summer went to answer it. As she opened the door, butterflies erupted in her stomach at her first glimpse of Chance. He hadn't shaved today, so he had stubble on his face.

And stubble on Chance Blackstone was sexy as hell.

He stepped to her, brushing a soft kiss against her lips.

"Dang, you look good, Sutherland."

"I was thinking the same thing about you. Come on in."

She led him to the great room, and they sat together on the loveseat.

"I cheated," he told her, and her belly tightened at his words. "I've already drunk part of my latte." He handed her cup to her. "You were right. It's really good. I better watch it, or I'm gonna get a taste for these frou-frou drinks. The boys will never let me live it down."

"I think you should buy a coffee machine for the bunkhouse," she told him. "They might like frou-frou, too. Do you even know what one of those is?"

"I'm not a heathen. I worked in offices which actually had them. You pop in a pod and have a cup of coffee a minute later. I tried them a few times, but I usually went back to the pot of coffee sitting on the hot plate in the break room."

Chance stroked her cheek with the back of his fingers. "But I guess I could get used to a fancy coffee machine, especially with Tammy leaving. Whoever gets up first always makes us a pot of coffee. We each drink a couple of cups. It would go to waste now if I keep that up."

"Then we'll go shopping for one," she told him.

Summer took a sip of her latte, savoring it, feeling the caffeine rush ripple through her. Chance entwined her fingers with his.

"So, I see your laptop over there. What have you been working on if not your book?"

She took a few minutes to explain to him about her author whose husband was undergoing chemotherapy treatments.

"Celia was one of my favorites to work with, and she knew she couldn't meet her upcoming deadline. It's this next Monday. Celia only has three chapters to go, two regular ones, along with a short epilogue, which will wrap up things. She's already outlined those three chapters."

Understanding filled his eyes. "You're the one who's going to write those three chapters for her, aren't you?"

Summer nodded. "I feel I owe her, Chance. Celia became a friend over the course of us working together for several years. She's a wonderful lady and a terrific writer. She's on the cusp of breaking through and moving from midlist author to hitting the bestseller list. I know I can't go back and do this kind of thing for all the other authors I edited, but Celia is one I'm choosing to help because of her situation."

"You have a big heart, Summer. That's one of the things that appeals to me. So, where are you and Sawyer going to eat tonight? I know you told me, but it's hard to think of other things when I'm looking at you," he admitted.

"Great Steak," she told him, secretly pleased at his words. "Have you eaten there before?"

"Once. After West moved back to Hawthorne, we met

there for dinner one night. It's pricey but really good. Make sure you get the truffle mac and cheese. It's out of this world. And the beer batter bread is pretty terrific. Comes with honey butter."

"Duly noted," she said. "I'm sorry I'm tied up with Sawyer tonight, but I really owe him."

"He helped you with this New York thing. Leaving your job, didn't he?"

"I can't violate the NDA I signed, or else I'd tell you everything, Chance. It's already hard enough not to talk about it with anyone, but especially you. Let's just say that I was put in the hot seat by the lady who ran Liberty House. She and the in-house counsel were trying to force me out the door. I called their bluff and asked Sawyer to look over the documents they were pressing me to sign."

"What did Sawyer think about them? You don't have to go into detail," Chance assured her. "Just give me an overall impression."

"Some of it was pretty standard industry practice, but he thought with a few of the clauses, they were jerking me around. He countered their offer and emailed it to them. Called me after he did so, and once we talked things over, he asked me to put him on speakerphone. Sawyer's darn good at what he does, and they capitulated to his demands on my behalf. But I had to sign the non-disclosure agreement, which is preventing me from giving you any more information."

"That's how you were able to pay in full for that shiny new Rogue," he surmised.

"Yes," she admitted. "I had no savings because living in New York is terribly expensive. I didn't want to be tied down with a car payment and all that interest. I had asked Sawyer about it, and he thought paying for a car would be a good use of my money. I don't plan to blow any of the rest of it, though.

I'll be as frugal as possible. It's that money which is letting me try my hand at being a full-time novelist. I told Autumn that I'll give it a year. If it's not working out, I'll keep writing, but I'll need to get a full-time job to support myself."

She saw his brow crease in worry. "Doing what?" he asked.

Summer shrugged. "I'm not going there yet. I don't want to think about failure when I'm just starting out. This time next year, I'll assess my financial situation and see what needs to be done. Don't worry, I'll keep you in the loop about my decision."

Chance's gaze pinned hers. "I'm hoping by this time next year that we may have come to some kind of understanding, Summer," he said huskily. "I know you've said you don't want to rush things, so we won't talk about it now. Just keep it on the back burner, will you?"

He squeezed her fingers, and Summer hoped that she had both a career as a full-time writer and a life with this man the next time spring came around.

# CHAPTER
## Twelve

Chance had welcomed Zeke and Maria Benevides to Blackstone Ranch, along with their eight-year-old son, Matteo, and five-year-old daughter, Luna. The couple expressed their gratitude to him for hiring them, and they were flabbergasted when he took them to the cabin which would become their new home. Zeke told him they couldn't accept something so grand, but Chance, along with Tammy, insisted this was where the family was to stay, hopefully for many years to come.

He had allowed Tammy to take over from there, and she had asked Chance if Joaquin, the children's uncle, could watch them for the afternoon. He readily agreed, and Joaquin set off with the kids, taking them to see the horses and cattle, as well as the chickens. Tammy took Zeke and Maria to both the big house and the bunkhouse and walked them through everything which would need to be done at both places to keep them clean. She also went over the times meals were to be provided and had drawn up menus for a month in order to smooth the transition.

Tammy also took the pair into Hawthorne, introducing them to where they would shop for groceries and cleaning supplies, and then to Hawthorne Elementary School, where they enrolled Luna and Matteo in kindergarten and third grade.

He knew Tammy wouldn't be home for dinner this evening, remaining with Zeke as he cooked for the ranch hands and then having dinner with the Benevides family, so Chance had asked Summer if she wanted to have dinner with him. He suggested they eat in town, but she was eager to try out the pork chop recipe Tammy had shared with her before Tammy left town. Summer told him she would bring everything she needed to cook dinner for them at the ranch.

Chance told her to come at five. He'd returned to the house around one after being in the fields and showered before heading to his office to deal with the never-ending paperwork of running a cattle and horse ranch. He finished up a few minutes before five, opening a bottle of red wine in order for it to breathe.

The doorbell rang, and he hurried to answer it, eager to see Summer. It was crazy how fast he had become addicted to her. Her smile. Her scent. Her rich laugh. Her warmth and wit. Everything about her told him that she was the one for him. When Summer had mentioned the possibility of getting a job a year from now, panic had flooded him. He doubted she could be a book editor in Hawthorne. The thought of her going back to New York and the fifteen hundred miles which would separate them was unthinkable.

That's why he'd pushed a little, telling her in as few words as possible that he saw a future for them. Together.

Summer hadn't mentioned it since then. Neither had he. But it was in the back of his mind. The sooner he could slip a ring on her finger, the happier he would be. In a way, it was funny. He'd always been a physical man. Sex had been a healthy part of his life. He'd had plenty of it, with all kinds of women. Yet here he was, in love with a woman he'd only kissed.

Chance stopped in his tracks, only a few feet from the front door.

*In love?*

He admitted to himself that he was. That he'd been bitten by the love bug. He knew he loved Summer Sutherland.

Now, all he needed was for her feelings to catch up to his.

Opening the door, he smiled at her. "Let me take those," he said, grabbing the handles to the shopping bags she held.

After he had them in hand, he leaned in for a kiss. Summer, her hands now free, framed his face with them and made the kiss a long, thorough one.

"Now, that's the way to greet a man," he said cheerfully, taking the bags to the kitchen.

She followed him, asking, "Are you sure Tammy doesn't mind me invading her kitchen?"

"She's happy you're going to test the pork chops on me," Chance told her.

"I told Autumn if they turned out right, I was going to see if we could get together this weekend with everyone and let me cook."

"Not this weekend," he said, setting the sacks on the over-sized island and reaching in, pulling out items. "You and I have plans on Saturday."

"We do?"

"You told me you've finished the two chapters for Celia. All you have left is the epilogue."

"True."

"Tomorrow's Friday. Can you wrap it up by then?"

"I planned to," she replied. "Then I'll read through what I've written and tweak it before I send it off to Celia. She can copy and paste it to the end of what she's written and read over it to see if she likes it."

He kissed the tip of her nose. "She'll like it. You're really helping her out in a big way, finishing up these last few chapters of her book for her."

"I was happy to do it. In fact, it's cemented the idea to me that creating an outline after I do my character sketches is the way to go. I do better with an outline. I've got fifteen pages of plot outlined for this second book I'm starting in my series." She giggled. "I know pantsers would hate that idea."

"Pantsers?"

"As in fly by the seat of your pants. Some writers only have a vague idea about their plot, but I know I would waste a lot of time if I didn't do some pre-planning. I always create character sketches and work out major plot points. Then I divide up those big events and work in smaller events between them. I section out the book that way, so I pretty much go into a chapter knowing what I need to write about in those pages. I can't imagine just sitting in front of a blank screen and starting to type, not even knowing who my characters are or where I want to take them."

"It's interesting that others work differently than you do," Chance said. "I guess I'm a planner and a never pantser, as far as the ranch is concerned. Even with all my planning, though, I've learned that I have to be flexible. You never know when weather can be a factor and throw a monkey wrench into things. Getting too much or too little rain. A tornado damaging a barn or tearing down a fence. Part of the herd escaping through that hole. Or even some type of sickness spreading through the herd. I plan as best I can and move ahead—with caution."

Summer smiled. "Well, I have dinner all planned out. I'll tell you up front that I've never been a cook. I had my stack of takeout menus sitting on the kitchen counter in Brooklyn and used the same places frequently. Or sometimes, I'd stop by a deli for a sandwich or salad or a pizzeria and grab a few slices of pizza on my way home from work. So, this cooking stuff is new to me. Tammy walked me through the pork chop recipe, though, and last night, Autumn had me help her make mashed potatoes and roasted vegetables. I think the hardest thing will be to get down the timing so that everything turns out about the same time."

He snagged her waist, pulling her closer, and dropped a kiss on her lips. "You've got a great sous chef in me. I'm a talented breakfast maker and can make a mean sandwich, but I've always left dinner up to Tammy."

She turned on both the ovens to preheat and removed the cellophane from a package of four plump pork chops. "I may have to see those breakfast skills sometime. Right now, you can peel these potatoes for us."

Summer took out three large potatoes, and Chance got to work on them while she washed vegetables and found a baking pan for them. She lined the pan with foil and patted the vegetables dry with a paper towel. He continued watching her as she mixed olive oil and lemon juice, adding a good amount of salt and pepper.

"I'll set that aside for now," she said more to herself than him. "Need to get the pork chops seasoned before they go into the oven."

He watched her moving efficiently. Even though Summer had never cooked before, he saw that she had a talent for it as she prepared the chops and placed them in the top oven, setting a timer. She put a large pot of water on to boil and had him cut the potatoes into chunks.

"Not too big and definitely not too small," she warned. "Like this."

She took the knife from him and cut into one of the potatoes.

"Got it," he said.

They continued to putter around the kitchen. He poured them each a glass of pinot noir, and they sipped on it as she drizzled the seasoned oil over carrots and zucchini, which she spread out on a cookie sheet. He got the potatoes into the water and lowered the heat as she instructed.

"Okay, we can sit for a minute," she told him, taking a seat at the kitchen table with her wineglass.

Chance followed, and he told her about his day, meeting Zeke and Maria and their kids.

"They were really excited about having the cabin to live in. Tammy took them around the ranch and let them know all what they'll be responsible for. She's made lists for them both to follow. Me, too. She's always paid the bills and insurance on the house and cars and trucks."

He chuckled. "I've got a Tammy to-do list of my own to follow."

When it came time, she took the meat out to rest as he retrieved milk and butter and the masher for the potatoes. She seasoned them and watched the amount of milk and butter he added, getting him to add a touch more milk. Summer took the roasted vegetables from the lower oven.

"I think I'll do it like Tammy and have us fix our plates without putting everything into serving dishes."

They did so and enjoyed a leisurely meal in the kitchen. Chance thought about how they had worked as a team, preparing this meal, and how both that and their conversation was easy and comfortable. He could see similar nights in their future. Cooking together. Talking. Laughing.

Chance dabbed his mouth with a napkin. "That was a delicious meal. If that's the only thing you learn how to cook, you've accomplished more than most people."

"I'd love to make it for the group. Not this Saturday, since we have mysterious plans. Maybe the next, though. Could we have everyone over here? It's just that after tonight, I'm familiar with where things are, plus you've got plenty of room at your dining table."

"I'd be happy for us to host." He pulled out his phone. "I've got a group text with everyone on it. Well, all but you. Let me fix that."

He added her to the chain. "What time?"

"I think early. Maybe have everyone come at six? Eat at six-thirty?"

Chance typed a message and pushed send. "Let's clean up."

They wrapped the leftovers and then placed the dirty dishes into the dishwasher. He wiped down the counters while she cleaned the table.

"Looks as good as when you got here," he told her. "Do you have time to sit a bit?" He looked at her hopefully. "To entice you, there might be kissing involved."

"Then I'm definitely in," she told him.

He took her hand and turned out the kitchen light, leading her into the den.

"Have a seat. I'm going to light a fire."

"Oh, don't go to any trouble."

Laughing, he said, "It's just a simple flip of a switch these days. Tammy got tired of the mess that burning real logs makes. She didn't even ask Dad. She just had an electric fireplace put in. Of course, he fussed about it. Then he saw how easy it was. He never griped after that."

They sat on the sofa opposite the fire. Chance slipped his

arm around her shoulders, and Summer snuggled into him. Yes. This felt right as rain.

"What's going on Saturday?" she asked. "I can't help it. I'm curious."

"We're going to Dallas to see the Stars play the Nashville Predators."

Her face lit up. "Are you serious? I've never seen them play in person." She paused. "You asked me about sports I liked, and I mentioned hockey. You remembered that."

Summer touched her palm to his cheek. "It's nice to be seen. To be heard."

He framed her face in his hands. "I know I never saw you before. I don't think I was supposed to all those years ago. I was pretty wild. I needed to get out of Hawthorne and do some living. Now that I'm back here, though, and you're here, too? It seems as if the timing is perfect. Absolutely perfect."

Chance kissed her. "I hope you feel the same way."

"I do," she said softly, her turquoise eyes shining, flames from the fire reflected in them.

They engaged in what he would've called in high school a make-out session. All they did was kiss, but each kiss was better than the previous one. He kissed her long and slow. Hard. Deep. Kissed her brow and her cheeks. Her eyelids. Grazed his teeth against her ear and nibbled on it, moving to her throat. He found her pulse point, throbbing wildly, and licked and kissed it. He took tiny little nips along her neck, feeling her shivers as he soothed the love bite with a swipe of his tongue.

Then he worked his way back to her mouth. He teased it open, his tongue plunging inside, sweeping against hers. He needed her closer and lifted her to his lap, and she wrapped her arms about his neck. They kissed for a long time.

And he was happy doing just that. With any other

woman, he would have stripped her bare and enjoyed having sex with her. Summer was different. *He* was different with her. He would wait as long as she wanted, and when they came together, Chance knew it wouldn't be sex. He would be making love to the woman he loved.

The one he wanted as his wife.

Summer broke the kiss, breathing heavily. "When is the game?"

"It's actually an afternoon game. At two on Saturday." He kissed her again. "I thought we could go to dinner after."

"And after that?"

He brushed his thumb along her lower lip. "Then come home." He grinned. "Make out some more."

She ran her fingers through his hair, causing his scalp to tingle. "What if I want more?"

Chance swallowed. "How much more?"

Her fingers tightened in his hair. "I'd say you better have a few condoms on hand."

Surprise rippled through him. "Are you sure?"

"Sure that I want you inside me—or sure that we'll need at least a few?" she teased.

He growled, seizing her mouth again, kissing her until they were both out of breath.

When he finally broke the kiss, he said, "I'll be sure to stop at the drugstore tomorrow."

Summer burst out laughing. "Then I'll tell Autumn not to expect me home on Saturday night."

"You know Tammy is leaving Saturday morning. We'll have the place all to ourselves." He kissed her. "I'm going to enjoy making you scream my name, Sutherland."

# Thirteen

Chance went downstairs to the kitchen, finding Tammy already sitting at the table, a pensive look on her face.

She looked up at him, giving him a wistful smile. "Last coffee time together."

He swallowed the lump in his throat. Going to the coffee pot, he poured himself a cup and then joined her at the table. She held out a hand, and he took it. They drank their coffee in silence, holding hands the entire time.

Finally, he said, "You have meant the world to me. I hope you know that. That I love you more than I could ever say."

Her eyes glittered with unshed tears. "You and Kelby—and this ranch—have been my entire world for so many years. I love you with all my heart, Chance." She smiled gently at him. "And I think I'm leaving you in good hands."

He knew she spoke of Summer. Tammy had shared that she had gifted Summer with her handwritten recipe book. Knowing how precious it was to Tammy, it had surprised Chance, yet it had moved him at the same time.

"She's the one," he confirmed. "I don't know how soon

it'll be before we're hitched, but I'm already committed to her." He grinned. "I'd like to do with her what you're doing with Tommy. Simply go to a justice of the peace. No fuss. But Summer may want more than that. A wedding with all the trimmings."

"You'll work that out between you," Tammy assured him.

The kitchen door swung open, and Kelby entered, carrying a white bakery box. Chance saw his sister's eyes already misting with tears. She put the box on the kitchen table, and Tammy rose, enfolding Kelby into her arms. The two cried for a little bit, happy tears, but tears, all the same.

They took a seat at the table, and Kelby said, "There's already such a hole in my heart, Tammy. I've depended upon you for everything my entire life. Don't get me wrong. I'm thrilled that you and Tommy have found one another again. I know you're going to have this happy, amazing life with the man you love. I guess it's just the end of an era, so it's a little bittersweet."

Tammy patted Kelby's hand. "It is. But you have West—and that sweet baby girl who'll make her appearance pretty soon. You know I'm coming back for that."

"And bringing Tommy," Kelby prompted. "We're all dying to meet him."

A tap sounded on the door, and it opened again. This time, West and Darby came into the kitchen. Tammy rose and hugged both of them.

"We had to come say goodbye," West said. "Darby and I spent so much time here at the ranch over the years. I still can't bite into an oatmeal cookie without thinking of you, Tammy. You always brought Chance and me plates of cookies and tall glasses of ice-cold milk."

"I remember all the late-night talks with you," Darby added. "When I would come to spend the night. You've always listened to all of us, Tammy. We love you and will miss you terribly."

Chance poured a cup of coffee for West. Darby and Kelby asked for glasses of ice water, and Kelby opened the box on the table, saying, "I had to bring kolaches from Luscious Layers one last time." She chuckled. "I thought we'd eat a couple of the dozen I brought, and then Tammy could introduce Tommy to them since they're the best kolaches in Texas. Seeing who's here now, I don't know if any will be left."

They all laughed, and Chance heard the doorbell ring. Frowning, he rose. "I'll get it."

When he opened the door, Summer stood on the porch, a book in her hand.

"I had to come and tell Tammy goodbye," she said. "I hope I'm not interrupting anything."

He pulled her to him and kissed her lightly. "Not at all," he assured her. "Come join the party."

Chance took her hand and led her back to the kitchen.

"I'm so glad you came," Tammy told Summer.

She looked around at those gathered. "I'm sorry I'm late. I didn't know all these people would be here."

"We had to come to say our goodbyes to Tammy," Darby said. "She has been such a part of our lives here in Hawthorne."

For the next hour, they reminisced about their years growing up. They talked of birthday parties which had been held at the ranch. Learning how to ride a horse. Slumber parties. Each of them had memories of advice Tammy had given them, helping them through a tough time in their lives.

Finally, Tammy said, "It's time for me to hit the road. I told Tommy I'd aim to be in Waco before noon." She hugged each of them tightly.

As they began to leave the kitchen, Chance saw Summer hand the book to Tammy and whisper something to her. Tammy nodded and went to Kelby. He saw Tammy pass the book to his sister, and they embraced one another again. He wondered what it was and decided he would ask Summer about it later.

They all walked Tammy out to her car, which Chance had helped to pack last night. Tammy looked at those gathered.

"I'll be back. For the baby and other times. I want you all to meet Tommy. He's heard so much about everyone from me. He already thinks of all of you as family."

"We're looking forward to that," he said.

Tammy placed her purse and the bakery box, which still held two kolaches, inside her car. She turned and took his hand and Kelby's, squeezing tightly.

"Thank you for being such a wonderful part of my life. Kate would be so pleased to see how well her children turned out."

"You had a huge hand in making us who we are, Tammy," Chance said, his voice breaking.

They both embraced her again, and then Kelby said, "Get in that car, or we may never let you go. And text when you get there. We want to know that you made it safely."

"I'll do that," Tammy said. "And thanks to the three of you for coming to see me off, too."

Chance had asked if Tammy were going down to the bunkhouse to say goodbye, but she told him that she'd said her goodbyes to the ranch hands yesterday. Still, it moved him when he saw the group of cowboys riding up on their horses, lining the drive. As Tammy's car drove past them, she waved. They each took off their hats and placed them over their hearts.

Kelby wiped the tears from her cheeks. "I'm a blubbering mess. Being pregnant only makes it worse."

Darby came and put an arm around her best friend. "Want to come back to our place, Kel?"

Kelby sniffed. "Right now, I just want to go home and curl up with an afghan Tammy made for me. Come home with me, Darb. We can sit on the couch and drink hot chocolate and binge-watch something."

"I'd love to."

The two women and West said their goodbyes. Summer said she also needed to leave.

He walked her back to her SUV and asked, "What book did you give Tammy?"

"It was a book of all her recipes. She gave it to me when I came over that day for the pork chop recipe."

Chance knew it had been Tammy's way of welcoming Summer into the Blackstone family, even though they had no official understanding between them yet.

"Why did you give it back to her?"

"My heart told me that Kelby was the one who should have it passed down to her, so I took pictures of every recipe inside it. It's a treasure trove of all kinds of foods. I plan to buy myself a blank recipe book, and then I'll record all of Tammy's recipes in it and learn to make every one of them."

"That was incredibly thoughtful of you to do that so Kelby could have it."

"I knew it would mean a lot to her. I need to go now. I sent the last pages of what I've written to Celia Cameron yesterday afternoon. She was going to read over them last night." Summer glanced at her watch. "We've got a call in an hour to talk about it." She smiled. "Then I'll see you for our big date later today."

He placed his hands on her waist, his thumbs stroking her

ribcage. "You haven't changed your mind about anything, have you?"

"No," she said softly. "Game. Dinner. And then home with you."

"What did Autumn say?"

"She grinned like a fool and told me to enjoy myself. I didn't ask her to keep quiet about it, Chance. At the very least, she's going to tell Eli."

"I don't care if she tells the world, Summer. I can't wait to be with you tonight. I'm half-tempted to skip the game and go straight to the good stuff."

She swatted at him playfully. "Not a chance, Blackstone. I've never seen the Stars play in person, and I'm looking forward to seeing the team on the ice. Watching all those hot hockey players will get me worked up. For you."

He kissed her. He could have kissed her all day, but he knew that he had to let her go.

*For now ...*

"Okay. I'll pick you up at eleven-thirty as planned."

"I can't wait," Summer said. "And you know I'm eager to be with *you*. The game is just some sweet icing on what I think will be a very fulfilling cake."

"Summer Sutherland, stop flirting with me, or you're never going to get out of here."

Chance opened her car door for her, and she climbed behind the wheel. He leaned in for one, swift kiss. "See you soon."

He stepped back and closed her door, watching her drive away. He was eager for the day when she would be here with him and never have to leave. It was impossible to think of his life without Summer in it. The sooner he could make her his, the better.

Chance went back into the kitchen and cleaned up,

putting everyone's mugs and glasses in the dishwasher. The house seemed so empty without Tammy's presence. It was going to take some getting used to, not having her around, but he was genuinely happy for her and the new life she was going to.

He went and saddled Rebel and rode aimlessly for an hour, memories of Tammy swirling through him.

When he returned to the house, he showered and shaved, taming his hair as best as he could. He still had a little time and decided to get on an auction site to view some of the upcoming horses for sale. He entered his office and saw two envelopes propped against the computer's keyboard. Tammy's familiar handwriting was scrawled across both. One was addressed to him and one to Kelby. He would drop his sister's letter off on his way to Summer's.

Sitting in his desk chair, Chance opened the envelope, pulling out a single page.

*Chance –*

*I learned when I was in high school that I could never have children. I was in a bad car wreck my sophomore year, and I suffered some pretty severe injuries. By the time I had gotten to college, I had reconciled myself to the fact that children would never be a part of my life. Truth be known, it was the biggest reason why I let Tommy go. I knew he wanted children, and I would never be able to give them to him.*

*Having your mom as my college roommate was simply fate. We had both gone with potluck and wound up with one another. Kate became my closest friend and confidant, the one person I could always depend upon.*

*I'm sorry you never really got to know her, Chance. Kate was the kindest person I ever knew, with the biggest heart in Texas. When she knew she wasn't going to make it, she asked me to look after her two babies. She loved you both so much. She told me to be a mom to you for both of us.*

*I never forgot her generosity of spirit. Her thinking of the two of you—and me—as the life faded from her. I may not have given birth to you and Kelby, but you are the children of my heart. If all I had ever done was raise the two of you, I would be completely content.*

*You are a good man, Chance. You've taken on a heavy burden with the running of Blackstone Ranch, but you're managing things beautifully. You also have a wonderful opportunity now to have lasting happiness of your own with Summer. Just watching the two of you together lets me know that you'll take good care of one another.*

*This isn't goodbye—only farewell for now. I expect regular phone calls from you, young man, and I hope to be in your life for many years to come. I want to see you married, Chance. See you loving Summer and having children with her.*

*Take care, my sweet boy. I love you with all my heart.*

*Tammy*

Chance placed the page on his desk and used the backs of his hands to wipe away the tears which flowed freely. He was the lucky one for having Tammy in his life. He knew his mom had also been fortunate to have such a wonderful friend, trusting Tammy with her two young children.

More than anything, Chance wanted a family, and he wanted one with Summer.

He didn't want to scare her off, but tonight he was going to tell her that he loved her.

# Fourteen

Summer didn't bother to contain her excitement as she and Chance entered the area surrounding American Airlines Center. The atmosphere was charged, with fans moving about the zone. Some watched the usual street hockey game which took place before the game inside the arena started. Others were playing cornhole or ordering items from local food booths.

"This is incredible!" she told Chance, who just grinned at her.

"Wait until you see where our seats are," he teased. "Let's just say that Jace has started repping two players with the team and when he heard that I was taking you to a Stars game, he made a little magic happen."

She hoped that didn't mean sitting in a suite. While it would be nice to have access to terrific food and comfortable seats, Summer wanted to be down in the midst of the crowd, caught up in the action.

"That was thoughtful of Jace," she said instead, deciding

that it didn't matter where they sat. She was with the man who held her heart.

And they were going to make love for the first time tonight.

That alone caused her heart to race. Being at this hockey game was just an added bonus to what she hoped would be a wonderful day—and night.

They wandered about the plaza for a few minutes, and she was glad that Chance had gifted her with an official Stars NHL hockey jersey when he picked her up. Everyone seemed to be wearing Victory Green, whether it was player jerseys or T-shirts. Of course, Chance was in his usual flannel shirt, jeans, and boots. Today's shirt was a deep blue in color, which seemed to make his gray eyes even darker.

"Thank you again for my jersey," she told him. "I feel as if I really fit in with all the fans."

"Any time, babe," he said, pressing a kiss against her temple.

Just the slightest touch from him caused goose bumps to crop up. Summer forced her thoughts away from how he would touch her tonight because she wanted to soak up everything at this game.

"There's Victor E. Green," she said excitedly.

"Who?"

"The Stars mascot, silly," she said, dragging Chance toward where Victor E. Green, the cute and cuddly green monster mascot stood, a line formed in front of him. "We've got to get our picture with him."

Chance laughed. "If you insist. Better yet, you stand next to him, and I'll take the photo."

"Nope. You're not getting out of it. I want both of us in the picture as a reminder of today."

They joined the line, which moved quickly, and ten

minutes later, they were at the front. Summer handed her phone to an employee for the Stars, and they quickly got on each side of Victor E. Green.

"Smile," said the employee, and they beamed at her.

"Thank you," she said to the mascot and the woman who handed her cell back to her.

Immediately, she brought up the picture and saw that two pictures had been taken. One showed the entire length of them, while the other zoomed in from about the waist up. Summer saw how happy Chance and she looked.

"This is my new lock screen picture," she declared, quickly changing out the picture on her phone for the new photo. Holding it up, she asked, "What do you think?"

"I think I'm here with the most beautiful woman in Texas," he drawled, winking at her.

"You're laying it on pretty thick, Cowboy," she shot back, wondering if he really thought she was pretty.

"Don't second guess yourself, Summer," Chance said. "I see a little doubt in your eyes. You're beautiful. Period."

She smiled happily. "Okay. I believe you. Should we go inside? I need to soak up everything inside the arena."

"Sure. Let's go."

Once inside, they walked an entire lap around the concourse, seeing what food was offered, as well as Stars merchandise.

"We should grab something to eat," he told her. "The last thing I ate was a couple of those kolaches Kelby brought by this morning. What sounds good?"

"I'm happy with a hot dog or nachos."

"We'll get both," he decided.

Once they had food and drinks, he steered her to their section. They kept walking down, down, down the steps until they were on the row next to the ice.

"Are you kidding me?" she asked happily, following him into the row and taking a seat. "These are amazing! And here I was worried we'd be stuck in some suite."

"Actually, Jace offered that first, but I told him that I know my girl, and she'd want to be in the middle of everything."

A warmth filled her. "I like hearing that. You calling me your girl."

Chance shrugged. "Well, you are. And I know you."

As they ate, the players skated onto the ice for warmups. More fans began pouring into the arena, and the place became electric by the time pre-game player introductions began. The light show and pounding music had the crowd amped. Summer was impressed by the video boards and graphics, snapping a few pictures to show Kelby.

When play began, she leaned forward in her seat, her heart racing as one side of the arena chanted *Dallas*, followed by the other side shouting *Stars*. It amazed her how sitting so close to the action was different from watching at home on TV. The players' speed seemed even faster as they sped by, and everything was louder, from the body checks along the boards to the slap shots. She was immersed with every hit and shot, admiring the skill of these professional athletes up close and how precise every move they made was.

She could feel the vibrations of the pounding music during stoppages. Sometimes, it was rock and other times pop or electronic. It added to the excitement as the crowd cheered loudly. Sitting on the front row meant no one stood in front of her, obstructing her view. That had been one thing she hadn't liked when she went to see West play at A&M. The student section stood the entire time during football games, and she sometimes missed a play because of that.

Leaning over to Chance, she shouted in his ear, "I could get used to seats like these."

He merely smiled and nodded. Summer had no idea if he might be a hockey fan, but he seemed to be enjoying the game.

Then the Stars scored, and the place erupted in cheers. People beside and behind them high-fived them, and the traditional Pantera song *Puck Off* came over the loudspeakers. She was enough of a fan that she knew the song, which had been written during the Stars' Stanley Cup run back in 1999, was always played after the home team scored a goal.

The Predators came back within two minutes and scored a goal of their own before the end of the first period. Summer could feel her face flushed with excitement.

"You're having a good time," Chance observed.

"The best!" she told him. "Thank you again for bringing me. It's a really different game in person than watching on TV. And these seats really make the whole experience even more intense. Every time players check each other into the glass near us or the puck slaps against the boards, it's so loud. I can even hear the scraping of the blades on the ice when they change direction. It's fantastic."

Summer leaned in and kissed him lightly. "I appreciate you remembering how much I like hockey."

"I want to remember everything about you," he said into her ear, his tone husky.

No scoring happened during the second period, but a scrum happened right in front of them, with players shoving and jostling for position, trying to get control of the puck. A stick battle broke out, turning into a fight. She could see the intensity in these players' eyes and realized just how physical a game hockey could be.

In the final period, the Stars scored, causing the crowd

to erupt. Ahead now two-to-one, she hoped her team would hold their lead. Then her favorite player, one of the co-captains, drove commandingly down the ice, slamming the puck past the opponent's goalie. Again, the arena went insane, with fans jumping up and down and cheering wildly.

The game ended, and Chance turned to her. "Happy?"

"Deliriously," she replied, her heart still pounding

*Because now the real excitement would start.*

They waited a few minutes, letting some of the crowd disperse before they made their way up the stairs and out onto the concourse. It took several more minutes before they reached the parking garage.

"As good as the tickets were, we really have to thank Jace for the parking pass," Chance said.

"We need to do something nice for him and Darby," she said.

"Well, we're already having them over next Saturday. Remember, you're cooking your famous pork chops for everyone."

"I wouldn't call them famous. They're Tammy's chops."

"But you have learned how to make them. That means a lot to me. You listened to me when I said they're my favorite meal."

They stopped at his truck, and Chance added, "I always want us to listen to one another. Really *hear* one another without being distracted. I know I'm not much of a talker, but conversations were meant to be heard. Not ignored."

Summer smiled up at him. "I agree. And you don't seem quiet to me anymore. Not like how you were growing up. You barely said anything to anybody."

He cupped her cheek. "Maybe I only have a lot to say to you."

Chance kissed her, and she tasted the promise of what was to come.

He helped her into the truck, and they joined the line of vehicles snaking their way out of the garage.

"Would you like to grab a bite to eat while we're in Dallas, or would you rather go home?" he asked.

"I'm still a little full from what we ate at the game," she admitted. "Let's wait."

"Fine by me."

He took her hand, holding it the entire drive back to Hawthorne.

When they reached town, he pulled up at a stoplight and said, "We could stop and pick something up. Take it home with us."

"To be honest, I don't have food on my mind right now."

His head whipped around, and he looked her in the eyes. "Same," he said softly.

The driver behind them honked, and Chance looked back at the road. The light had turned green, and he started up his truck.

"I seem to only be aware of you," he said, his voice a bit raspy.

"Same," Summer said, her heart speeding up.

They drove down Main Street and came out the other side of Hawthorne. Blackstone Ranch was only a few minutes north of town. Suddenly, she wondered if she would please him.

"What's wrong?" he asked, ever in tune with her.

"I'm a little worried," she said, her voice small. "You have been with a lot of women, Chance. I'm not upset with that. I know that was before, but I'm feeling a little uncertain. I have experience of my own, but not a lot recently. I became a workaholic my last couple of years at Liberty House."

He chuckled, bringing her hand up and kissing her fingers. "I already told you before. I dived into work when I came back to the ranch. Have put in even more hours since Dad passed. It's been a while for me, too, Summer. But this is one horse I know I can climb back on and not miss a beat."

Chance paused. "I just want everything to be good for you."

As he turned into the front gates of Blackstone Ranch, Summer said, "It will be. I'm hoping it will be good for us. I know a lot is riding on tonight, Chance. We're compatible now, but tossing sex into the mix might change things."

"Have no fear, my dear," he said teasingly. "We're gonna fit together just fine. Like those jeans you're poured into now. Have I told you how long your legs look in them? Or how they make me want to cup your buttocks?"

She felt herself blushing. "I'm glad you kept that to yourself. If you would have said that earlier, I never would have been able to focus on the game."

He stopped the truck in front of the big house and cut the engine. Turning to her, Chance said, "The hockey game is over now, but we've got a few new games to play with one another. Are you ready?"

His words caused a chill to ripple along her spine.

"Ready," Summer replied, hoping that she would be enough for him, trying to push away the doubts wanting to squeeze in.

She loved him—and would try to show him tonight just how much she did.

C hance hadn't watched the hockey game as much as he had watched Summer watching it. The pure pleasure on her face made his heart sing. He had wined and dined his fair share of women over the years, but none of them took such joy as his girl did. He had escorted women to parties with movers and shakers. Taken them to Michelin star restaurants. Concerts with famous artists. Broadway touring productions. Yet most of them had been bored at whatever event they accompanied him to.

And he had been bored being with them.

Summer was a hometown girl, with the same values and interests he had. She enjoyed sports. Family life. She was dedicated to her writing and worked tirelessly at it. He couldn't imagine sharing his life with a better partner. That included in the bedroom. He could be adventurous at times, and he didn't want to overwhelm her. Already, he enjoyed kissing her more than he had any other woman from his past. He hoped they would mesh well sexually.

Tonight, he would find out.

They entered the house, which was dark.

"Sorry. Forgot to leave any lights on since I walked out of here this morning," he apologized.

He turned on a lamp in the entry way and then another which lit the stairs. Already, Chance's heart was pounding, anticipating making love with Summer. He had told her he'd lived like a monk the past couple of years. While he'd taken care of his needs on a regular basis, he hadn't been with a woman since he'd returned to Blackstone Ranch. He told himself to take his time, for both their sakes, as they slipped off their jackets.

They moved up the stairs, his hand wrapped around hers. Chance almost led Summer into the bedroom which had been his for so many years, but two days ago, he'd finally moved down the hall, into the primary suite. With Tammy removing everything which had belonged to his dad, he'd been able to fill the drawers and closet with his own things. Putting his toiletries in the bathroom had seemed odd, though. While he had spent little time in the actual bedroom, he had visited his dad many times in the bathroom, watching Big Jim shave. They'd had some of their best talks in this bathroom, and he wondered if someday his own son—or daughter—might come to him for advice as he lathered his face and slid a razor across his cheeks, ridding himself of stubble.

Need was building in him, and even though no one was in the house but the two of them, Chance closed the bedroom door as he turned on the overhead light. It was harsh, though, causing them both to blink. He hurried to the lamp sitting on the nightstand and switched it to low, coming back to Summer, who had slipped her purse from her shoulder and set it on the dresser before turning off the bright overhead light.

Desire now filled him, and he crowded her so that her back touched the bedroom door. Hungrily, his mouth took hers, his hands sliding down her arms, encircling her wrists. He kissed her as he never had anyone else, loving her taste and her scent. He lifted her arms, pinning her wrists to the door, high over her head, his body pressing against hers.

He kissed her until they were both breathless, his body rubbing against hers. He moved her wrists so they were stacked and captured them with one hand. With his free one, he slipped it around her nape, kissing her again, feeling her wriggle against him.

Lifting his mouth, he said, "You do know that when you move, it's a huge turn on for me."

She bit her lip. "I can't help it."

"Good. I don't want you to."

As he kissed her, his hand stroked her neck and then moved to her throat. She wore the jersey he'd gotten for her, and underneath it was a V-neck sweater. He slipped his hand under the sweater and brushed his fingers along her ribcage. She gasped, but he didn't let up, kissing her harder, wanting to possess every inch of her.

Fortunately, her bra closed in the front, which made it a lot easier to open with one hand. He did so, pushing the cups away, his fingers grazing her nipple. Slowly, he stroked it back and forth with the pad of his thumb, feeling it pebble in need. She moaned softly.

He broke the kiss and dragged his lips along her throat, feeling her pulse beating wildly. His hand palmed her breast, squeezing it, massaging it, playing with the nipple again, tweaking it. She writhed more, struggling to bring her hands down, but he kept them pinned to the door.

Then he slid his hand to her smooth back, moving up and down the satiny skin before heading lower. He cupped one of her buttocks, squeezing, feeling her body tremble. He moved his hand again, stroking her core, hating that she still wore the thick, skintight denim jeans.

"These have got to go," he said, finally releasing her wrists.

Her fingers plunged into his hair as he undid the button and slid the zipper of her jeans down. They fit her like a second skin, and it took him a minute to work them over her hips and slide them down to her ankles.

Pressing his body to hers again, he stroked her along the seam of her sex, finding her panties damp.

"You're wet for me," he murmured, kissing her.

"Yes," she said, panting. "Yes."

"I'll have to do something about that."

"Yes," she said, more urgently now, her fingers tightening in his hair.

Moving quickly, he captured her wrists again, returning them above her head, continuing to kiss her mouth and stroke her core. Then he slipped a finger beneath her panties, pushing it inside her.

"Yes!" she gasped. "More."

He stroked her deeply, feeling the tremors run through her as he did so. He couldn't touch her as he liked and was too impatient to remove her jeans and underwear. Instead, he yanked hard on the scrap of material, tearing it away from her. Breaking the kiss, he gazed deeply into her eyes.

"I want to watch you as you come."

Her eyes widened, but she nodded.

He did just that. Caressing her. Pushing a second finger inside her. Feeling her juices flow for him. She began writhing. Whimpering. His eyes never left hers.

And then she began calling his name, pushing against him, and he quickened his pace. Suddenly, she erupted with a scream, and he covered her mouth with his, feeling her orgasm rip through her. She rode it, and he reveled in the pure pleasure he gave her.

Finally, she stopped moving. He gentled the kiss and broke it, looking at her.

"That was ... powerful," she said, her voice full of wonder.

He was ready to explode himself, and that was the last thing he wanted. He needed to make love to her with more than his fingers.

"I want you inside me," she said haltingly. "*Really* inside me."

"I bought those condoms, just like you told me to," he said, watching the corners of her mouth turn up in a smile.

"Then we better make sure you get your money's worth."

"Oh, I plan to, babe."

Quickly, they began undressing one another. He pulled the jersey and then sweater over her head. She undid his buttons and opened his shirt, leaning toward him and kissing his chest. Her lips scalded his skin. Before he could stop her, she'd latched onto his nipple, teasing it with the tip of her tongue, causing desire to spike within him.

Easing her back up, he said, "That felt wonderful, but I don't want to come yet. Not until I'm inside you."

He stepped back, pulling off her shoes. Knowing the jeans bunched around her ankles would present more of a challenge, he picked her up and placed her on the bed, working the faded denim over her feet. Then he pushed the straps of her bra from her shoulders and rid her of the last piece of clothing she wore. He looked down at her.

She was spectacular.

Those long legs went on forever. Her waist was small and her rounded breasts were an average size, but they suited her frame. He nudged her to her back, her legs hanging off the bed. Hovering over her, he placed his mouth on one of her breasts, licking her, his hand working her other breast, tweaking her nipple. She locked her legs around his waist, pulling him closer to her.

"Wait. Let me get the rest off. Then I promise I won't go anywhere."

She watched him pull off his boots and jeans and then his boxer briefs and socks.

"Wow," she whispered. "Just ... wow."

"You approve?"

She grinned. "I more than approve. And I want to touch. A lot."

He climbed onto the bed, nuzzling her neck. For a long time, they explored one another's bodies. With fingers. Lips. Tongues. Her every touch pushed him higher and higher, until he was flying high and ready to explode.

"Wait," he gasped, climbing from the bed and opening the drawer to the nightstand, removing a foil packet. He tore it open and quickly sheathed himself.

"Ready?" he asked, gazing down at her, wanting her to truly be his.

"Ready, Cowboy," she said huskily, causing him to fire on all pistons.

He hovered over her now, his fingers parting her. He slipped a finger inside her, seeing she was ready for him. Taking his time, he pushed into her slowly, hearing her sigh. Her legs came up, wrapping around his waist, and he began moving in and out, keeping the pace slow and steady. She pulled on his nape, bringing his mouth to hers, and his kisses mimicked his lower motions, moving, stroking.

He deepened the kiss, thrusting into her now deeply, moving faster, his heart beating wildly. She clung to him, meeting every thrust. And then he erupted, like a volcano, roaring her name, even as she called out his, her body reverberating.

Collapsing atop her, he quickly rolled to his side, bringing her with him, not wanting to crush her. He rested his forehead against hers, their breathing heavy. Chance could feel her heart beating and knew she could feel his, too.

He kissed her tenderly. "That was amazing."

She smiled. "It was out of this world. You are incredible, Blackstone. That was the ride of my life." Summer paused. "I hope ... that it was good for you, too."

He gathered her in his arms. "Babe, it was the best ever. *You* are the best. The one who makes my heart sing."

Chance kissed her hair, gathering his courage. It was now or never, and he knew now was the perfect time.

"I love you, Summer Sutherland."

She stiffened, and he cursed inwardly.

It had been too soon. It was too much. He was going to lose her.

No, he couldn't. It would kill him.

Summer burst into tears, surprising the hell out of him. Chance had no idea what was going on, but he knew he needed to comfort her. He held her tightly to him, murmuring to her that everything was going to be okay. He rubbed his hand up and down her back, wondering how he could have gotten things so wrong.

"I'm sorry," she said. "I didn't mean to start crying." She gazed up at him, her luscious mouth trembling. "Do you really mean that, Chance? Or is it something you just say whenever you finish having sex with a woman?"

He smoothed her hair. "I've never said those words to another soul, Summer. Only you. And while I've had sex with a lot of women, I've only made love with one.

"And that's you."

Fat tears rolled down her cheeks again, but she was smiling.

"Really?" she asked.

"Really," he assured her.

"I love you, too, Chance," she said softly. "I can't believe I feel this strongly so soon, but I do. I've never said that to anyone, either. I've never felt so much a part of someone than when we came together."

Summer wiped away her tears. "I'm afraid this is the best dream I've ever had—and I'm going to wake up and all the happiness and love I feel will be gone."

"You're awake now. Everything is absolutely real. I'm not going anywhere, Summer. I can promise you that. I've found the woman I love. The one who completes me." He smiled. "You're never going to get rid of me."

Her eyes misted with tears. "Good. Because I could get used to having you around, Cowboy."

# Sixteen

Summer awoke, enveloped in warmth. Chance's scent surrounded her, and she luxuriated in it and the feel of his body wrapped around hers. She had spent the night at the ranch as she'd planned.

Now, she never wanted to leave it. Or him.

After they'd made love, they were both ravenous. He'd called in an order to Pizza Palace, both of them agreeing to pepperoni, sausage, and mushroom. When it arrived, Chance had thrown on a robe and paid the delivery driver, bringing the pizza and a bottle of wine back to bed. He'd shed his robe, and she couldn't help but admire his body, hardened with muscle, thanks to the physical labor he put in on the ranch.

They'd eaten pizza. Drank wine. Made love again. Slept. Awoke and made love once more.

Now, it was morning. Or she guessed it was. The curtains were drawn, keeping out any light. Then again, dawn may not have occurred yet.

Chance stirred, his arms tightening about her. Slowly, he

began stroking her bare belly, causing her skin to pucker with goose bumps.

"You awake?"

"Yes," she told him, savoring his touch.

"I'm still here. I told you I wasn't going anywhere."

"I know," she said, smiling to herself.

"Hungry?"

"For you? Or food?" she flirted.

His hand slid lower. A finger pushed into her, and Summer arched her back.

"Is this a new kind of wake-up call?" she teased, her breathing quickening.

"A new, exclusive, personal service. Only available to the woman I love."

He continued caressing her, heat rippling through her. She felt the orgasm coming and gave into it, toppling over the edge into sheer bliss.

Then he was kissing her everywhere, and she reveled in the feel of his callused hands against her skin. He took his time, slowly exploring her body, allowing her to do the same to him. Already, she was becoming familiar with it. The muscles. A few scars. How he sucked in his breath when her fingers lightly danced across his abs.

When he finally thrust into her, she knew this was the man she had been waiting for. She was becoming a strong, confident person because of him. He gave her the courage to soar.

He fell against her, his body driving her into the mattress. She welcomed his weight, wrapping her arms about him.

"I don't want to crush you," Chance said, easing from her.

He turned her so that her back was against his chest and pulled her to him, their limbs entangling. She liked nestling against him. It was as if he had always been a part of her.

They lay quietly, savoring the moment. Her thoughts scattered.

Then the silence was broken by a low growl.

"Did that come from you?" he asked. "You must be awfully hungry."

Summer wasn't even embarrassed. At one time, she would have been mortified, but this was Chance. Everything was easy between them.

"Is that offer to make me breakfast still good?"

"I told you I'm the king of breakfast. Whatever you want."

"It doesn't matter. But I am starving."

She wriggled from his arms and started to hunt for her clothes.

"Wait," he said.

Going to the closet, he pulled out a worn flannel shirt. "Here. Put this on."

She slipped into it, the fabric whisper-soft against her bare skin. It struck her mid-thigh. Chance buttoned the front.

"There. Now you're warm, but I can admire those long, luscious legs of yours."

"Luscious?" She giggled. "I've never heard legs called luscious before."

"Okay. Then I'll go with spectacular. I can't wait for warmer weather so I can see you in shorts." He grinned. "Then again, it was awfully fun peeling those jeans from you."

"Keep looking at me like that, Cowboy, and it may be tomorrow before I claim that breakfast."

Chance laughed and threw on his robe. She came to him, belting it for him.

"That's a pretty fancy knot, Sutherland. I'm not sure I'll know how to get this off."

She smiled. "I can help get you out of it."

He caught her in his arms, a low growl coming from him, and buried his lips against her neck. She felt her body coming alive again. Then both their bellies yowled noisily, and he released her.

"Breakfast coming right up."

He took her hand and led her downstairs, telling her to sit at the table.

"I can help," she protested.

"Nope. I want to make breakfast for my girl."

She watched as he worked efficiently. Brewing coffee. Flipping eggs and pancakes. Turning bacon. Buttering toast.

He set plates down for both of them and poured them each a cup of coffee.

"This looks amazing," she praised. "I'm used to toasting a bagel in Brooklyn or pouring milk over cereal at Autumn's. You're going to spoil me."

Taking her hand, he kissed it. "I want to spoil you, Summer. I love you. I want to do everything for you."

"Even write my latest romance?" she asked, coquettishly batting her eyelashes at him.

"I don't have the skill to do that." He brightened. "Then again, I could be real handy with the research. You know, working out things between your couple. I'm ready, willing, and able to step in for the hero and help you work out any scenes you need help with."

Summer laughed. "I'm glad you're willing and able to be so helpful."

They finished breakfast and put the dishes in the dish-washer. Chance started it, and they returned to his bedroom.

Seeing it the light now, she asked, "Is there a reason it looks so sterile? It's almost like a hotel room. So impersonal."

"I only started sleeping here a couple of days ago," he

admitted. "It was Dad's bedroom. Tammy tried to get me to move down the hall into it after he passed. It didn't feel right then, so I stuck to the room I've always had."

"What changed your mind?" she asked, curious.

"You," he said, a crooked grin emerging. "I wanted to start making memories with you here."

He took her into his arms and kissed her. "Everything I do, I'm always thinking about you, Summer."

"Same," she said. "I was afraid to tell you that I loved you. You're in my head. My heart. My soul."

"Don't ever be afraid to tell me anything," Chance said. "I think it's important that we're always open and honest with one another."

He kissed her again, and Summer felt she had come home in every way imaginable.

* * *

SUMMER SAT cross-legged on the bed, Autumn across from her.

"I've never seen you look so happy," her twin said.

She shook her head. "It's hard to believe how much my life has changed in such a short time. I had such a crush on Chance when we were growing up. He was Mr. Everything. I remember kissing my pillow, pretending it was him."

"Even if he had noticed you, West would've shut things down," Autumn said.

"You think so?"

"Absolutely. Chance was a player then. From what little I know, he was that way in college and after. But he matured by the time he came home. He's been serious about his obligations to the ranch. The times we've gotten together, he's never brought anyone with him."

"He hasn't really dated since he came back to Hawthorne," Summer confirmed. "He's been all about the ranch."

"He was waiting for you," Autumn said matter-of-factly. "Even though he didn't know he was. *You* didn't know you'd be returning here. It's as if you two were the last pieces in a thousand-piece puzzle. The picture is now complete—and you complete each other."

"I love him so much, Autumn. I never knew I could have this kind of love in my heart. It's growing so fast. Filling me up."

Her sister smiled, her hands coming to her belly. "You'll find your love for Chance will grow even more once you become pregnant. I didn't think I could love Eli any more than I already did, and then this little peanut came along. Already, I'm madly in love with him or her, and my love for Eli has grown even deeper. I can't imagine what it'll be like once we're holding the baby we made in our arms."

"I hope Chance wants children," Summer said. "It's so early for us. We haven't talked about kids."

"He will," Autumn assured her. "He'll want to pass Blackstone Ranch on to the next generation of Blackstones."

She glanced at her watch. "Chance will be here soon. We're going to have dinner with West and Kelby tonight. He wants to tell them about us."

"They'll be pleased," her twin said. "They both want the best for their siblings. You two finding one another will make them happy. Mom and Dad will also be glad. You know how much they've always liked Chance."

"I know."

Chance arrived and came in for a few minutes. Autumn hugged him tightly, and Eli gave him a big smile.

"I hear you've got a new lady in your life," Eli said.

He slipped an arm about Summer's waist. "She's the last new lady in my life."

"Until you have a little girl," Autumn predicted. "It's always you tough, silent types that go all mushy inside when you have a daughter."

Chance gazed into her eyes. "This one already has me wrapped around her little finger. I'm going to be in a heap of trouble if we have girls."

Autumn and Eli laughed, and Summer said, "We need to get going."

Once they were in the truck, she asked, "Do you really want children? Or were you just kidding around in there?"

He reached for her hand, threading his fingers through hers. "I had never thought about it too much before you. Now, all I want is a life with you *and* our kids, Summer. I don't want to rush it, though. I want some time to ourselves before we even think about starting a family."

"I'm glad you do want them," she said. "And I don't mind waiting for a while. We need to be together, and then we can think about babies."

"But not too long," he said. "I'm already thirty-three. You're thirty. I don't want to wait more than a couple of years, okay?"

"Okay."

Truthfully, she would be happy to become pregnant tomorrow with Chance's baby. Then again, they hadn't even talked marriage yet. It just seemed assumed. She wanted to enjoy the here and now for at least a little bit before she talked to him about settling down permanently.

They had a nice dinner with West and Kelby. West grilled steaks, while Kelby prepared baked potatoes and a Caesar salad. It was hard for Summer to believe how her siblings had returned to Hawthorne and were both happily married, with babies on the way. She was glad she would be here for those births and hoped that she would add a baby or two to the mix. It had been fun growing up with Darby and Sawyer in Hawthorne, and she wanted her own kids to enjoy time with their cousins just as she had.

After a slice of pecan pie, Chance and West left the kitchen. West wanted to show Chance some new plays he'd drawn up for spring football practice. She and Kelby cleared the table and then sat.

"I never thought I would see Chance settle down," Kelby began. "Then again, I get now that the right woman had to come along for him to want to do that. You're certainly that woman, Summer. I've never seen my brother so happy. The way he looks at you makes me feel so happy for the both of you."

She patted her large belly. "And it'll be great for all the cousins to play together. They'll be each other's first friends."

"I was thinking that very thing," Summer admitted. "None of this would be possible if we all hadn't come back to Hawthorne."

Pulling out her phone, she said, "I wanted to show you some of the graphics from the Stars game we went to. Their video board is incredible. I thought you might get some ideas for branding."

"I do have a couple of new clients," Kelby told her. "West has cautioned me not to take on anymore. I've actually poked around on LinkedIn, trying to see if there's someone looking for a job that would be a good fit for Social Synergy Creations. Tammy told me that even though I want to be a working mother, I'll fall madly in love with this baby and want to spend a lot of time with her. That means I've got to hire someone to help with all my clients. I don't want to let any of them down."

They scrolled through the pictures Summer had taken and batted around a few ideas the pictures inspired. Then her phone rang. She saw it was a FaceTime call with Jen.

"I'll decline. I'll call her later."

"Who's Jen?" Kelby asked.

"My closest friend and fellow editor at Liberty House."

"Answer it. I'll make some tea while you two talk."

"Okay. Thank you."

She swiped to answer, Jen's face appearing. Her puffy, red, I've been crying face.

"What's wrong?"

Jen's eyes welled with tears. "I did it. I quit."

"You quit Liberty House?" Summer asked, shocked.

Her friend nodded. "I'd had it up to here with Millicent. She kept piling more and more work on me. On everyone. She didn't even bother replacing you, just dispersed your stable of authors to everyone."

"I hate hearing that," she said sympathetically. "I know how heavy the workload is."

Jen dabbed at her eyes with a tissue. "At least I don't have to wait to come and see you. Is that all right? I hate that I'm inviting myself, but I really need to get out of the city." She sniffed. "I guess Texas is about as far away as I can get."

"You're always welcome. I'm staying with my sister now. She's only got the one guestroom if you don't mind sharing. We'll talk through everything and figure things out, Jen."

Kelby gestured to Summer and mouthed, "She can stay here."

Nodding to Kelby, she focused on the screen again. "Are you going to apply for work at another publishing house?"

"The witch'll probably blackball me," Jen said morosely. "It doesn't matter. I don't think I could edit now. I'm so burned out. I've spent all weekend trying to decide what my next step is in my career. I love to read and edit. I also enjoy writing. I've thought maybe searching for jobs in advertising or marketing. You know I've got mad skills when it comes to creating graphics, and I'm really tech-savvy. Marketing might be my next chapter."

"What?" Kelby said, waddling over to the table and taking a seat. She placed her hand around Summer's and turned the screen so she could see Jen.

"Hi, Jen. I'm Summer's sister-in-law. Kelby. And you might just be the answer I'm looking for."

Summer gave up her phone, and Kelby tilted it down to her belly and back up.

"As you can see, I've got a baby on the way. She'll be here in about two months. I own my own company. I'm literally the only person employed by Social Synergy Creations."

Quickly, Kelby explained to Jen what SSC did, everything from branding to writing mission statements, creating and maintaining websites, and handling social media accounts for a wide range of clients.

"SSC is growing really fast. I want you to look at some of the accounts I handle." Kelby provided her website. "If you're interested and would like to talk more about coming to work with me, I'd be happy to talk the nitty-gritty details once you arrive in Hawthorne."

"This is fantastic," Jen exclaimed.

"I'm giving you back to Summer now," Kelby said. "Let me know if you have any questions."

Summer took her phone again, and she saw the excitement on her friend's face.

"When can you come to Texas?" she asked.

"Anytime. Tomorrow?"

"Sounds good to me," Summer encouraged. "Book it. I'd

love to see you. I want you to meet Chance. You'd also be able to talk with Kelby in person."

"I'll look at flights right now," Jen told her. "I'll let you know when I'm coming. Oh, Summer, you don't know how much I need to see you."

"I understand."

They ended their call, and Kelby said, "This seems like fate. Your friend needing a job. Me desperately needing full-time help at SSC."

"It would be terrific if things could work out."

Her phone chimed, and she read the text from Jen.

"She can get a ten-thirty flight on American to DFW tomorrow morning. She said she'll rent a car. Just for me to send her the address," Summer said.

She texted back to book the flight and then gave her West and Kelby's address, along with Autumn and Eli's, telling Jen she was staying at the latter and that Jen would be a guest of West and Kelby's.

"I sent her your address," she told Kelby. "Autumn wouldn't mind having another guest, but I think it would be good for Jen to stay here at least a couple of days. Since you work from home, she could really shadow you, and the two of you could see if she might be a good fit."

"Let's go tell the guys," Kelby said.

As they left the kitchen, Summer hoped that Jen would soon become a permanent resident of Hawthorne.

# *Seventeen*

Summer dropped Atticus at the vet's. He was due a few shots and was going to be bathed and groomed. She had not been able to have a pet in her Brooklyn apartment, and it had been nice living with Autumn and Eli and getting to enjoy Atticus' company. She wondered if Chance might consider getting a dog once they got married.

Since Atticus would be ready at noon, Summer decided to stay in town. She had already gotten in a few hours of writing this morning and decided to stop for a coffee at Coffee Hour as a reward. Her laptop was in her backpack just in case the coffeehouse didn't have many sippers inside. Of course, it would be hard to concentrate, knowing Jen was now in the air. They had talked again early this morning. Summer had volunteered to pick up her friend at the airport, but Jen was from the Midwest and enjoyed driving, something she hadn't done in New York. She told Summer she was eager to get behind the wheel of a car again and would rent a vehicle to drive to Hawthorne.

As she entered Coffee Hour now, she saw half a dozen

others scattered about the coffeehouse. That was in addition to the old-timers at the back, having their usual fun. She wondered down the road if she and Chance might be a part of a group such as that, friends for decades with others. Already, she enjoyed getting together with her siblings and cousins and their spouses. Then she wondered if Jen did stay in Hawthorne, would she be a good match for Sawyer? Like Chance, Sawyer hadn't really dated since returning to Hawthorne. Her cousin was such a kind, decent man, and she knew he would make for a wonderful husband.

She approached the counter, where another barista worked alongside Ben. He spotted Summer and smiled.

"Back again? I'm sorry so many people interrupted you the other day, Summer. You were so polite to everyone, but that had to be frustrating."

"It was a little tough," she admitted. "But I've been writing at my sister's house. I'm staying with her and her husband. And Chance has also offered to let me come to his ranch and work."

Ben nodded knowingly. "Chance is a fine fellow. Saw the two of you hitting it off."

"We knew each other when we were younger. He's my brother's best friend."

The coffeehouse owner smiled. "But he didn't pay any attention to you back in the day, am I right?"

"Not a bit," she said, laughing. "But things are certainly different now."

"I like Chance. Don't know him well. He keeps to himself when he comes in here, but he seems rock solid."

"He's one of the good ones," she shared. "We're seeing one another now."

"Good for you, Summer," Ben said, his smile wide. "Oh,

by the way, Becky's here. Maybe you'd like to go and talk to her. You said you wanted to meet her."

"She's not in school?" She looked over her shoulder, skimming the customers inside the coffeehouse.

"She's over by the window," Ben said proudly. "That's my Becky."

He referred to a woman who was in her mid-forties. She was dressed in navy slacks and a cream sweater. Her hair was cut in a stylish bob, and she was slightly overweight.

She was also one of the plainest women Summer had ever seen.

She recalled how Ben had mentioned how beautiful Becky was. Even now, she heard the pride in his voice when he referred to his wife.

"Let me go and introduce you two. I told Becky all about you. She loves reading romances, and she's eager to meet you."

Ben came from behind the counter, leading Summer across the coffeehouse. He bent and brushed a kiss on his wife's cheek, saying, "Guess who came in? Summer Sutherland."

Becky stood and shook hands with her. "Oh, it's wonderful to meet you, Summer. Please, have a seat."

She did so, and Ben asked, "What can I bring you?"

"How about a cinnamon dolce latte?"

"Coming right up." Ben dipped his head and left them together.

"I hope I'm not interrupting you," Summer said, seeing several folders sitting on the table, some of them open.

Becky closed her laptop and set it aside. "Just catching up on paperwork. I know it sounds crazy, but I take off one day a month. Sometimes, it's so hard getting everything done at work because I counsel so many students during the day. I like to spend my time with Ben and not on school stuff when I get home. I have well over a hundred unused sick days, so Ben suggested I take a day off each month. I catch up on all my paperwork because I don't have anyone interrupting me."

"Like me?" she teased.

Becky laughed. "I'm able to get everything done, and I still have a little time for myself. Sometimes, I'll read a book. Take a walk. Do a little shopping. Not grocery shopping or anything needed. Fun shopping, like for shoes or a new purse. It's a me day. A gift I give myself, thanks to my husband's encouragement."

"Ben certainly loves you. When we met, you were right at the top of our conversation."

"His first marriage would've been successful if he would have put the time into it. Ben was too busy making money and saving the world back then. I do feel sorry for his first wife. By the time I met him, especially after his heart attack, he was a different person. He'd already learned to stop and smell the roses."

Ben reappeared, placing Summer's mug on the table. "Enjoy. And don't say too many bad things about me."

"As if I could even think of anything bad," Becky said, smiling indulgently.

After Ben left, Summer asked, "Why Ben? What attracted you to him?"

Becky sighed. "I liked everything about him. His zest for life. He believes he was given a second chance. A new lease on life after his heart attack. He cut out smoking. Lost weight. Took up hobbies. We do puzzles together. Paint birdhouses. Go for walks. Even take fitness and yoga classes."

The counselor's gaze met Summer's. "You can tell I'm not much to look at. I'm not ugly. Just homely. I never had a date before Ben. Not a single one. When I was young, the guys I knew were all caught up in a woman's looks. That certainly left me out of the party. As I grew older, I found myself in a profession where I didn't meet many men. The few I did showed no interest in me. Ben was the first person who saw me. He thinks I'm beautiful, and he tells me that every day. We started out as friends, and I quickly fell in love with him. I was terrified because I was afraid of opening my heart. Of giving myself. I was afraid our relationship was like a house of cards, and the slightest breeze would send it tumbling down. Instead, Ben showed patience with me. He loved me and was willing to wait until I truly believed in the two of us together."

"That's incredible, Becky. I'm writing a small-town romance series, and I would like to take bits and pieces of your love story and incorporate into my Panhandle town."

Becky blushed. "Oh, that would be so nice, Summer. I've read romance novels from the time I was thirteen. I would put myself in the heroine's shoes and fall in love with each hero I read about, never knowing one day I would find a real-life hero of my own." She frowned. "But would readers want to read about two older people such as us?"

"I think so. There is a small but growing market for more mature romances. Not every heroine can be eighteen and making her come-out."

They both laughed at the usual storyline for a Regency romance.

"Seriously, Becky. I would like to feature an older couple in this series. I don't know if I would devote an entire book to it, but I plan to sprinkle a few secondary romances into the series."

"We would be honored to be a part of your writing, Summer," Becky assured her.

Summer realized that looks faded, but Ben had been

smart enough to discover Becky's kindness and warmth. She knew their love story would live on as long as they did, and that was what she wished to capture.

They talked about the town where she had set her series for several minutes, and Summer asked, "Would you care to do any beta reading for me? My sister has offered to do so, but Autumn will just tell me she likes whatever I write. Since you're a true romance reader, I would be honored if you would look at my work."

Becky's face lit up, and Summer could see why Ben had fallen in love with this woman.

"I would be honored to."

"I only ask that you don't share it with anyone since it's not published yet. If you'd like, I can send you the first book. It's already completed. I'm starting the second one now."

"I'd be delighted. Let me give you my email address."

They exchanged cell numbers and emails, and then Summer said, "I'm going to let you get back to those folders so you can wrap up things and have time to yourself."

"I'll be done in an hour or so," Becky told her. "Maybe by then, you'll have sent me your manuscript. I can't think of anything better than to sip on some hot tea and read all afternoon."

"I've got to pick up my sister's dog at noon. I'll head home then and send it to you," she promised.

Summer said goodbye and went to pay for her coffee. Ben shook his head.

"Just seeing my Becky enjoying her conversation with you is payment enough."

She thanked him and returned to her SUV, placing her backpack inside the car. Instead of trying to write for her current story, she wanted to think about Ben and Becky's romance. That meant taking a walk.

An hour later, she returned to the car, a good bit of the plot having come to her. She definitely had enough material for an entire book, based upon her brainstorming. She had captured her ideas on her voice memo app and would type them up later. Now, she needed to pick up Atticus.

She arrived at Dr. Bridges' practice and spoke to the receptionist.

"Oh, Atticus is such a love. The entire staff thinks he's the best boy ever." She handed over a printout. "This has the shots he received today. I'll have him brought up to you."

Atticus arrived with a dark blue bow around his neck, grinning from ear to ear.

She bent and hugged him. "You look so handsome, Atticus." Rising, she took the leash the tech offered to her. "Thanks so much."

"Atticus is a favorite. He's welcome back any time."

Summer took the pup to her SUV and got him settled in the back seat. Autumn had told her to place a blanket down, and Atticus would ride in peace.

She drove to Triple H, where Atticus went to work with Eli several times a week. The patients got a kick out of him visiting, and Eli said the staff was always asking about the dog. Kelby had started an Instagram account for Atticus, and he had several thousand followers. She took a couple of shots of the dog and forwarded them to Kelby, hoping she could use them.

Before they went inside the hospital, Summer waited until he peed in a bush, telling him, "No going outside and working up a sweat. You look good for Eli now, so let's keep it that way."

They rode the elevator up to Eli's office, where they were greeted by Eli's assistant.

"I'm Nancy Nichols," she said, offering Atticus a treat

and then shaking hands with Summer. "It's so nice to meet you. Eli tells me you're an author."

"Hopefully. I'm working on a series now."

"I'm a voracious reader. Mystery. Romance. Thrillers. I gobble up everything."

Though she already had Becky as a beta reader, Summer thought it wouldn't hurt to add one more.

"I don't mean to put you on the spot, Nancy, but would you consider doing some beta reading for me?" she asked, explaining what it would entail.

"Absolutely," Nancy told her. "That would be so much fun."

She got Nancy's email address and promised to send her completed manuscript to her. As she headed home, Summer was glad she'd found a couple of true readers who would hopefully give her good feedback. She still didn't know if she wanted to pitch the series or publish it on her own. No decision needed to be made yet, though. She needed to get much more written before even thinking about publishing.

Summer arrived back at Autumn's and made herself a sandwich, then emailed both Becky and Nancy a copy of her first completed manuscript. Then she read over the last three chapters she'd completed and did some editing on them.

The doorbell rang, and she looked at her watch. It had to be Jen.

Hurrying to the foyer, she opened the door. Jen fell into Summer's arms, and they danced a jig.

"I'm so glad you're here in Hawthorne."

"Not half as happy as I am to be here," Jen replied. "The moment the plane took off and we were in the air, it was as if everything weighing me down just floated away. I hope you don't mind that I came here first. I just had to see you."

They hugged again. "Let me get my purse. We'll go over

to West and Kelby's. I think you're really going to get along with Kelby."

Summer retrieved her purse and locked the door. On the way, she took Jen by the town square, pointing out various places to her.

"I grew up in a small town," Jen revealed. "Okay, maybe not as small as Hawthorne, but it had about fifty thousand. New York seemed so huge when I got there. D.C. was the only big city I'd ever visited before. I'll tell you now, it's nice to be somewhere like Hawthorne after spending several years among all those skyscrapers and concrete."

She texted Kelby that they were on their way and then said, "If you're not ready to take a new job just yet, it'll be okay. And if you aren't interested in the work SSC does, there'll be something out there for you. I think it's important to take your time and not rush into anything new too soon."

"After I booked my flight, I spent a couple of hours on Kelby's website," Jen said. "I also looked at websites she's built for her clients. Took a look at different social media accounts she handles. I'm excited about this opportunity, Summer. Really excited."

They arrived, and Kelby greeted Jen warmly. Kelby took them to the kitchen, where she plied them with homemade oatmeal raisin cookies and herbal tea. Talk immediately turned to Kelby's company and the homework Jen had done. Soon, the pair was speaking as if they were old friends, finishing one another's sentences. They pitched ideas back and forth, and Summer saw that Jen really would be an asset to SSC if Kelby extended a job offer to her.

Kelby showed Jen her home office and some of the accounts she was working on. The two women's enthusiasm bubbled over as they continued firing ideas at one another.

Finally, Kelby said, "If you decide not to come to work

with me, I'll understand. I may have to kill you, but I do understand."

Jen laughed. "Are you making me an offer?"

"Absolutely." Kelby named a salary and briefly mentioned some benefits, which Summer thought were very generous.

"How soon can I start?" Jen asked eagerly.

"Are you serious?" Kelby asked. "I'd have you start tomorrow if I could. I know you want to visit with Summer, though. And you still live in New York."

"Summer works during the day on her novel," Jen said. "I'm not going to pass up this opportunity to begin working with you immediately. Besides, who knows when that baby will decide to make an appearance? I want to be well-grounded in everything about SSC so you won't have to worry about business while you're on maternity leave."

"Well, I will be in the house, so if you did have any questions, I could help. All while feeding and burping the baby, of course."

They all laughed, and Jen said, "If I could, I'd like to stay with you for a week. Get my feet wet with everything SSC is about. Visit some with Summer. Then I'll go back to New York and shut down my life there. My apartment came furnished, so I only have my clothes and a few personal items to pack up, and frankly, there isn't much of either of those. I'll also need to find a place to live."

"Believe when I say this, Jen. You can live with West and me for a couple of months. That way, you can take your time in finding a place to live. We have a lot of room here."

"I can't impose," Jen protested.

"You aren't," Kelby assured her. "This house is huge. You can take a room upstairs and see as much or as little of us as you wish. We can set up an office for you upstairs, as well.

Then when I have the baby, you can work from there or from my office. We'll work out the details later. Can I hug you?"

Jen embraced Kelby. "You have made my dream come true. This is such an exciting opportunity, to be on the ground floor of a new company."

"Well, I get Jen tonight," Summer said. "After she unpacks. I want her to have dinner with Chance and me."

"I'll go get my suitcase now," Jen said. "I'll unpack and then take you home again." She smiled. "I am very interested in making the acquaintance of this cowboy who's stolen your heart."

"Watch it," Kelby said, laughing. "That's my brother you're talking about."

Half an hour later, Jen drove them back to Autumn's house, where Summer went to the kitchen and packed up what she needed to make dinner for the three of them at the ranch.

"I didn't know you cooked," Jen said.

"I'm learning to. You're getting pork chops tonight, one of the few things in my repertoire. They're Chance's favorite."

"So, that's how you landed him. Through his stomach."

"It didn't hurt," she joked. "But the sex isn't bad either."

Her friend's eyes widened. "Summer Sutherland, we *really* have a lot to discuss."

"Yes, we do," Summer said. "More than you could ever imagine."

# Eighteen

Chance kissed Summer. "Have fun with the girls tonight."

"I will," she told him. "It's really great to have such a terrific core group of women. I'm glad everyone has welcomed Jen into the fold. I'll be back tomorrow morning for breakfast. Don't forget that you promised me an omelet. And I want the works. Mushrooms. Onions. Ham and cheese."

"Yes, Your Highness," he teased, closing her car door. He watched her drive away and knew the time had come.

*It was time to marry this woman.*

Yes, it was way too soon to think that way, but he wasn't one to leave anything to chance. Summer already spent several nights a week with him at the ranch. He didn't see any need to waste time. They loved one another. They should be together all the time.

Chance decided a visit to Joe and Meg Sutherland was in order.

He went to his truck, not wanting to call ahead. The

Sutherlands had hosted them for Sunday lunch last weekend, and he had noticed both of them watching how Summer and he interacted with one another. Chance hoped he would get their permission to wed their daughter, but if he didn't, it wouldn't stop him from proposing.

On the way, he rehearsed what to say and then decided he wouldn't remember any of it by the time he got to their place. He would merely speak from his heart.

Ten minutes later, he found himself on their doorstep, his heart beating slightly faster than normal. Chance rang the doorbell, and Meg Sutherland answered, giving him a warm smile.

"Why, hello, Chance. It's good to see you. Come on in."

He stepped into the foyer. "I hope you don't mind that I didn't call before coming."

"Oh, honey, we don't mind at all. It's a Friday night, and we're both tired after a long work week. Joe has already had his dinner and watched *Jeopardy*, so you're not interrupting anything."

She walked him to the den, a room he'd sat in hundreds of times over the years. He and West had watched plenty of ballgames. Played video games. Even a few parties had been held here. He saw Joe sitting in his chair, reading glasses perched on his nose as he held a book in his hand.

Spying Chance, he closed the book and set it aside, rising to greet him. "Hello, Chance. You lonely with the girls having their night out? Or in, I should say. Autumn said it was a potluck and didn't know what they'd be eating."

"Have a seat," Meg offered.

He took one, and they talked about how Jace had taken West and Eli to New Orleans today. The Final Four was being held in the Big Easy this year, and the three would attend the two semifinal games scheduled for Saturday. Jace would stay on to watch the championship Monday night, while West and Eli would return on Sunday in time to go to work on Monday.

Finally, Joe said, "I know you have better things to do on a Friday night than spend it with us. What's on your mind, Chance?"

"Your daughter," he responded. "I think you know how much I care for Summer. It's hard to think now that I never really paid much attention to her all the years I spent coming over here."

"You had your eye on other things," Joe said. "Sports. Girls your own age."

"You're right. I never thought of Summer as anything other than West's little sister. His rather talkative little sister," he added, causing the couple to laugh.

"Yes, Autumn was the quiet one," Meg said. "But Summer could talk your ear off. She really blossomed after the braces came off and she began wearing contacts. If I recall, you were gone away to college by then."

"Yes, ma'am. I know I saw her a couple of times before she graduated from college and moved to New York, but again, she was only West's sister." He paused. "She's a lot more to me now. That's why I'm here."

He took a deep breath and slowly expelled it. "I'm in love with your daughter. Summer is the only woman I've ever loved. The only one I ever will love. She makes me happier than I ever imagined possible. I'd like your permission to ask her to marry me."

The Sutherlands exchanged a glance, and Meg teared up as Joe said, "We think the two of you are meant to be together. It's obvious, just watching you, how crazy you are about one another. Normally, I would be hesitant, thinking a marriage wouldn't be a success because your relationship has happened lightning fast, but we've known you your whole life, Chance. I trust you and Summer know what you're doing."

Meg took his hand and squeezed it. "It's sweet that you came to ask us, but you don't need our permission. Summer is an adult with a mind of her own. She'll be the one to decide if she wants to marry you or not. But there's not a doubt in my mind what she'll say."

He raked a hand through his hair. "Boy, that was harder than I imagined it was going to be, but I sure do appreciate your support."

Joe offered Chance a hand, and he shook it.

"You're already like family, Chance. A brother to West. And with your sister married to our son—and now you and Summer getting hitched—we truly are family. How about a beer to celebrate?"

"Sounds good to me," he replied.

Meg wound up bringing them beers and making a bag of popcorn. They sat and reminisced about events over the years, and Chance knew he was blessed to have this couple as his future in-laws.

"I better head home and hit the sack," he finally said. "Summer and I are going riding tomorrow."

"She said she's been riding with you a few times," Meg said. "I know she hadn't been on a horse since high school. I hope she's coming along all right."

"I have her riding Duchess. She's a roan with a gentle spirit, and she and Summer have taken to each other. Nothing to worry about," he assured them. "Summer's at home in the saddle."

"Do you know when you'll ask her to marry you?" Meg asked. "Not that I'm pushing for you to do it soon. It'll just be hard to look at Summer, knowing what we know and not letting the cat out of the bag."

He grinned, recalling that Meg was known for not being able to keep a secret. "I'm planning a picnic after we ride tomorrow. I'll ask her then. I'm sure she'll be talking to you about it soon. What kind of wedding she wants."

"Do you have any preferences?" Meg asked.

"Soon would be my only preference," he replied. "But I know girls sometimes have an idea of what their wedding should be in their head. Summer can take all the time she wants."

"She'll appreciate that," Joe said. "Good luck with your proposal. And we'll act very surprised when Summer tells us about it," he joked.

Chance drove back to the ranch, his spirits soaring. He might not have his own parents alive to witness the ceremony, but Tammy would be there, and he knew he was getting a terrific set of in-laws.

He sent a text to Summer, telling her he hoped she was having fun and that he couldn't wait to see her tomorrow. It took him no time to fall asleep.

And his dreams were all about the woman he loved.

* * *

SUMMER DRESSED in jeans and boots for her morning ride with Chance. Although she'd enjoyed spending time with the girls last night, she was more than ready to see her man.

She came downstairs and found Autumn sipping herbal tea. Her sister's baby bump was already showing.

"How is it, giving up coffee?" she asked.

"Not bad. I tried a half-coffee and half-decaf mix, but to be honest, the taste of coffee doesn't sit well with me anymore. I've bought a variety pack of herbal teas which are caffeine-free. Blueberry. Pomegranate. Citrus. Orange spice. They're really good. Want a cup?"

"No, thanks. I'm heading over to the ranch now. Chance is making breakfast for me. He may not be able to cook anything else, but he's a master chef when it comes to making breakfast foods."

"How is your cooking coming along? I barely see you since you're at the ranch all the time."

"I'm working my way through Tammy's recipe book. I've had some hits and misses, but I'm really enjoying cooking. I'm even thinking of making a future character a chef."

"That reminds me. You haven't sent me anything new for a week now."

Autumn had read her first novel in one sitting, giving Summer some much needed feedback, and she was reading this second one a few chapters at a time, the same as Becky and Nancy were doing.

"Let me go email you now in case you can get to it this weekend, especially with Eli gone until tomorrow afternoon."

Autumn smiled. "You know how much I'm enjoying it. You are so talented, Summer. I really believe that this series is going to sell well."

"Let's hope."

She went upstairs again and quickly sent the updated manuscript to her twin and two beta readers and then came back downstairs, saying, "I sent the new pages to you, Becky, and Nancy. You don't know how much it's helped, getting this feedback from the three of you. And I'll be back by dinnertime this evening. I'll show off my new cooking skills to you."

"Don't you want to be with Chance?" Autumn asked.

"Eli's gone. We have to take advantage of that. We can

have serious twin talk time. We'll have dinner. Yak. Watch a mushy Hallmark movie. It'll be fun."

Her sister smiled. "I'd like that. I'll see you later then."

"Bye."

Summer left and headed straight for Blackstone Ranch. She looked forward to their ride this morning. Though she hadn't been on a horse in forever, she was enjoying time in the saddle. Duchess was such a gentle mount, and it was refreshing to be outside and get some exercise in a fun, unique way.

Besides, it gave her time with Chance, and she was all about that.

He came out on the porch as she pulled up, giving her a sweet kiss.

"Have I told you lately that I love you?" he said, his voice low and seductive.

"Why, I believe you did last night when I left."

He wrapped his arms about her. "Then let me start with today." He kissed her brow. "I love you, Summer Sutherland." He kissed the tip of her nose. "I love you." He kissed both cheeks. "I really love you."

Then he gave her a long, lingering kiss, causing her toes to curl and the butterflies in her belly to take flight.

"I love you very much," he finished. "Come on inside. I'm starving."

Chance already had all the ingredients chopped and diced for their omelets.

"I hope you don't mind a little green peppers added in."

"Not at all," she replied, watching as he melted butter in two different skillets, ready to watch and learn. "Medium heat?"

"Nope. Medium high."

Chance added everything but the eggs into the pans and

began to stir, saying, "It takes about five minutes for the onions to soften up enough. And for the ham to caramelize."

As they waited, he cracked eggs into a bowl and stirred rapidly, telling her not to over stir them.

Reducing the heat to medium-low, he poured some of the eggs into each frying pan, pushing around the other ingredients with a spatula so everything was evenly distributed. He seasoned both with salt and pepper and then ran a spatula around the edge of both omelets.

"Now, it's time to add the cheese," and he did so, sprinkling grated cheese liberally into the cooking egg mixture.

"It takes another five minutes or so to finish," he shared. "You want the top wet but not runny."

When done, Chance folded the omelet over and plated one for each of them as she poured orange juice for them both, along with cups of coffee.

After her first bite, Summer said, "This is heavenly. You could open a diner and serve only breakfast foods, and there'd be a line out the door."

"I'd rather be a rancher," he drawled.

Once they'd finished eating and cleaning the kitchen, they headed to the stables. Chance saddled Duchess for her and Rebel for him, and they set out. Over the next couple of hours, they rode the entire perimeter of the ranch, finding several patches of bluebonnets growing wild.

"I love bluebonnets," she told him. "I missed seeing them during those years in New York. Mom would have Dad take her on a drive so she could send pictures to me of patches of them along the highway. New York is good about reserving green spaces in the city. You can see all kinds of flowers, no matter what the season, but I missed my bluebonnets."

"Remember that song they taught us in elementary school?" Chance asked, and he begin to sing.

*Though I love dear Texas in summer and fall*
*But bluebonnet time is the best time of all.*

"I didn't know you could sing, Chance," she said. "You have a really nice, rich voice."

"Thanks. I sing to the cattle sometimes. It soothes them."

She smiled flirtatiously. "You can sing to me anytime, Cowboy."

They came to an old oak, and Summer saw something sitting at the base of it.

"Let's stop here," he said, dismounting and tying Rebel's reins to a nearby bush. He did the same with Duchess' reins and then led Summer to the old oak.

"We're going to have a picnic," he declared. "I was going to make us the food, but Maria told me she would do it. She put everything in a basket and got a blanket, too, and had Zeke bring it out here."

"You're lucky to have her and Zeke. They really have stepped in and taken up the slack."

"I miss Tammy, but you're right. Zeke and Maria have fit in really well with everyone. And it's nice to have kids on the ranch again. Joaquin is teaching the kids to ride, and Matteo has already told me that he wants to be a cowboy when he grows up."

Chance unfolded the blanket and snapped his wrists, letting it unfurl before resting it on the ground. They set a rock on each corner to keep it in place, and then he began pulling out their lunch from the basket. Maria had made chicken salad sandwiches and had included a fruit salad and bags of chips. Two mason jars containing iced tea were also in the basket. When they finished their sandwiches, Chance pulled out a container with chocolate chip cookies.

He talked about how he had recently promoted Buck

Overton to be Blackstone Ranch's manager and how that would change things.

"Change how?" she asked. "What will Buck be involved with?"

"He'll have a helluva lot more responsibility than he previously did. He'll manage the feeding and breeding programs. Administer vaccines to both the horses and cattle. Be in charge of predator and feral hog control. Maintain all the equipment himself or oversee the help in doing so. That kind of thing."

"That's quite a bit. What will you do? I know you've been in charge of overseeing the ranch."

"More paperwork. I'll keep the records in Cattlemax, which is a software program. Buck will use it, too, to keep track of things on his end. I use it for financial information. Sales and purchases. The ranch's income and expenses. The software helps you make more informed decisions and can even predict ranching income. I'll also be solely responsible for handling salaries, workers' benefits, insurance. That kind of thing. In essence, I'll be the face of the ranch, working on marketing, sales, shipping, and storage, while Buck will manage the hands, the herds, and the hauling and equipment. He'll generate weekly reports for me, so I'll continually be in the loop."

She frowned. "It sounds as if you'll be more of a businessman than a rancher."

"It's true that I won't be out on the land as much, but it's time for me to give Buck the responsibility and title of ranch manager, as well as the salary. He's put in the time and deserves it. I've made plans to build him a cabin of his own. A ranch manager needs to be separate from the ranch hands. Kelby has been shouldering a lot of the marketing for me ever since Dad passed. While she'll still maintain our website and social media accounts, I need to take some of what she's been doing off her plate, especially with the baby coming around the corner."

"Will you be happy doing this?"

He leaned over and brushed a strand of hair from her cheek, tucking it behind her ear. "I can always get out on the land when I want to. Or when I'm needed, especially at times like branding. That's an all hands on deck situation." He smiled. "I'm hoping it'll give me more time with you. The ranch is important—but you're more important to me, Summer."

Hearing him say that made her spirits soar. He had become the most important thing in her life, but to know that Chance felt the same way let her know she was on the right path to a future with him.

They packed everything back into the basket, and she thought they would resume their ride, but he leaned his back against the tree and told her they had all the time in the world. Chance stretched out his legs and pulled her down so that her head rested in his lap. As they talked, he absently combed his fingers through her hair. It soothed her, yet at the same time, it was very sensual. They talked about everything, from the latest pages she had written to how Jen was settling in, working with Kelby. She thought today was absolutely perfect. The mild weather. Being in one another's company.

Then Chance looked at her in a way that told her he had something important to say.

"You've been spending a lot of your nights at the ranch," he began. "I like that. A lot. But I'm ready to make things permanent."

He paused, looking down at her with love shining in his eyes. "I'm not a man who spouts flowery words, but I know what's in my heart. I love you, Summer Sutherland. I want to spend all my nights with you. Forever."

Chance lowered his lips to hers, the kiss tasting of the future they would live.

In love.

He broke the kiss. "So, what do you say, my little ray of sunshine? Are you ready to start a new chapter of your life with me? Be my partner and my love?"

She beamed up at him. "I've never been happier in my life. *You* make me happy, Chance. You make me believe that I can do anything. And that we can do anything together. Yes, I will marry you. A thousand, million, bazillion times *yes!*"

Chance lifted her, placing her in his lap. He gave her the sweetest, most tender kiss they had ever shared.

"I'm ready whenever you are, babe. Just say the word. Whatever kind of wedding you want. Big. Small. In-between. Wherever you want it to be, I'm with you every step of the way."

Summer kissed him. "I don't want fancy. I'd like to be married here at Blackstone Ranch. To speak our vows in the place we'll live for the rest of our lives. I hope we can do it soon. I'm not someone who needs a lot of frills. Just a simple ceremony." She grinned. "And maybe a really big party afterward."

Chance kissed her enthusiastically. "I knew I was marrying the right gal. How about we get hitched right here, under this old oak tree?"

"I like that idea. It's very sentimental. And we can come here whenever we want and celebrate our love. I wouldn't mind getting married here as quickly as possible. After all, Kelby will be having the baby soon, and we both want her here. I only want one attendant. Autumn."

"And I want West as my best man. Just a few close friends and family then."

He pulled out his phone. "I know we'll need to find someone to officiate the ceremony."

"Oh, I'll bet Judge Stowe, Dad's golfing buddy, would find a spot in his calendar for us. Let's check with him before we make any more plans."

"Sounds good to me." He gave her a lingering kiss. "Want to head back to the house? I think our engagement calls for a celebration."

She smiled. "Would this celebration be happening in bed?"

Chance shrugged. "In bed—if we make it that far."

Summer laughed as he brought them both to their feet.

"Let's see just how creative you can get, Cowboy."

A slow, sexy smile spread across his face. "You're on."

# CHAPTER
## Nineteen

Chance met with the architect he had hired, along with Buck Overton, seeking his new ranch manager's input on the house being built. They agreed upon the final plans, and Chance told Buck that he would now hire a construction manager and crew to complete the house.

"I can't thank you enough for this opportunity, Chance," Buck told him. "Having a house come with the new position is more than I would have expected."

"I'd originally wanted to give you the cabin Zeke and Maria are living in, but with them having Matteo and Luna, I knew they would need separate living quarters from the bunkhouse. I'm glad we've got things settled now and can break ground on this place for you."

He walked the two men to the front door, shaking hands with them both, and then he returned to his office. He had been working for an hour when Maria tapped at the door, an anxious look on her face.

Rising, Chance went to the door. "Would you like to clean in here?"

"No," she said, shaking her head. "Mr. Chance, you have someone here to see you. They came just as I was leaving."

"Who?"

"She wouldn't give me her name. She only said you'd want to see her. I told her she could wait in the living room."

Annoyed, he said, "I'll handle it, Maria. Thank you."

She smiled uneasily. "There's a chicken casserole in the fridge. For you and Miss Summer. I left the instructions on heating it on the counter."

"I appreciate that. I'm sure it'll be delicious."

He went to the living room, a little used room, watching Maria head out the front door. It puzzled him that she'd first mentioned *they*, but then Maria had only mentioned a *she*. Chance hoped this wouldn't take long. He had a list as long as his arm of things he wanted to get done this afternoon before Summer arrived for dinner.

As he entered, Chance saw a tall, thin woman with her back to him staring out the window. Something about her seemed familiar. Then she turned, and he recognized her.

*What in the hell was Astrid Powell doing in Texas?*

"Hello, Chance. It's been a while."

It certainly had been. He'd met Astrid through one of his co-workers in Seattle. Chance had taken Astrid to dinner one night, then a night later, they had attended a party together, where he'd gotten rip-roaring drunk. They had taken a rideshare back to her place afterward, and he had spent the night. The next morning, Astrid had told him that she didn't care to see him again. He'd left and hadn't given her a thought since then, especially because he'd left Seattle a few weeks later, returning to Hawthorne.

"Three years," he replied. "I have to wonder why you're in Texas, at my ranch."

"I won't mince words, Chance. We have some business to attend to."

Astrid took a seat on the sofa and looked expectantly at him. Reluctantly, he sat, wondering why she would have come all this way.

"I know we saw each other a couple of times. I can't imagine what kind of business we'd have, though."

"It's about your daughter."

Chance shot to his feet. "What the hell? Is this some kind of shakedown?"

"Sit," she commanded, steel in her eyes.

Once more, he took a seat, wary now.

"You do remember that we had sex, don't you?" Astrid asked crisply.

"I do. You told me you were on the pill."

"I was." She hesitated. "But I wasn't always good about taking them every day."

He cursed under his breath. "And you think this .... girl ... is *mine*?"

"I know she is. I didn't have sex with anyone after I broke up with Rufus. Other than you, that is."

Vaguely, he recalled her mentioning that she had been dating Rufus Wheeler, a wealthy investment adviser he was acquainted with.

"Rufus and I had been seeing one another, and then he got the opportunity to open a new office in London. I had no interest in living abroad. I'd already done that. My parents divorced when I was young, and I was shuffled back and forth between them for over ten years. Mummy married a man who had homes in England and Switzerland. Daddy never liked staying in one place for long, and every time I went to live with him for a few months, we were in a different country. Brazil. France. Japan."

Astrid stood and began pacing. "When I was fourteen, I was fed up with it. With them. Neither of them really wanted me, and I rarely saw them when I did live with them. I finally convinced them that I wanted to live with my maternal grandmother in Seattle. I think they were both relieved to wash their hands of me. So, I came home to the States and swore I'd never go abroad again unless it was for a short vacation."

She returned to her purse, which sat on a table, and reached inside, pulling out a pack of cigarettes.

"Not in here," Chance warned, still off-balance after her pronouncement about him fathering a daughter.

"Suit yourself," she said, cramming the pack back into her purse.

"Get to the point, Astrid."

She returned to her seat. "I still loved Rufus when I slept with you. And then I found out I was pregnant. You had left Seattle by then. I asked around and heard you'd come back to Texas to help run your family's ranch. I thought there was a slim chance the baby might be Rufus' child, so I went ahead and gave birth to her."

Astrid laughed bitterly. "She came out looking exactly like you. Thick head of dark hair. Those gray eyes."

His gut clenched. It became hard to breathe.

"I had a lock of hair that Rufus had let me cut. Had the kid tested, just to be certain. She wasn't his," Astrid said flatly. Then she looked into his eyes. "I've tried, Chance. I really have. But just like my parents before me, I don't want her. I don't want kids, period. I have no patience with her. I know she senses how I feel about her."

Astrid began fidgeting. "I've been in touch with Rufus ever since he left. Casually, at first, then things really ramped up a few months ago. He told me it was a mistake, letting me go. He's done in London and will be put in charge of his firm's New York office next month. I plan to join him there.

"Without Daisy."

*Daisy* ...

"That's why I've come to see you," she said, her tone now all business. "I hired a lawyer, who advised me to establish residency in Texas since the father lived here, and it would make this whole process easier. I've filed an affidavit to voluntarily relinquish my parental rights. Foolishly, I named you on the birth certificate, so I have to notify you regarding my actions. You can sign away your rights, too. Right now, Chance. My Texas attorney is sitting in the car out front, and he has all the paperwork. You can complete it, and Givens will file it today."

He thought her heartless, cruel, and immensely selfish.

"I'm not signing a damn thing, Astrid. I can't believe you are."

Her eyes flashed with anger. "I can't make it any clearer to you, Chance. I had a child I never wanted. I haven't bonded with her. I hate spending time with her. I don't like her—and I will never love her. She deserves to go to someone who will. Don't be selfish. Just sign. That way, she can be adopted."

"No," he said firmly. "I want to see her."

Astrid sniffed. "Robert thought you might say that. Daisy is in the car with him. I'll get them."

She left the parlor and went outside. Chance moved to the window and saw her go to the car and open the door. She said something, and after a moment, he saw her unbuckling a child and lifting her from a car seat, setting her on the ground.

*His daughter.*

Astrid's attorney also got out of the car, but Chance only had eyes for the little girl. She looked small and lost and as lonely as anyone he'd ever seen.

She was also a dead ringer for Kelby at that age.

"Come on," he heard Astrid call as she turned her back and walked up to the porch.

Even though he didn't have kids, Chance knew you didn't treat a toddler like this. Quickly, he rushed out and knelt before the girl.

"Hi, Daisy. Do you want to come inside?"

She studied him with large, gray eyes, reminiscent of his own. Then she nodded.

"Okay. Take my hand. I'll help you up the porch steps."

She did so, trust in her eyes, and Chance knew he would never let this little girl be taken from him.

They entered the house, and he sat in a wing chair in the parlor, leaving Astrid and her attorney the sofa. Daisy looked at him solemnly, and he lifted her, placing her in his lap.

"I'm Robert Givens, Mr. Blackstone, representing Miss Powell's interests."

"Who's representing Daisy's?" he asked.

The attorney looked startled and didn't bother to answer his question. "Ms. Powell has filed for an Original Petition to Terminate the Parent-Child Relationship, as well as paying the filing fee. In Texas, it is not enough for her to sign this affidavit, which voluntarily relinquishes her parental rights. The court determines what is in the child's best interests, and the judge must sign a court order to end Ms. Powell's rights forever. I gather Ms. Powell asked you to sign away your rights, as well. Since we're sitting here, I suppose that you are considering taking the child."

"The child has a name. Daisy," he said firmly. "And yes, I

will not terminate my rights. I will be exercising them and will take custody of my daughter."

Chance glanced down, wondering if Daisy understood anything about what was going on.

"I advise you to seek counsel then," Givens said. "Someone who is experienced in family law."

"I can have my attorney here in fifteen minutes."

Without waiting for the lawyer's response, Chance called Sawyer.

"It's an emergency. Can you come to the ranch right now?"

"Sure, Chance. Has something happened to one of your ranch hands?"

"No. The mother of the child I never knew I had just showed up out of the blue," he said, glaring at Astrid. "She wants to terminate her parental rights. I want to take custody of Daisy immediately."

"I see," Sawyer said evenly. "On my way."

While they were waiting, he asked, "Does Daisy have any allergies?"

"No," Astrid said. "Why?"

"Because we're going to go and have ourselves a snack," he replied. Looking to his daughter, Chance asked, "Would you like some milk and peanut butter crackers?"

The little girl's eyes lit up, and she nodded.

"Good. Let's go find some."

In the kitchen, he got out the milk. Since he didn't have a sippy cup, he only poured half a cup of milk into a plastic cup, placing Daisy on the counter next to him as he smoothed peanut butter on a couple of crackers.

As she ate, he dialed Maria's number, and she answered on the first ring.

"Maria, I need some quick help. Can you come back to

the big house? I have a little girl named Daisy who needs to be watched while I do some business."

"Yes, Mr. Chance. I'm coming now."

Maria beat Sawyer there. Chance asked that she keep the girl occupied, and the housekeeper opened the canvas bag she carried.

"When you said a little girl, I brought a few things with me."

She handed Daisy a doll, and the girl hugged it to her tightly. Maria smiled, patting Daisy's head, and told Chance, "I also brought some crayons and paper. Some Play-Doh."

"You're a lifesaver, Maria."

She smiled encouragingly at him. "We'll be fine, Mr. Chance. You go do your business."

He headed back to the parlor but was interrupted by the doorbell. After admitting Sawyer, he briefly told him everything he'd learned from Astrid and Givens.

"You really want to assume custody, Chance? It's a big responsibility, taking on a child. And you need to think about Summer, too."

He kicked himself mentally. He hadn't given Summer a thought because he was so angry at Astrid and ready to do whatever it took to get Daisy away from her.

*What if Summer didn't want to raise a child he'd had with another woman?*

Chance decided he would have to address that later. The most important thing was Daisy and her well-being.

"Go in there and do whatever it takes to make certain that Astrid Powell will never have a thing to do with my daughter ever again."

Sawyer nodded. "I understand. Let me speak with this Givens and find out if they already have a court date. If not,

I'll press for one as soon as possible." He hesitated. "Are you ready to take on your daughter right now? This very moment? Because I think that's what it'll come down to."

"I'm ready," Chance said. "Go kick some ass, Sawyer."

# Twenty

Sawyer had previously told Chance that, being in Hawthorne, he was mostly dealing with family law matters. This situation certainly fell into that category. He listened now as Robert Givens walked Sawyer through everything Chance had learned from the attorney, plus additional information.

Sawyer asked for the court date, which Givens said would be this upcoming Thursday.

"And my client will then be able to obtain full, legal custody of Daisy at that point?" Sawyer asked.

Chance saw Givens and Astrid exchange a look, and she nodded to the attorney.

Givens then told them, "Yes."

"Where will Daisy be staying until the court hearing?" Chance interjected, worried about his daughter's well-being, and staring at Astrid pointedly. Her confession of not liking the child and having no patience with her had him truly concerned.

"Since you're going to take her off my hands, I think she should go ahead and stay with you now," Astrid told him. "She might as well get used to you. And if you see what a little brat she is, you could always change your mind and sign the papers and present them to the court at the hearing."

He hated the callousness in her tone, and Chance knew the sooner he got Daisy away from this woman, the better.

"I can come to where you've been living and pick up Daisy's things," he said.

She shrugged. "Actually, I have a diaper bag in the car with her things in it."

He cursed loudly and then said, "One diaper bag? It has everything of hers?"

Astrid shrugged nonchalantly. "I've known for long time that I wasn't going to keep her. I didn't see the point of buying her a lot of clothes or toys."

It took everything Chance had to remain in his seat and not knock the fire out of her. He had never struck a woman before. Had never even thought of doing so. But Astrid Powell was sorely testing him. Again, he knew the best thing for Daisy would be to have a fresh start.

*Starting now.*

Chance rose, and Sawyer followed suit.

"Let's go to the car and get Daisy's things," he said, his voice tight.

They went outside to the black Lincoln, and Astrid handed over the diaper bag.

"I assume Daisy isn't potty-trained yet."

Astrid wrinkled her nose. "No. That takes a lot of time and patience, and I didn't want to invest any more than I had to in her."

He unzipped the diaper bag and looked inside, seeing

one ratty-looking stuffed bear. No books. No other toys. Only a few items of clothing and some diapers. Disgust filled him.

"We'll take the car seat, too," Sawyer said, leaning into the vehicle and removing the car seat.

Though he didn't want to ask this, Chance said, "Would you like to tell Daisy goodbye?"

"No," Astrid said. "I'll see her on Thursday. I can say goodbye then." She looked to her attorney. "Let's go, Robert."

Chance watched them drive away and then turned to his friend.

Sawyer shook his head. "I've dealt with some bad people in my time, but your ex takes the cake."

"Let me be perfectly clear. I want to clear up any misunderstanding. I went out with that woman twice. Twice. We had sex. Once. That's it. I never saw her again because I didn't particularly care for her, and she seemed to feel the same about me. The fact that she kept Daisy from me makes me want to rake her over the coals. I've missed my little girl's first smile. First steps. First words. I'll never be able to get that time back."

"You're going to need to buy a lot of things for Daisy. I don't know much about kids, but I'll bet Kelby can clue you in on what you'll need."

Chance knew absolutely nothing about children. But he did know that he already had a lot of love in his heart for his daughter.

"We should be fine, regarding the hearing. Thursday should go smoothly for us," Sawyer assured him. "Especially with Astrid wanting to cut all ties. I've never seen a colder woman in my life."

"From what she told me when she arrived, she had broken up with a guy she really loved before we went out.

He'd been transferred overseas, and she didn't want to go. She decided to have the baby because she thought it might have been his. Now, he's been reassigned by his office to New York, and it seems they're getting back together. She wants a new life. Nothing to do with Daisy. And I'm glad of that. I know someday I'll have to tell Daisy about her mom, but I just want to focus on loving my little girl right now."

"You'll need to fill Summer in on what's happened. It's going to affect her as much as it will you. Maybe more so."

Chance's heart sank. He decided he couldn't marry Summer. He couldn't drag her into this mess. Daisy was going to need one hundred percent of his attention, and she deserved every bit of his focus. The same was true of Summer. Whoever she married needed to be completely devoted to her.

He couldn't be that man right now. Maybe never.

Because of that, he had to let Summer go.

"Could you keep this under your hat for a while, Sawyer?"

"Attorney/client privilege, Chance. That goes without saying." Sawyer's gaze bore into him. "But you're going to have to tell Summer the truth. She deserves to know."

"I'll talk with her after I have complete, legal custody of Daisy."

They went into the house and discussed going to Dallas on Wednesday since the hearing was at nine o'clock on Thursday morning. Sawyer offered to book rooms for them, and Chance agreed.

"We can get together Wednesday night after Daisy has gone to bed and go over any questions that you might have," Sawyer said.

"Thank you. Both Daisy and I thank you."

"That's what I'm here for," his friend said genially. "Call in the meantime if you have any questions. I'll text you the hotel information."

Chance took the diaper bag upstairs, taking everything out of it and placing it on his bed. It was pitiful how little was inside it. He would make certain he'd shower Daisy with everything she could ever need.

As soon as he could figure out what all of that was.

He went downstairs and found Maria playing with Daisy in the kitchen. The housekeeper looked at him questioningly, rising to her feet and coming to him.

"Daisy is going to be living with me," he informed her. "I don't know anything about a two-year-old. I'm going to need some help, Maria. I know you were hired to clean, so I'll have to get someone else to watch Daisy while I'm working, but I'd appreciate if you could tell me a little bit now about what I need to get for her."

"Of course, Mr. Chance."

During the next half-hour, Maria talked about some of the things Daisy had already experienced and what was to come. He learned about pull-ups versus diapers, and Maria gave him tips on potty training. She told him that Daisy seemed a little behind in her language skills, but other than that, she seemed very healthy.

"She can eat pretty much whatever you do, Mr. Chance." She grinned. "Just a lot less of it. Be sure to cut everything up into tiny bites. You don't want her to choke."

"Do I buy a crib? Or does she sleep in a bed?"

"She's ready to get out of a crib at her age. You can put her in a twin bed and push it against the wall. They have a guard you can slip under the mattress which will keep her from falling to the floor on the other side. I think it would be good for her to be around other kids, though, Mr. Chance. You should see if they have a preschool in town. I've tried to sing a few songs with her. *Itsy-Bitsy Spider. Row, Row, Row Your Boat. The ABCs.* She doesn't know any of them. Being around other little ones, she'll learn quickly."

"Thank you for your help today, Maria. I don't know what I would've done without you. Would you show me how to change a diaper before you leave?"

"Sure, Mr. Chance. It's easy."

Daisy was sitting on the floor, playing with a bowl and a wooden spoon. Plastic mixing cups were scattered about her. She seemed happy playing with these, and he would remember this in the future. He recalled how he and Kelby used to love playing inside big cardboard boxes. He'd look for one of those tomorrow, as well as getting her some new toys and books. Definitely books. He wanted the world for his daughter, and it would open to her through the magic of reading.

Maria showed him how to change a diaper. Thank goodness, it wasn't complicated.

"What size of clothes should I buy?"

She checked the tag inside Daisy's shirt. "This is eighteen months. It's a little tight on her. You should get a 2T. That's a size two for a toddler," she emphasized. "I'd also take her to a doctor, Mr. Chance. Make certain everything is all right with her."

"That's a great idea, Maria."

Chance decided to wait on that until he had full, legal custody of Daisy so that no one would question anything.

He picked up his daughter and carried her out of the kitchen, saying, "Let's say goodbye to Maria."

The little girl waved and softly said, "Bye-bye."

Those were the first words she had spoken, and it caused his eyes to mist with tears.

"One more thing, Maria. I didn't know about Daisy. The woman who brought her here? I only saw her twice before today. If I would've known about Daisy, I would've brought her to the ranch right away."

Maria placed a hand on his forearm. "I know that, Mr. Chance. You're a very nice man. You're doing the right thing for Daisy."

After Maria left, Chance wanted to devote all his time to Daisy. With dread, he pulled out his cell and called Summer. Just hearing her voice when she answered crushed his soul. He would need to talk to her in person to end things. Not now, though. Daisy was in a strange place and needed him.

"I'm going to have to take a rain check on dinner tonight," he told her.

"Why? Did something come up?"

"Yes, something pretty big that can't be put off. I'm going to have to go out of town for the next few days. I have some legal matters to attend to."

"But we had an appointment to see Judge Stowe tomorrow morning," she protested. "Can you put things off until after we've seen him?"

Stowe was supposed to officiate at their wedding. Chance didn't have a clue how to tell Summer they were no longer going to go through with their plans.

"Cancel it," he said brusquely. "I'll be gone until late Thursday or Friday morning. Then we'll need to talk."

"Chance, is something wrong? You know you can tell me anything."

His heart ached as he said, "I promise we'll talk come Friday."

She sighed. "I guess we won't be getting married this

weekend. Well, let me know how things are going in the meantime."

"I'm going to be pretty tied up with business. We'll talk later, Summer."

He ended the call before she could press him any further, tears stinging his eyes. He loved Summer more than anything and hated hurting her, but Daisy had to be his chief priority. He needed to build a relationship with his daughter. Make her understand that she was safe with him. That he wasn't going anywhere and neither was she. Introducing Summer into the child's life would only further confuse her, and he would have trouble shifting his focus from Daisy to Summer. He couldn't ask Summer to become an instant mother to a child she'd never seen before. It wouldn't be fair.

*He had to let her go.*

"Are you hungry, Daisy?" he asked, pushing aside thoughts of Summer.

The little girl nodded.

"Well, let's find us some dinner," he said cheerfully, a smile on his face. Chance didn't want his gloom transferring to Daisy.

"What do you like to eat?" He began looking around the kitchen. "I've got grapes. Bananas. Apples."

"Nana," she said. "And cheese."

He took a banana from the bunch and found string cheese in the fridge, something Summer liked, which caused his heart to ache. He peeled open the banana and held it to Daisy. She took a tiny bite and he praised her.

"Good girl."

Chance let her eat half the banana and realized she didn't have anything to wash it down with. Maria had said juice was too sweet and bad for teeth, so he should stick with milk or water.

"Would you like some water to drink? Or milk?"

"Milk," she said decisively, and he filled a cup half full. He would need to buy cups and plates for her. Small little forks and spoons. His head was spinning, knowing how little he knew. At least he could get online and read about how to raise a child.

*His child ...*

He looked down at Daisy, seeing it was obvious that she was a part of him. Her dark hair and unique gray eyes were only two things that gave away the fact she was his daughter. Daisy also had his same nose. Even his lips. He knew the more he was around her, the more he would see of himself in her. Once again, love washed over him. It had been instant. Fierce. Possessive.

And he would do anything for his child.

He peeled off a string of the cheese and gave it to her. She studied it carefully and then ate it slowly, saying, "Mmm" a couple of times.

He better start a grocery list. Maria had told him some of the things that Luna and Matteo had liked at Daisy's age. Yogurt. Applesauce. Animal crackers.

Chance took her into the den and held her in his lap, singing to her as she gripped her bear. Maria had mentioned two kids' songs, so those were the first two he tried out. It was obvious that she didn't know either tune. He also sang *London Bridge is Falling Down* and *Twinkle, Twinkle, Little Star.*

After he finished with *Twinkle,* she said, "Again," so he repeated it seven times in a row.

Much to his delight, Daisy started chiming in on the fourth time around, letting him know that she could learn quickly and most likely would be eager to do so.

Then Chance told her about the ranch.

"We'll go see the horses tomorrow. The cattle. Even the chickens. Do you know how a chicken goes?"

Daisy shook her head, so he clucked. He kept clucking until she joined in. Then he started mentioning different animals. A cow. Dog. Cat. Lion. Pig. Each time, he would make the noise that animal made, and his daughter imitated him. Chance couldn't wait to buy books for her so he could show her different animals. Colors. Shapes. A whole world was waiting for her to learn about, and he was ready to get started and make up for lost time.

Daisy yawned noisily, and he asked, "Are you sleepy?"

"Sleepy," she echoed, yawning again.

He took her upstairs to his bedroom and set the bear on the bed before he removed her clothes, thinking he should also change her diaper so that she would have a dry one to sleep in. He couldn't leave her alone and decided she would sleep in bed with him.

Drawing back the covers, he placed her on the pillow and handed her the bear.

"What's your bear's name?" he asked softly.

She shrugged. It broke his heart that Astrid had not even taken the time to help her name her only toy.

"Let's call him Teddy, okay?"

"Teddy," she repeated, nodding, a smile appearing on her face.

Chance looked at her and said, "And I'm Daddy. Can you say Daddy?"

Timidly, Daisy whispered, "Daddy."

"That's right. I'm your daddy. You're going to live with me from now on, here at Blackstone Ranch. We're going to play together. Eat together. Do everything together. Would you like that?"

Daisy nodded, another big yawn coming out.

"Okay, kiddo. Time for sleep. Close your eyes. Daddy will be right here with you." He smiled gently at her. "Daddy loves you. Daddy loves Daisy."

She looked at him a long moment, then her eyes drooped. But Chance heard the words she whispered as she fell into sleep.

"I love Daddy."

# Twenty~One

Chance took Daisy out of the car seat, having quickly become familiar with all the buckles and inserts. Yesterday morning, he'd taken her with him to Walmart in Decatur, not ready to shop in Hawthorne and face questions about her presence. He'd bought items such as baby shampoo and bath essentials, along with hooded towels and washcloths. Even a white noise machine and baby monitor. Pull-ups and diaper cream were tossed into his shopping cart, as were plates and eating utensils. He got several sippy cups, too, going heavy on the Disney Princess theme, knowing Kelby had been mad for them when she was Daisy's age.

He also picked up a thermometer and medicine for coughs and fevers before hitting the clothes section. He held up a few shirts and pants to Daisy and agreed with Maria that a 2T would be the right size for the toddler too wear. A few long-sleeved shirts went into the basket, along with more short-sleeved T's. Then some pants. Lots of shorts. A few dresses, including one she had on now, for the court hearing. Two sets of PJs, one with Winnie the Pooh characters and another with Ariel from *The Little Mermaid* on it. The final item was a swimsuit. Although it was still too cool to swim, he couldn't pass up a pink Minnie Mouse swimsuit with a ruffle along the bottom. He was girl-dadding, all the way.

Maria had told him as he walked out the door to also buy Daisy pretty panties. When he asked what those were, she had laughed and told him all little girls' panties should be called that. That way, when he began potty training Daisy, he could encourage her not to mess up her pretty panties. Maria said it had worked for her when she was young, and she had used the same tactic on Luna.

Then he'd hit the toy section, pushing a second cart by that time. He'd gotten dolls. Stuffed animals. Things that made music. Blocks. Simple puzzles with only five or six pieces. Books came next, and Chance had picked out some of his favorites from long ago, such as *Goodnight, Moon*, along with some that might be a little young for Daisy. Then again, since Astrid hadn't worked with the girl on things such as colors, numbers, or letters, these easier books might come in handy, helping Daisy to catch up on things.

He left Walmart an hour later, not having gotten a bed or dresser or anything like that for her. It struck him that some of Kelby's old furniture might still be in the attic, and he would need to look up there. Tammy would know, but he wasn't ready to speak to her—or anyone else—about Daisy.

Especially Summer.

Sawyer met them in the courthouse lobby. "Any trouble getting here?"

"No."

"Daisy looks nice. You do, too, Chance."

He raked a hand through his hair, trying to smooth it down more. "We've been busy shopping," Chance said. Grinning, he added, "It'll probably be the only time we do so where she doesn't have an opinion on clothes. I have a feeling she's going to be a strong, tough girl with a mind of her own."

"Then she definitely takes after you in more than looks," his friend said, laughing. "Kelby, too."

Sawyer escorted them to the elevators, and then they entered the courtroom.

"We've drawn Judge Penland. I've argued before her a couple of times. She's tough but fair. I don't foresee any speed bumps. Just answer her questions truthfully."

"I'll have to testify?"

"I'm not certain. She may want to hear from you. She may not. Don't panic. You're here for Daisy. Your heart is in the right place. It'll turn out fine. Have a little faith, Chance. In me and the system."

Sawyer had them take their place at a table. He glanced over and saw Astrid and Givens at the other one.

Then the bailiff announced Judge Penland, and they stood, Daisy still snug in his arms.

"Be seated."

Judge Penland looked at Daisy and him, then her eyes swept to Astrid and her attorney. She looked back at them.

"It's good to see you again, Mr. Montgomery. I'd heard you'd left the D.A.'s office."

"I did, Your Honor. I've moved back to my hometown of Hawthorne and couldn't be happier."

Her eyes fell back to the pages in front of her. "I see this is a most unusual case. I have before me an Original Petition to Terminate the Parent-Child Relationship." The judge glanced now at Astrid. "I believe you, Ms. Powell, are voluntarily seeking this parental connection to be severed."

"I am, Your Honor," Astrid responded.

"Hmm. Usually, when these petitions are brought before me, they involve child abuse or neglect. Abandonment. It is the court's responsibility to consider what is in the best interest of the child, in this case, Daisy Blackstone."

Chance hadn't realized that Astrid had given Daisy his surname.

"I see that pre-hearing procedures were waived. Since I don't see a representative of the court petitioner seeking termination, I need to hear opening statements from each side so that I can grasp what exactly is going on in this matter."

Robert Givens rose. "It's fairly straightforward, Your Honor. My client wishes to voluntarily terminate her parental rights to one Daisy Blackstone. Because of that, none of the usual evidence has been collected, such as medical records, police reports, or social service records because no neglect or abuse has occurred. Therefore, no evidence will need to be challenged."

Judge Penland frowned. Looking to Sawyer, she asked, "Give me your impressions, Counselor."

Sawyer came to his feet. "Chance Blackstone, my client, is Daisy's father. Until a few days ago, Mr. Blackstone had not been informed of the child's existence. When Ms. Powell notified him that he was Daisy's father and had been thus named on the child's birth certificate, Mr. Blackstone was upset that his daughter's birth had been hidden from him. He is more than ready to step up and take full, complete legal custody of Daisy."

The judge's gaze met Chance's. "I'd like to hear from you, Mr. Blackstone."

Chance cleared his throat. Daisy touched his face, and he told her, "It's okay. Daddy needs to talk to the judge."

To Judge Penland, he said, "I sowed a lot of wild oats in my twenties, Your Honor. I met Ms. Powell and basically had a one-night stand with her. I never saw her after we had relations. In fact, I left Seattle a couple of weeks later and moved to Texas. I settled myself down and began helping my father run our family ranch. Dad passed on a year ago, and I'm in charge of the ranch now. I'm more mature than I used to be, thanks to the responsibilities I hold. I deeply regret missing the first two years of my daughter's life.

"But I'm ready to step up and be her father now. If you'll allow that, Your Honor."

The judge looked to Astrid now. "Ms. Powell, do you have anything to add to what Mr. Blackstone has told the court?"

She wet her lips. "I have never wanted children, Your Honor. I had just gotten out of a long-term relationship when I slept with Mr. Blackstone. Once. After I discovered I was pregnant, I thought it was possible that my former boyfriend was the father. It was the only reason I had the girl."

Astrid looked across the aisle at him. "She came out favoring Mr. Blackstone strongly. To make certain, I had a DNA test run, and she is definitely his child."

She turned her attention back to the judge. "I don't want to be a mother. I have no connection to Mr. Blackstone and no feelings for his daughter."

"She's also *your* daughter, Ms. Powell," Judge Penland pointed out.

"I don't want her," Astrid said flatly. "I want to waive all rights to her. I only notified Mr. Blackstone because I was legally required to do so and offered him the chance to sign the same parental termination rights documents that I had. I never dreamed he'd want her." She shrugged. "It seems he does want to keep her. I'm fine with that. I plan to move to New York and be with my previous boyfriend. We have plans to marry, and those plans don't include the girl."

"I see," Judge Penland said, her tone cold. "This is a

highly unusual case, especially since parental rights termination usually involves both parents. However, I see that Ms. Powell is determined not to have anything to do with her daughter, while Mr. Blackstone seems eager to step into the role of being a parent to Daisy Blackstone."

She looked to Chance. "It won't be easy, young man. Raising children is hard work."

"I've never been afraid of hard work, Your Honor. I may not know a whole lot about toddlers, but I'm a fast learner. And I love Daisy." He glanced down at her. "I love her a lot."

The judge nodded. "That's all I need to know. Ms. Powell, your termination petition has been granted, and your relationship with Daisy Blackstone will be legally severed. Since Mr. Blackstone is Daisy's natural, legal father, this court will not require a post-termination plan for the child's future."

Judge Penland scrawled her name on the documents, and said to Chance, "I wish you all the best with raising your daughter, Mr. Blackstone." She paused and then smiled at him. "And as a grandmother, I can recommend *Sesame Street* and *Paw Patrol*, with a dash of Disney thrown in for good measure."

She rapped her gavel against the bench. "This matter is now resolved. Next case, bailiff."

Sawyer told Chance that he would receive copies of the legal documents granting him sole custody of Daisy, as well as ones terminating Astrid's parental rights. He nodded and looked up, seeing Astrid striding from the courtroom with her attorney.

"She didn't even bother to say goodbye," he mused aloud.

"Daisy deserves better—and she got you," his friend said. "It's time to return to Hawthorne and your new life with your daughter."

Chance stood. "We're going home," he told her.

"Home," she said, nodding in approval.

The only thing left to do was let Summer know that things were over between them.

* * *

SUMMER OFFERED to help with the dishes, but Eli told her he would take care of them.

"I think I'm going to go for a walk then. Clear my head. Work on some plot points," she lied, knowing that writing was the last thing on her mind.

"Enjoy your walk," Autumn said, going and wrapping her arms around Eli as he stood scrubbing a pan at the sink, resting her cheek against his back.

Summer turned away, bile rising in her throat. She was truly happy for her twin. After a terrible first marriage, Autumn was now blissfully happy with Eli. Her new job. The coming baby. Summer didn't want to be jealous of Autumn, but she saw everything her sister had—which she wanted—slipping from her grasp.

The last few days had been absolute torture. Chance hadn't texted or called a single time while he was out of town. She hadn't told anyone about the dread building within her. Somehow, she knew that things were over between them.

And she hadn't a clue why.

She had gotten no work done the past few days. Everything she had written, she wound up deleting. How was she supposed to write about love and happiness when she herself was miserable?

Her phone rang, causing her heart to leap. She pulled it from her pocket.

It was Chance. Finally.

Summer took a deep breath and answered. "Hello?"

"I wanted to let you know that I'm back in town," he said tersely. "Would you be able to come by tomorrow morning and talk?"

He didn't say that he had missed her, much less that he loved her. Chance didn't even invite her for breakfast. Her heart sank.

"What time is convenient for you?" she asked, as if she were scheduling an appointment with a stranger.

"I have a lot going on because I've been gone. Is eight o'clock too early?"

He knew it wasn't. She was an early bird, the same as he was.

Her voice tight, Summer said, "I'll be there at eight."

A silence followed, long and drawn out. Stubbornly, she decided she wouldn't be the first one to hang up and let it drag on.

Finally, Chance said, "I'll see you then."

He hung up without even saying goodbye.

Tears sprang to her eyes. She willed herself not to cry, though. She was strong. Confident.

And she would fight like hell for the two of them and what they had.

# CHAPTER
## Twenty~Two

Summer hadn't been able to eat anything this morning. She was afraid if she did, it would come right back up. She dressed carefully, wearing a shirt Chance had complimented her on because it brought out the deep turquoise hue of her eyes. If he planned to break up with her this morning and wouldn't listen to reason, she was going to keep her head high and look damn good as she walked away.

She came downstairs, knowing Autumn and Eli had already left for work. She drank a cup of water because her mouth was dry and then went to her car. Usually, she turned on an oldies station and sang along to whatever tune played, but today her spirits were low, and she drove in silence to Blackstone Ranch, the windows down since it was such a pretty day.

When she arrived, she took three deep breaths, letting them out slowly. She had done everything to prepare herself for the worst. Summer couldn't begin to wonder what Chance might say, but she loved him and was willing to fight for him.

It was odd to ring the doorbell since she usually just walked right in. Moments later, he opened the door, a grim look on his face.

"Come on in," he said, and she warily stepped into the large foyer.

He closed the door and stood a moment, looking at her, almost drinking her in as if he were memorizing everything about her.

That confirmed what she suspected.

They were over. Whatever she said wasn't going to make any difference.

"Say it," she said sharply. "You called me over here to look me in the eye when you told me, so do it. Tell me you don't love me anymore. That you aren't going to marry me."

His apologetic gaze met hers. "Summer, I don't want to marry you."

Even though she thought she'd prepared herself, she almost crumpled at hearing those words. But instead of sorrow, she allowed anger to boil inside her.

"I thought I knew you. Apparently, you aren't the man that I thought you were. Did the idea of settling down with me turn your stomach so sour that you couldn't handle it? Have you gone back to catting around like you used to? You used me, Chance. Badly. And now you're tossing me and everything we had away. Throwing away our love. I gave you my heart. My body and soul."

Summer glared at him, daring him to speak. To offer some kind of explanation. He merely remained grim-faced.

"I'm sorry that I hurt you, Summer. Whether you believe it or not, I did love you."

*Past tense.*

Nausea filled her at that realization. "Well, you certainly have an odd way of showing it," she said harshly. "I didn't know you could love someone and turn it off as easily as turning off a faucet."

Anguish filled his eyes. "I still love you," he admitted, his voice breaking.

Her mouth opened, but nothing came out of it. She could only stare at him.

"Something has happened," he said, his words suddenly coming in a rush. "Something I didn't know about. I had no control over it. But I had to step up and do the right thing." He swallowed hard. "But it's my problem. Not yours."

He raked his fingers through his hair in frustration. "No, it's not a problem. It's a blessing. Still, it's going to change my life. Turn it upside down. And I can't ask you to go through those kinds of changes with me."

She shook her head. "Chance, you're talking in riddles. Nothing makes sense. You say you still love me? I love you. We can get through anything. Together."

"No. I refuse to thrust things on you. The life that we had planned together, Summer, isn't the one that we would have."

Chance reached and took her hands, and she could feel him trembling.

"I want the best for you. I want you to have someone who makes you happy. Who can devote himself to you. Who can give you the life you've always dreamed of."

He released her hands. "I'm no longer that guy."

Her anger returned. "You've told me you love me, yet you say we can't be together. Because things have changed. Why won't you share with me what has changed? Maybe I would be happy with that change. Maybe I love your thick skull so much that I want to go through this change with you."

He looked at her wordlessly, his eyes filled with tears. "I can't. I can't do that to you. I have obligations now to meet. A priority bigger than you."

Before she could demand an answer from him, movement caught her eye. Summer looked over his shoulder and saw a little girl, no more than two years old, heading toward them. She had hair black as a raven's and the Blackstone gray eyes.

*Chance had a daughter.*

He must have seen she was distracted and looked over his shoulder. Hurriedly, he went to the girl, who was obviously his, and scooped her up.

"Daddy! I make a cake," she happily told him.

"That's wonderful, sweetie. I'll come try some in just a minute. Go back to the kitchen and stay with Maria now."

Chance set her down, but the little girl took a step toward Summer. She knelt so that she would be on the child's level.

"Hi. I'm Summer. What's your name?"

"Daisy. Daisy Blackstone."

Summer reeled at the words but kept a smile on her face. "Well, it's nice to meet you, Daisy Blackstone. I'm a friend of your daddy's."

"Daddy's my friend. And Teddy," the little girl added.

"Oh, do you have a Teddy Bear?"

Daisy nodded enthusiastically. "I show you."

She ran from the room, and Summer slowly came to her feet.

"I gave you my heart, Chance Blackstone. Loved you with everything I had. Shared my hopes and dreams with you. Yet you kept this secret from me."

Summer began to tremble. Chance reached out to touch her, but she jerked away.

"You said your life was changing. I assume Daisy and her mother will be coming to live at the ranch. That you're marrying her instead of me." She swallowed. "Or are you already married?" she accused.

"It's not what you think, Summer."

"What am I supposed to think, Chance?" she said angrily. "You leave town on some mysterious business. You tell me to cancel the appointment we have with Judge Stowe. Either you're already married to Daisy's mother and you can't marry me, or you've decided to marry your baby mama instead of me."

Chance looked at her pleadingly. "Let me explain."

"You really are going to explain? Now? I've been begging for an explanation. I went days without hearing from you, hoping to get one. Now, I'm here and all I'm getting from you are half-truths."

Daisy ran back into the room, a shabby Teddy Bear in her arms. She came to a halt, looking back and forth from Summer to her father, sensing the tension between them.

Quickly, Summer composed her features and smiled brightly at the child. "Is this Teddy?" she asked, dropping to her knees again. "Why, I had a Teddy Bear when I was a little girl. About as old as you are. Do you know how old you are, Daisy?"

"I'm two," the girl said happily. "Two," she said again for emphasis, holding up two fingers.

Maria appeared, looking stricken. "I'm so sorry, Mr. Chance. Daisy, come back with me. Let's finish your cake. You still have more of the bowl to lick."

"Okay," Daisy said happily. She skipped toward Maria and then turned and looked at Summer. "Bye, Summer."

Her heart ached. "Bye, Daisy."

After Maria and Daisy had left, she looked at Chance. "I guess there's nothing more for us to say."

Summer turned and opened the door, running down the stairs and to her SUV. She put her hand on the handle to open it when Chance's hand covered hers.

"Don't go," he pleaded. "Not like this."

She stood there, feeling the warmth of his body against hers. The scent of leather and cologne invading her senses.

"I have to," she said, her voice breaking. "You don't trust me enough to tell me the truth. Back away, Chance. Please. Let me go."

Summer meant physically, but she also meant the words emotionally. She needed to be freed so that she could start the process of cutting Chance from her heart and life. She had no place in his life anymore. It was going to be hard enough to see him around town with his new wife and child. She would also have to see him on holidays and other family get togethers. After all, her brother was married to his sister. It would be impossible to avoid him completely.

The thought of no longer having Chance in her life shattered her heart.

"Let me go," she said again, her voice but a whisper.

Dropping his hand from hers, he took a step back. She escaped into her car. It took three times before she could get the seatbelt buckled. Her eyes were filling with tears as she started the car. She had to get away from here. Now. Before she fell apart in front of him.

Summer put the car into gear and looked up, only to see Chance standing in front of the SUV, blocking her way. She kicked the car into reverse and pushed hard on the gas pedal, the vehicle quickly moving back. Though she turned the wheel to move forward now, Chance had rushed to the side of the car.

"Open the door, Summer. We're not done yet."

She refused to do that and hit the gas. He ran along beside the car, yelling at her to stop. She didn't let up on the gas, and the car sped away, leaving him behind.

Summer then heard him call out, "Don't be a coward!"

His words infuriated her. Riled, Summer slammed on the

brakes. She threw the car into park and unbuckled her seatbelt, leaving the car and storming back toward him.

"I'm not the coward. You are!" she shouted at him. "You didn't tell me you had a daughter. You didn't tell me you were involved with someone else. I truly think you did feel something for me. Maybe it was love. But you already had a commitment, Chance. Not to me. To Daisy and her mother."

He took her by the shoulder and looked her in the eyes. "I didn't even know Daisy existed until Monday afternoon."

His words stunned her. Summer's jaw dropped.

"Yes," he nodded. "I slept with her mom. One time. I never saw her after that. She thought the baby was her ex's, and she went ahead with the pregnancy. Much to her surprise, Daisy came out as my spitting image."

His hold on her gentled, but Summer was still too stunned to speak.

"Astrid showed up with Daisy in tow a few days ago. She's gotten back with her ex, and she wants no part of Daisy. She filed papers with the court to terminate her parental rights."

He swallowed hard. "Since Astrid had named me as the father on the birth certificate, she had a legal obligation to notify me. She wanted me to sign away my rights, too. Give Daisy up to the system."

Chance looked at her earnestly. "I couldn't do that, Summer. It was obvious she'd been terrible to Daisy. She didn't abuse her physically, but she hadn't showed Daisy a bit of affection. Daisy only had a couple of outfits and that one, ratty bear. No toys. No books. And definitely no love."

Finding her voice, Summer asked, "How could someone be so cruel?"

"I wasn't about to give away my little girl," he said stubbornly. "I want to teach her the ABCs and how to ride a bike.

And a horse. I want to give her everything she's never had. Most of all, I want to love her. I want her to know she's loved. Hell, I fell in love with her from the first moment I saw her."

"Why didn't you tell me about this? I can't believe you've gone through this alone."

Anguish filled his eyes. "I couldn't ask you to be a part of this, babe. I have to make Daisy my top priority now. I wouldn't want you marrying me and having to raise some other woman's child."

She cupped his cheek. "Daisy isn't some other woman's child. She's *your* daughter, Chance. The woman who gave birth to her is long gone. Daisy will never see her again. Yes, she's going to need her daddy's love, but she'll also need a mommy, too. I'd like to be considered for that job."

His hand came up and touched hers. He pulled it from his cheek and laced his fingers through hers.

"Are you serious, Summer? You'd be willing to start our marriage with a third person already in it?" he asked huskily.

Tears swam in her eyes. "Absolutely. You aren't the only one who fell in love with Daisy at first sight. Chance, I love you. With all my heart. And I already love Daisy, too, because she's a part of you. It would be a blessing to become a family."

"I'm sorry I pushed you away," he apologized. "That I didn't trust you. I had a picture of what we were supposed to be in my head. Then Astrid arrived with Daisy, and I was thrown for a loop. I knew my allegiance was to my little girl above all else."

"I'm not so selfish that I would claim all your attention," Summer assured him. "I understand that I won't have your complete, full attention. But I know you have enough room in your heart to love the both of us." She hesitated. "And more children. If you want them."

He beamed at her. "Of course, I do. I always saw myself with you and lots of kids." He wrapped his arms about her. "Summer Sutherland, let's try this again. Will you marry me —and Daisy?"

Tears misted her eyes. "You bet, Cowboy."

Chance kissed her, and all the hurt dissolved, being replaced with an abiding love that would be ever true.

*Epilogue*

Summer slipped the bow in Daisy's hair. "There. Now you're all set to go. Are you ready to drop the flowers like we practiced?"

"Uh-huh," Daisy said, wrapping her arms around Summer's leg.

"You're good with her," Tammy observed.

She laughed. "For not having any experience with kids, the past week has been a crash course in parenting."

"The first one is always learning on the job," Mom said, smoothing Summer's hair. "Even though Autumn was the one who babysat all the time, I knew you'd also make for a good mother."

Love filled Summer's heart. Her parents had openly accepted Daisy, and she knew they would consider the little sprite to be as much a granddaughter to them as the babies Kelby and Autumn now carried.

Kelby came over. "Would you like me to take Daisy with me? That way, you can make any last-minute adjustments."

"Thanks, Kelby." She knelt and told Daisy, "Go with Aunt Kelby. I'll be there soon."

"And then we get married?" asked Daisy.

She and Chance had told Daisy they were getting married and that she could call Summer Mommy. Daisy had taken it to mean that the three of them were getting married. Not only would Daisy serve as their flower girl, but they would include her in the vows they spoke to one another.

"Yes, then we'll get married."

At first, Summer had balked at the idea of Daisy calling her Mommy. Then Chance reminded her that she would be the only true mother Daisy would ever know. It would be odd if Daisy called her Summer, while all their other children called her their mom. He told Summer that she had already agreed to be Daisy's mom, and she should take the title that came with it. Jokingly, he had teased that she might reconsider during the teenage years, causing her to laugh.

Summer insisted that as soon as Daisy was old enough to understand, she be told about her birth mother. Chance agreed, but he said that was a long time off. For now, Summer would happily accept being called Mommy.

They had also talked about having children of their own. Chance said that he wanted them to get started soon, not wanting too big a gap between their firstborn and Daisy. She had happily agreed, her nurturing nature springing forward as she helped care for Daisy. Chance had thrown out his box of condoms, and they hoped she would turn up pregnant in the next few months.

Kelby left with Daisy, and her mom, Tammy, Darby, and Jen went with them. Only Autumn remained behind. Her twin spritzed Summer with perfume and fiddled with her hair one last time.

"You're perfect," Autumn said. "And Chance is perfect

for you, just as Eli is for me. I'm so happy for you, Summer. You're back in Hawthorne for good. Your writing is getting stronger with every chapter. I know by this time next year, you'll have sold your series. Maybe the first book will already be out." Her twin grinned. "And maybe you'll be pregnant or already have another baby."

"That's the plan," she confirmed. "Chance and I are eager to start our family. No, we already have a family. We're ready for another baby. Of course, since we weren't around Daisy when she was born, we'll have a lot to learn."

But she knew they would be good parents. She thought that when she saw Daisy sitting in Chance's lap as he read to her. When she and Daisy went for a walk, holding hands, looking at everything in nature. Although they'd missed out on Daisy's first two years, she was their first child. Already, the bond between Daisy and them was strong, and Summer knew that closeness would only grow stronger over time.

"I'm ready," she told her twin, accepting the bouquet Autumn handed to her. "Let's go down to the old oak tree and make things official."

When they exited the big house, Buck stood near a golf cart. He grinned at them.

"We don't use this often, but it'll get you where you're going quicker than walking," the ranch manager said. "Climb aboard."

Autumn took the seat next to Buck, letting Summer sit in the rear, facing out. She held on tightly as the golf cart rumbled along, getting them to the place where Chance had proposed to her. She allowed Buck to help her down and skimmed the small crowd. Eli stood with Jace and Darby, her mom, Jen, and Sawyer next to them. Tammy and her Tommy were also present. Everyone already loved the kind, good-natured Tommy, who treated Tammy like a princess. West leaned down and kissed Kelby and made his way to the base of the tree, where Judge Stowe was waiting for them. The ranch hands were among their guests, and everyone was smiling.

Her dad made his way toward them, Daisy's hand in his.

"Ready to start the next chapter in your life?" he asked.

"More than ready," she said fervently.

Dad handed the basket with rose petals to Daisy. "Walk to your daddy, Daisy," he told the toddler. "Drop the petals as you go to him."

"Okay," Daisy said, taking the first rose petal and dropping it on the ground as Autumn went to stand behind her.

Dad took Summer's hand and slipped it through the crook of his arm. "My last baby getting married."

"You sound like Mom, getting all sentimental on me."

He smiled at her. "I just hope you'll be as happy as I've been with your mom all these years. You'll have a few more bumps along the road, Summer, starting marriage with an instant family, but you are going to take to motherhood. You already have."

"I think so," she said. "Already, I can't imagine my life without Daisy in it."

He led her toward their guests. By now, Daisy had emptied her basket and given it to Kelby. She now stood next to Chance.

When she reached them, she handed Autumn her bridal bouquet and took Daisy's hand as Chance took her other one. They smiled at one another, and the love filling her heart spilled over.

Judge Stowe cleared his throat, and Summer turned her attention to the officiant.

"We're here on this beautiful spring day to unite Summer Sutherland and Chance Blackstone in marriage." The judge smiled down at Daisy. "And Daisy Blackstone is also a part of this marriage. A big part. I'd like to read a poem. The author is anonymous, but I think you'll appreciate the sentiment."

Stowe removed a page from his pocket and opened it, saying, "What is a family?"

> *A family is ...*
> *The sweetest feelings*
> *The warmest hugs*
> *Trust and togetherness*
> *Unconditional love*
> *The stories of our lives written on the*
>     *same page*
> *The nicest memories anyone has ever made*
> *Treasured photos*
> *Thankful tears*
> *Hearts overflowing with all the years*
> *Being there for one another*
> *Supporting and caring*
> *Understanding, Helping, Sharing*
> *Walking life's path together*
> *And making the journey more beautiful*
>     *because ...*
> *We are a family ... And a family is Love.*

Emotion filled Summer. She glanced to Chance and saw he was just as moved as she was by the poem.

"Now, let's get down to business," Judge Stowe told those gathered.

He went through the ceremony and paused so that Summer and Chance could speak the vows they had written together for one another.

"I, Chance Blackstone, take you, Summer Sutherland, to

be my beloved partner in life. I promise to love, honor, and cherish you until the end of time."

Chance lifted Daisy in his arms and looked at her, smiling. "We also commit ourselves to Daisy Blackstone, promising to love you and take care of you. To guide you through life."

Summer's gaze met his. "I, Summer Sutherland, take you, Chance Blackstone, to be my loving husband. For better or worse, I pledge to you my heart and my life. Let us now come together as a family. Father. Mother. And Daisy. From this day forward, I promise to love you both as long as we shall live."

The judge had them exchange rings. West handed Summer's wedding band to Daisy, who gave it to Chance. Balancing her in his arms, he slid the ring onto Summer's finger. Autumn then handed Chance's band to Daisy, who gave it to Summer, and she placed it on Chance's hand.

Judge Stowe smiled broadly. "By the power invested in me by the State of Texas, I pronounce you husband, wife, and child!"

Chance kissed Daisy's cheek, as did Summer, and then he handed Daisy to West. Then he took Summer into his arms. The kiss he gave her was incredibly poignant, letting her know just how much he cherished her and the life they would build together. As a couple—and as a family.

When he broke it, he gazed at her tenderly. "I'm glad you came home to Hawthorne, Summer Blackstone."

Hearing her new name for the first time sent a thrill through her. "Guess you can't call me Sutherland anymore, Cowboy."

"I'm guessing you're right, Blackstone. God, I love you so much, Summer. You. Daisy. Everything that's still ahead of us."

She felt a tug on her dress and looked down, seeing Daisy looking up expectantly. Summer picked up her daughter.

"How do you like being married, Daisy?" she asked.

Their little girl smiled. "Can we eat cake now?"

Summer and Chance laughed, and he said, "It's all about the cake. Come on, ladies. We've got some celebrating to do."

She set Daisy back on the ground, and their daughter ran to Tammy, taking her hand and pulling her along.

"It's cake time, everybody," Chance announced. "At least, that's what's on Daisy's mind."

Those assembled turned and began making their way back to the big house. Chance pulled Summer close for a long, hot kiss. Then he broke it and grinned at her.

"Let's go, Blackstone. Before our girl eats up all the cake."

Chance took her hand, and he and Summer walked slowly back to the house where they would live with their family. Where they would grow old together.

Where they would live in love.

## HEARTS IN HAWTHORNE

Heartstrings and Helmets

Heartbeat Harmony

Agent of the Heart

Hearts and Hooves

Hoops and Hearts

## LOST CREEK, TEXAS HILL COUNTRY

The Perfect Blend

Painted Melodies

Script of Love

Love in Every Bite

Whispered Melodies

## SUGAR SPRINGS

Shadows of the Past

Learning to Trust Again

A Perfect Match

A Fresh Start

Recipe for Love

## MAPLE COVE

Another Chance at Love

A New Beginning

Coming Home

The Lyrics of Love

Finding Home

## HOLLYWOOD NAME GAME

Hollywood Heartbreaker

Hollywood Flirt

Hollywood Player

Hollywood Double

Hollywood Enigma

## LAWMEN OF THE WEST

Runaway Hearts

Blind Faith

Love and the Lawman

Ballad Beauty

## SAGEBRUSH BRIDES

A Game of Chance

Written in the Cards

Outlaw Muse

## KNIGHTS OF REDEMPTION

A Bit of Heaven on Earth

A Knight for Kallen

## SUDDENLY A DUKE

Portrait of the Duke

Music for the Duke

Polishing the Duke

Designs on the Duke

Fashioning the Duke

Love Blooms with the Duke

Training the Duke

Investigating the Duke

<u>SECOND SONS OF LONDON</u>

Educated by the Earl

Debating with the Duke

Empowered by the Earl

Made for the Marquess

Dubious about the Duke

Valued by the Viscount

Meant for the Marquess

<u>DUKES DONE WRONG</u>

Discouraging the Duke

Deflecting the Duke

Disrupting the Duke

Delighting the Duke

Destiny with a Duke

<u>DUKES OF DISTINCTION</u>

Duke of Renown

Duke of Charm

Duke of Disrepute

Duke of Arrogance

Duke of Honor

<u>SOLDIERS AND SOULMATES</u>

To Heal an Earl

To Tame a Rogue

To Trust a Duke

To Save a Love

To Win a Widow

<u>THE ST. CLAIRS</u>

Devoted to the Duke

Midnight with the Marquess

Embracing the Earl

Defending the Duke

Suddenly a St. Clair

<u>STANDALONE ROMANTIC THRILLERS</u>

Leave Yesterday Behind

Illusions of Death

# About the Author

*USA* Today and Amazon Top 100 bestselling author Alexa Aston lives with her husband in a Dallas suburb, where she eats her fair share of dark chocolate and plots out stories while she walks every morning. She enjoys travel, sports, and binge-watching—and never misses an episode of *Survivor*.

Alexa brings her characters to life in steamy historicals, contemporary romances, and romantic suspense novels that resonate with passion, intensity, and heart.

**KEEP UP WITH ALEXA**
Visit her website
Newsletter Sign-Up

**MORE WAYS TO CONNECT WITH ALEXA**